reason

Other books by Berlie Doherty

BERLIE DOHERTY

reason

ANDERSEN PRESS
LONDON

First published in 2011 by
Andersen Press Limited
20 Vauxhall Bridge Road
London SW1V 2SA
www.andersenpress.co.uk
www.berliedoherty.com

Reprinted 2011 (twice), 2012

British Library Cataloguing in Publication Data available.

ISBN 978 1 84939 121 4

Printed and bound by CPI Group (UK) Ltd, Croydon, CR0 4YY

For Carolyn and George

The year is 1539. Henry VIII is King of England. All three of his wives, Katherine of Aragon, Anne Boleyn and Jane Seymour are dead. He has three children: Mary, Elizabeth and the long-awaited heir to his throne, Edward. Henry has broken away from the Church of Rome because the Pope would not allow him to divorce his first wife. Anyone who refuses to accept that he is the Supreme Head of the Church of England is accused of an offence that is punishable by death.

Treason.

The drowning

We jumped down from our horses and ran ahead of Father along the shore. Sand whipped into our faces. Waves hurled themselves against the rocks, sending cascades of spray high into the air, then rolled across the sand like hungry dogs, snuffling into every hole and hollow.

'I'll race you to the cave!' I gasped over my shoulder. Matthew strode on past me. An extra-high wave filled his boots and he jumped sideways onto a boulder, waving his arms to keep his balance. I scrambled up after him and we staggered from rock to rock towards the cave.

'Don't go any further!' Father shouted. He had his hands cupped round his mouth. 'The tide's too high. It's dangerous.'

We ignored him. It was too exciting to stop now. We were above the waves, but the water curled over our feet and bursts of spray soaked right through our heavy clothes.

'We'll never make it to the cave,' I panted.

'We'll have to,' Matthew laughed. 'We're surrounded. Can't go back. Have to go on.'

'Come back!' Father shouted again.

Behind him, where the sand was still dry, Ned Porritt,

the stable lad, stood clinging onto the reins of the horses. He was hopping from one foot to the other. 'Master Matthew, Master William!' he mouthed. 'Come back!'

Matthew laughed across at me. 'That's got them worried. Not scared, are you?'

'Of course not!'

'Then follow me. Onward, ever onward!'

'I still think we should try to go back,' I said. I turned to look at my father, and at that moment a tower of sea smashed against the rock, slamming me off balance. I flung my arms out as I toppled forward, and grabbed wildly at my brother's sleeve. Then we both plunged helplessly into the sea.

I was being rushed along in someone's arms. My eyes kept opening and shutting. I saw sky with huge clouds, and spatters of leaves and blinding sun, and black shadows. I saw the archway that led into the house, and the blue-painted wood of the ceiling above the stairs, and the dark curtains that draped over my bed. I saw my sister Margery's white, anxious face peering down at me. I saw light and dark and light again. I heard muffled voices, and Father, far, far away, saying, 'I tried to save him. I tried, I tried. I could only save one of them.'

But which one? I tried to say, and couldn't. *Am I alive, or am I dead?* The voices were spinning away from me, fainter and fainter.

'Master Willim, Master Willim, wake up now. Sit up, come on, I'll help you.'

I opened my eyes. Nurse Joan had pulled back the curtain from around my bed and was easing her arm under my shoulders. My head and my arms felt too heavy, my chest was tight and painful. I could hear myself moaning.

'That's a good boy. Have this food I've brought you, and you'll feel much better.' Joan pushed a cushion behind my back as I struggled to sit up. I took the wooden bowl and spoon and tried to swallow the salty gruel, but it came back up my throat again. I pushed the bowl away and sank back onto the pillow. Something had happened. I tried to remember what it was, and couldn't. Nurse Joan watched me gravely, as if she was waiting for me to speak. I couldn't find the words. What was it? What had happened?

She sighed and stood up. 'I'll send Stephen in to clean you up,' she said.

'Where's my father?'

'In chapel. Praying with Brother John. They've been there all day, and the vigil will go on all night, so don't ask for him.' She waited again as if she expected me to say something, and then turned to go.

'And Matthew?'

Nurse Joan stifled a sob and hurried out of the room, leaving the door open for the old servant Stephen. But it was Margery who ran in, as if she had been hovering outside the door all the time.

'Don't you know? Hasn't she told you?' Tears were streaming down her cheeks.

'What? What's happened?'

'Matthew's dead. He's drowned, Will.'

'You are alive'

In the weeks that followed, I hardly saw my father. I wanted to be with him; I wanted him to comfort me, to tell me it was all right, to make things better again. But it wasn't all right, and it never would be again, and Father kept away from me. Matthew hadn't been found, and Father went down to the shore every day, alone, watching. He loved Matthew more than any of us; we knew that. Nurse Joan told us he was breaking in half with grief.

There was a weight of silence in the old Hall, and when Father came home in the evenings he walked on his own in the dark gardens as if he couldn't bear to be in the house with us. He had scarcely spoken to me or to Margery, hardly even looked at us. Our meals were sent to us in our rooms. I had to look across at the empty bed that Matthew and I used to share. I drew the curtains round it, but then the stillness scared me so much that I opened them again. The house was so quiet without his boisterous laughter that Margery and I hardly dared speak to each other, hardly dared cross the creaking floorboards between our rooms.

After the first month, Brother John asked me to go and see him in the rose garden outside the chapel. He was my father's cousin, and he used to live in a monastery,

4

before King Henry closed them all down and took their land and money to pay for his war with France. He was our tutor now. Matthew and I used to meet him in the rose garden every morning after Mass, before our lessons started.

'The fresh air will bring colour to your cheeks and light to your eyes,' he always said, in Latin. 'Healthy boys make healthy scholars.' He liked us to talk in Latin most of the time, but it was very hard, especially before breakfast. Sometimes he would notice how much we were struggling and he'd drop into English and tease us with a riddle.

It was still winter, and the grass was sharp and fat with ice. Brother John was bending down, hands on knees, looking at something on the ground.

'Something here has made me think of a riddle for you,' he said. 'I swim, but am no fish. I have legs, but am no man. When I'm full-grown, I leap across the land, but am no hare. What am I?'

I wasn't in the mood for riddles. Besides, I wasn't very good at them. Matthew was always the one to guess the answer first. He used to whisper it to Brother John and then wrestle gleefully on the ground with me till I guessed the answer too, or until he shouted it down my ear.

'Come on, William,' Brother John coaxed.

'I've no idea,' I said at last. 'Tell me.'

'Ah no. It's no satisfaction if you're told the answer. Look at this now, what do you make of it?'

I squatted down next to him. There was a patch of ice across the path, but it was beginning to thaw in the pale sun. The surface ice was thin and hard, but underneath it moving water squeezed and bubbled in dark blobs.

'You'd think it was alive, wouldn't you?' Brother John said. 'You'd think it was full of living creatures squirming to be let free.'

I watched the black wriggling shapes. 'They look like tadpoles.'

Brother John clapped me on the back. 'Exactly! Nothing in this world is quite as it seems.' He stood up and looked down at me. 'Death is not the end, William. Your brother is with his maker. He will have eternal rest. You are alive, and you bring hope to your father.'

'My father doesn't talk to me any more.'

'He will. He will come out of his grief, and you will be the one to help him. You are *alive*. Remember that. Remember it always. While there's life, there's hope. Who said that?'

I fumbled for the answer. No Matthew to prompt me or to try to beat me to it. 'Cicero?'

'Exactly – one of the greatest Romans. Aha, but can you translate it?'

It had always been a tussle, between me and Matthew, to get there first. Even though he was three years older than me, I usually had a fair chance of beating him. But there was no race today.

'*Dum anima est, spes esse dicitur.*'

Brother John beamed down at me. 'Good, good, good! What a splendid morning this is turning out to be! Time for breakfast, and then lessons. I think I shall invite Margery to join us now, instead of pining in her room. What does she do all day, William?'

I shrugged. 'She spends most of the time with Nurse

Joan, reading or sewing or something. She plays Mother's psaltery, but she's not much good at it.'

'Then she has time to join us. What an excellent idea.'

He strode back to the Hall so quickly that I had to run to keep up with him. It made me laugh, because I knew Brother John was doing it deliberately. I tugged the edge of his sleeve. 'Stop! I've worked out the answer to your riddle!'

Brother John spread out his hands questioningly. 'And? What am I?'

'You're a tadpole!'

When I arrived in the library after my breakfast I was surprised to find Margery sitting there already, practising her handwriting with a new goose quill. Brother John leaned over her shoulder, peering at her script.

'You read and write beautifully,' he told her. 'And there's room in your brains for much more than that, Margery. I should like you to learn French and Latin and Greek, like your brother. There's a place for you now, where Matthew used to sit.' He looked across at me. 'It's better with two, isn't it, Will?' His kind brown eyes glittered as he spoke. 'I loved that boy,' he added quietly. 'We will never let him out of our thoughts.'

Then he smiled quickly at us, rubbing his hands together. 'Aha! I have a riddle for you both. This will get your brains moving. I have no sight nor hands, many ribs, a mouth in my middle. I move on one foot, I am swift as the wind. What am I?'

Margery giggled. 'Give us a clue of some sort,' she begged, but the monk shook his head, smiling, and pursed his lips.

'He never tells us the answer,' I warned her. 'We have to work it out for ourselves.'

'Here's an easier one. I am a thief in the darkness. I eat words. What am I?'

He looked brightly from one to the other of us. 'Quick now, quick.' His eyes flicked to the shelves and back again.

'Ah! I know!' Margery shouted. 'A bookworm!'

Brother John clapped his hands together. 'Exactly! And that's what I want *you* to be, Margery. Start chewing now!'

Is it wrong, I wondered? *Is it wrong to laugh and joke, when the rest of the house is so wrapped in grief for Matthew?* I saw how bright Margery's eyes were, and how her white cheeks were flushed with laughter, and how Brother John smiled. I imagined Matthew then, laughing and joking with us all. It made me feel a little better.

Up till that morning, it had always been Matthew and me: playing, riding, reading, joking, teasing, laughing, fighting. We were inseparable. Sometimes Ned Porritt, the stable lad, would be with us, especially when we went riding. And afterwards, when we were cleaning and brushing the horses together, Ned used to scare the wits out of us with ghost stories. And while the horses breathed and stamped in the darkness of the stables, Matthew used to hide in the shadows and suddenly jump out at me, making me yell with fright. And we used to run back to the Hall, clutching each other's sleeves, shrieking with laughter.

Margery was never part of that. She had a friend called Lady Catherine who used to come and stay

8

sometimes, and they used to play together at whatever it is girls play. But then Catherine moved to live in a fine mansion in London, too far away to visit us, and Margery wrote long letters to her. I suppose she was quite lonely, but Matthew and I never invited her to join in our games. But now she was having lessons with me, and I liked it. We shared the huge hole in our lives that Matthew had left. But we couldn't talk about it. We didn't know how. And still Father was hardly ever seen. He spent his time on the shore or in the chapel, praying.

'Come with me and sit with Father in chapel,' Margery sometimes said, but I didn't. I desperately wanted to talk to him, but how could I, when he wouldn't even look at me? It was as if he didn't want to know me any more.

So nobody mentioned Matthew, except Brother John.

'Remember, children, Matthew is in heaven now. There's no need for grief. Pray for his soul, that he may have eternal rest,' he said.

But I couldn't imagine where Matthew's soul might be, except rolling backwards and forward at the bottom of the ocean. How could it ever have rest, when the tides moved it constantly, when fish drifted around it, day after day, night after night?

One day Margery and I went riding together. We cantered over the moors, setting the skylarks skittering away from us. And then, without really meaning to, we came up to the edge of the cliff and looked across the bay. The sea was winter blue and calm, with hardly a fleck of white. We stared down at it.

'Hard to believe,' said Margery at last.

'I know,' I agreed.

'I was watching from up here,' she said slowly. 'Nurse Joan was with me. We saw it happen. It was awful. I saw Father plunging in after you. He dragged you out, and then he went in again. He stayed in the water for ages and ages. Ned brought you back, but Father stayed, walking back into the sea, and running along the shore, and going back in again.'

I couldn't remember any of that, nothing at all. There was an empty place in my mind between clutching at Matthew's sleeve and waking up in my own bed.

'He wishes it was Matthew that he'd saved, not me.'

Margery turned her head slowly towards me, biting her lip. 'Don't be silly,' she said. But she didn't deny it. Then she kicked her pony's side and cantered back down to the house.

The heir to Montague Hall

A couple of months after Matthew's death, Brother John told me that Father wanted to see me after lessons. I couldn't finish my work for trembling. Margery squeezed my hand as I left the library.

I hardly dared to knock at Father's door. I heard a voice telling me to come in, and still I dithered. Stephen saw me waiting and opened the door for me, but I hesitated until I heard Father's voice again.

'Come in, William.'

Although it was still cold outside there was no fire in the room. The light was gloomy. Father was sitting at his chair by the table, reading by candlelight. He didn't look up, and I waited just inside the door. We used to run over to him, Matthew and I, and stand each side of his chair. He used to get up and embrace us both, Matthew first, then me, and laugh at us because Matthew was getting so tall and I had a lot of catching up to do.

'Come over here,' Father said at last. He put his book to one side and gestured to me to come and sit by him. He looked at me, and then he looked away again and cleared his throat. 'We have had a most terrible loss.'

I nodded. I had no idea what I should say about what had happened in the bay; whether I was expected to apologise, or to try to explain, or whether to mention it at all. What I wanted to say was, 'It wasn't my fault. I couldn't help it.' But the words couldn't find their way out.

Father turned back to me and gave me a brief, weak smile.

'You are the heir to Montague Hall now, William. Two years ago I talked to your brother about his responsibilities here. What it meant to be a Montague, and what an honour it is for us to live here. I asked him to bear the name with pride and to carry it into future generations.' He cleared his throat again. 'Now I ask the same of you.'

I wriggled in my chair. I could hardly take in the words.

'You know that long ago your ancestor, Walter Montague, was a favourite of King Edward the second of England?'

I nodded. I had heard the story many times. It was in the fourteenth century, over two hundred years ago. The king gave my ancestor a massive estate stretching across several counties.

'When Montague lost favour with the king he was disgraced. And so his family moved here, to this old hall, which was ancient even then. This is all that remains of the power of Montague. But we have this hall, we have our name and we have this ring to remind us how beloved and wealthy he once was. And we should be proud of that. I wear my name with pride, and I wear my ring with pride.'

Then he took the ring from his finger and reached across for my hand. 'One day this will be yours, William. Look at it now.'

It was a signet ring. When I was little, Father used to let me press it into the hot wax that sealed his letters. It was big and heavy, with a broad band of silver and a high mounted plate, polished almost smooth with the years. It was just possible to see the shape of gryphons twisted round each other and the letters WM engraved into it; the family shield. The same device was carved into the arch over the entrance gate.

'Try it on.'

I did as he said, and slipped the ring onto my finger. It was too big, and slid round so the signet plate was on the inside of my palm.

'One day it will fit you, and it will be yours till you die,' Father promised. 'You will wear it with pride, and men will always honour you.'

'Yes, Father.' I swallowed hard, trying not to think that he had said all this to Matthew, and that the ring, and Montague Hall, and the pride in the name, should rightly belong to him. But Matthew had gone. Matthew was under the sea. Through the silence, I could hear the distant waves rolling, rolling across the sands.

Father rang the bell and asked Stephen to fetch Margery. We waited for her in silence. It was as if Father couldn't think of anything else to say to me. I slipped the ring off my finger and gave it back to him. Absent-mindedly he twisted it round and round in his hands. I noticed how big and strong they were, and how he had to push the ring over his knuckle to fit it back on. Margery came in smiling and breathless from hurrying. She went straight to Father and hugged him as she always used to do. I wished I could have done the same. But I was shy of him now, a bit

13

afraid of him. I didn't feel I had the right to hug him any more.

'I have something to tell you both,' Father said. He bid Margery sit and got up from his chair and moved across the room. Wafts of dust rose from the herb-strewn floor as he walked. It drifted in the pale sunlight that streamed through the window slit. 'I don't feel I can stay here any more.' He stood with his back to us. 'Much as I love Montague Hall, it holds too many memories for me. I can't be happy here. Your uncle Carew, my brother-in-law, has been immensely kind to me. He has offered me a position in court as his secretary. I'm leaving tomorrow.'

To me his words were like a flock of black rooks, but Margery sat up sharply on her stool and clapped her hands together. 'King Henry's court! Will you see the king?'

'Probably.' Father turned round and smiled briefly at her. 'But King Henry won't see me. He won't notice me, anyway. There are hundreds of people working in his various palaces – thousands. I will be very low among His Majesty's attendants. I won't even live in the palace. I'll have to find apartments nearby. But I'm very proud to be working for Lord Carew. He is so very close to the king, such a very, very important man. It's an honour for our family.'

'Oh, but tomorrow's too soon!' Margery jumped down from her stool and clutched his hand. 'We'll be lonely here without you.'

'You won't be alone. Your aunt Carew has kindly offered to come back here for a few months to run the house and to look after you.'

'Oh no!' Margery gasped. She turned her head and looked at me, screwing up her face. 'Not Aunt Carew!'

Neither of us liked our father's sister. She was like a hen, full of bustle and bossiness and cluck. The thought of having to live with her in our house was awful.

'Why does she have to come?' I asked. 'We're all right here, really. There's Brother John and Nurse Joan and Stephen and everyone.'

'Yes, we could manage,' Margery agreed quickly.

Father smiled again. He knew we didn't like her, and that she didn't like us. He didn't like her much himself. He once told us it had been a relief to everyone when she'd married Lord Peter Carew and gone to live in London with him. And when her husband became King Henry's adviser, at last she had everything she could wish for. Her dream had come true.

'Your aunt has plans for you both. Great plans, she says, and I believe her. I've agreed to leave it entirely to her to make all the arrangements she needs.'

Margery and I exchanged anxious glances.

'But we're fine as we are,' I started to say, and then I saw the pain in Father's eyes, and I stopped. We weren't fine at all. We had lost Matthew: laughing, playful, adventurous Matthew. He was gone for ever. Nothing would ever be the same again.

'Leave me now,' Father said. He sighed deeply. 'It's agreed. And that's that.'

Aunt Carew

It was hardly light, and we were still rubbing sleep from our eyes as we stood in the windy courtyard waiting to say goodbye. Ned Porritt was saddling Father's horse and I ran across the yard to help, as I always used to do.

'Shall we go riding after, Master Willim?' Ned asked.

I shrugged. In the old days we would be out for hours, racing each other along the cliff tops and over the scrubby headland. Matthew would always be in front, hollering at us to catch up with him. But I hadn't ridden for weeks now.

Ned smiled slowly. 'Your pony's nearly too small for you. You should be enjoying her, before Mistress Margery takes her off you.'

'I don't much feel like riding today, Ned.'

He nodded. 'You'd feel better if you do. We could have a race! Or we could go along the track with your father for a bit, to set him on his way.'

'I don't think so.' I turned away and walked slowly back to Margery.

Father was in the chapel with Brother John, and they came out together at last, wrapping their warm cloaks around themselves. Father hugged Margery, said goodbye to the servants and thanked Ned for his care with the horse. He hardly seemed to notice me. He and Brother John embraced.

'Goodbye, Cousin,' the monk said. 'God be with you on your journey.'

'Aye,' Father said. 'It's a cold day for travelling. I shall be glad to be in London, away from this damp air.'

His horse was stamping the cobbles, impatient to be off, snorting white air into the cold. Margery clutched my hand and edged me forward, and as if it was a sudden idea that had caught him unawares, Father leaned down from his horse and touched my shoulder.

'Young Master of Montague Hall,' he murmured. 'Take care of it. Take care of your sister.'

'I will, Father.' *Climb down, climb down,* my wild thoughts sang. *I want to hug you, like Margery did.*

But Father kicked his horse on and trotted briskly away, with his man Bailey following behind him. Soon the sea fret had sipped him up, and the muffled sound of hooves died away to nothing. Like one of Ned Porritt's ghosts, he had slipped away from us.

Brother John rubbed his hands as if they were leather shoes to be polished. 'And we don't want chilled bones and cold feet, do we, and runny noses for the rest of the day? Hurry inside now. Warm yourselves by the fire, and we'll have breakfast together, and then lessons. Stories today, from a great Roman poet. Nothing better than stories to take your mind off things.'

We stayed with him until late afternoon, reading aloud and listening in turns, while Brother John chuckled and nodded and smiled encouragement. His eyes shone with the wonder of the old stories we were reciting to him, as if he was hearing them for the first time. 'Don't you love that bit? Isn't it wonderful?' he muttered from time to time, shaking his head in disbelief, and then leaning back, closing his eyes to listen with every part of himself.

Suddenly we were all aware of a flurry in another part of the Hall; a woman's voice raised in sharp anger, feet pattering in the corridor, and the door to the library was flung wide open. Stephen stood egg-eyed with fright in the doorway, and then he was pushed aside. Aunt Carew, in a purple-red velvet gown crusted with pearls, stood in the doorway like a plum tree bursting with ripe fruit.

Brother John closed the book and motioned to us to stand up, but Aunt Carew walked straight past him, brushing him aside as if he were a low-born servant who had strayed into her presence by mistake.

'No one to greet me! Too busy reading!' she snapped. 'READING, if you please! And look at you both, dressed like peasants. Go up to your rooms at once and get the servants to put you into some respectable clothes, fit to greet a lady of the court. And DON'T run. Then come down and give me the courteous welcome I deserve after travelling all hours to this wretched place.'

We hurried out, heads down, stifling the nervous laughter that always seemed to trouble us when we were near Aunt Carew. Brother John started to follow us.

'Stay! I want a word with you,' Aunt Carew told him.

I closed the door behind us. Stephen was standing up against the wall, his arms folded, his head drooping like a dry old sunflower. Aunt Carew would shout at him for that.

'Shall we listen?' I asked.

'Of course!' Margery whispered.

We crept along the corridor and pressed open a door that was used by the servants, leading back to the very room we'd just left. A heavy tapestry hung across the door on the other side to keep the draughts out. It was moth-eaten and frayed in places, and we edged forward so we could just make out the muffled voices and fuzzy shapes of Brother John and Aunt Carew.

'Don't giggle!' I whispered.

Margery pressed her fist to her mouth, red in the face and eyes watering.

'I didn't expect to find you here,' we heard Aunt Carew say.

'It's my home again now,' Brother John said. We could imagine the smile of delight in his voice, and how his eyes would be shining. 'When King Henry closed the monasteries, Robert was good enough to write to me and invite me back to the Hall to tutor the children. Without his help I would be starving and homeless, as you well know.'

'He could be hanged for letting you live here,' she snapped. Beside me Margery gasped, and I clutched her arm. *Hanged!* 'King Henry broke away from the Pope in Rome completely so he could marry Anne Boleyn. He is the head of his own church now, as you very well know. I also know that your monastery refused to disband, refused to accept his supremacy as head of the Church in England. What are your views on that now, Brother John? Do you accept that King Henry is head of the Church in this country?'

'I do not, Cousin. And I never will.'

19

'Then that is treason. If my husband knew you were in this house you would be out on your ear, starving or not.'

'Oh, Elizabeth, Elizabeth.' Brother John's voice had a chuckle bubbling in it. 'We are still cousins. Nothing can change that. I've known you all your life! We were children together; we played and sang together in this very room. You had a pretty voice in those days.'

Aunt Carew huffed impatiently. 'A great deal has happened since then, Brother John. I grew up. I grew away from this draughty miserable barn of a house. I've spent the last five years in the houses of the aristocracy, learning how to be a true lady.'

'Congratulations,' Brother John murmured. 'All your hard work has been rewarded.'

Aunt Carew swung away from him angrily. She could tell that he was mocking her.

'I too worked hard and long to fulfil my dream,' he went on. 'I studied hard and gave my life to God. I looked after the poor and the sick in the monastery. We have lived very different lives, Cousin.'

'I hope you understand that I am deeply ashamed of being a member of this ill-bred Montague family,' Aunt Carew hissed. 'I am a Carew now, and proud of it.'

'Then it was good of you to pay us a visit. I hope your stay will be a pleasant one.' Brother John bowed, his hands clapping together silently behind his back. Perhaps he guessed we were there, watching and listening like a couple of mice behind the tapestry.

'I intend to remain till the summer,' Aunt Carew said.

I groaned. I couldn't help it. This time it was Margery who put a warning hand on my arm. Aunt Carew was very close to the tapestry now. We could hear the swish of her dress as she swept against it.

'My husband is building a magnificent house outside London for when he and I are away from court, and I will live there as soon as it's ready. And then I will be done with the Montagues for ever. Meanwhile, these children have to be protected in case they suffer the same fate as their brother. If I had children of my own I would never let them out of my sight! What was their nurse thinking of?'

'Their father was with them when the boy drowned,' Brother John protested, and was ignored.

'They are not allowed, ever, to go out of the grounds of Montague Hall. No more playing like a farmer's brats. Nor are they allowed, ever, to go into that ludicrous chapel with all its painted wooden dolls and popish frippery. I don't like it.'

'Madam, you overreach yourself.' It was the first time we had heard anger in Brother John's voice.

'Sir, I did not give you leave to interrupt me. For you to be here is to risk my husband's job, if not his life,' she snapped. 'We will not discuss it again. The boy is to study in the mornings, and you may continue to teach him until I can find someone more suitable. You may *not* pray with him.' She shook her head, making the jewels in her hair bob like bluebottles. 'I myself will teach him the manners proper to the nephew of Lord Carew. I have plans for him. Great plans. He will thank me with all his heart if my plans succeed. Likewise the girl. She may *not* study with you. She knows how to

21

read and write, that is enough. I will take on the difficult, near-impossible task of turning her into a lady instead of a plain-faced farmyard wench. My brother is a sick man. He nearly lost his mind when Matthew died. He has handed over the Hall and the children into my care completely.'

'No,' whispered Margery. 'Please, please, no!'

'It is not my wish, but I have agreed to do what I can to provide for William's and Margery's future. I have made plans for them. Now leave me.'

Wait, wait, wait

I hardly saw Margery after that, except at meal times. Brother John taught me for five hours every morning, and Aunt Carew was in and out of the library, listening, watching, frowning, scolding. There was no laughter there any more, though Brother John's eyes still shone with smiles whenever she wasn't looking, and he chirruped like a bird set free as soon as she went out of the room.

And in the afternoons, well, it was her turn. She turned me into a nobleman. She drilled me as if I was about to become a soldier and go into battle, but instead of marching and fighting with all the thrilling sound of trumpets and drums, I had to learn to bow and simper, to smile sickly smiles when nothing funny was being said, to praise her beauty – which was all in her imagination – and her charms and her massive gowns, and I had to watch her at all times. I had to learn to dance; slow elegant dances instead of the sweating jigs and reels we loved so much when the local people came to us for Christmas celebrations. I had to sing dreary court ballads about soppy love, instead of hearty village songs. When I went wrong or forgot or went into a daydream she slapped my face till it stung hot and sore. I had to murmur, never shout; never speak unless I was spoken to or was ordering the servants. I had to walk as if there were eggshells under my feet – stroll, just stroll – and never, ever run.

The worst thing was that I had to treat the servants like servants instead of like members of the family. I was never to chat to them or listen to Nurse Joan's gossip or sit in the kitchen eating warm tarts and hearing the cook's songs and the kitchen maid's old stories.

'Ignore them. At all times ignore them,' my aunt insisted. 'Never speak to them unless you are asking for something. They are low born. Never forget that, or they will take advantage of you.'

'Not even Ned?' I asked. 'He's my friend.'

She snapped round at me then, flashing her hand across my cheek. 'Servants are never friends.'

So I wasn't allowed to spend time in the stables with Ned Porritt, and when I went riding he would get my pony ready on his own while I stood and waited. As I mounted, he would smile his slow smile at me as if to say, *Let's race together! Let's have some fun!* and I wasn't even allowed to smile back. Dear old Nurse Joan was told to stay with Margery now, and I was given ancient Stephen, who could hardly walk up the stairs any more without creaking and huffing. He really belonged next to the fire in the kitchen, turning the spit and dreaming as he watched the yellow stars dancing in the logs in the great hearth. He had to wash me and dress me and he was so much of a snail that I was always late and always being told off. And his hands were as cold as ice too.

And then the day came when my aunt said I was ready.

'What for, Aunt Carew?'

'For life!' she snapped. 'Don't let me down, boy. Don't make the Carews ashamed of you.'

There were no more lessons with Brother John after that day. I had no idea where he was. I couldn't find him anywhere in the house. The chapel was locked, as it had been since Aunt Carew came, and his room was empty. I couldn't believe that he would go, just walk away, without saying goodbye to me.

In a panic I ran to find my aunt, and got told off for not walking.

'You cause a flurry of dust, boy, wherever you go,' she said, shuddering.

'Aunt Carew, where's Brother John?'

'His services are no longer required,' she answered sharply. 'Go to your room, William, and wait.'

I asked Stephen if he knew where Brother John was, and he stood with his long hands pressed together as if he was praying and said, 'I'm not allowed to say, sir.'

I ran to Joan, desperate now, and she shook her head, and pressed her lips together.

'Joan, where is he?' I demanded.

'I can't say, Willim. He's gone, that's all I know. Sent away by your aunt during the night. Told never to come back.'

'But he hasn't got anywhere to go!'

'No, Master, you're right. But what does she care about that?' Joan pursed her lips. 'And I would do as she says and wait in your room, or I'll be sent off next.'

But I couldn't give up. Not yet. Margery and I ran out along the lane, searching for a sign of him. Surely we could catch up with him and bring him back home.

'It's not fair,' Margery panted, jogging just behind me. 'He was brought up here too. He's a Montague, like us. It's his home as much as hers.'

'And she doesn't even like it,' I agreed. 'But nothing Aunt Carew does is fair, is it?'

Soon we heard the sound of hooves pounding along the lane, and turned round to see Ned Porritt cantering behind us on my pony.

'You've to come home, Master Willim,' he shouted. His voice bounced up and down with him. 'Your aunt has sent me to find you, and if I don't I'm in for a beating, so please come.'

He cantered up to us and slid down from the pony. 'Master Willim, Mistress Margery, why didn't you come to me first?' he whispered. He untied a piece of sacking from his belt. 'I don't know where Brother John is, but he left these in the stable and I found them this morning. I know they're for you.'

He fumbled inside the sacking and brought out two small bundles, which he slid into our hands. All the time glancing furtively over his shoulder as if he expected to see Aunt Carew quivering down the lane after him. One of the items was a wooden rosary. I had watched Brother John make it himself, fashioning little round beads out of the wood from a fallen hazel tree, polishing each one till it shone like a nut and threading them onto a lace of leather. He drew a tiny knot behind each bead, so we could count our prayers. He fastened a little carved figure of Christ on the cross where the ends of the lace tied together. I knew it was meant for me. The other present was a tiny carved statue of the

Virgin Mary, in a painted-blue gown. It just fitted into Margery's palm. She gazed down at it and closed up her hand, hiding it.

'I'll keep her for ever,' she said.

'Come home now,' Ned pleaded. 'You two ride the pony, and I'll walk.'

So we went with him, and I did as I had been told and went straight up to my room and waited. I sat gazing out of the window slit across the yard. I could hear the voice of the sea, sighing, growling. It spoke to me all the time. *Wait, wait, wait*. Sometimes I would hear a long, sad cry. Was it one of those great, white sea birds, or was it the voice of my brother, rising out of the bed of the ocean?

I spent three days waiting, just waiting, for my life to begin. And then I heard the sound of a horse trotting up the lane, and saw Ned running out to take the reins. It wasn't until the rider dismounted and turned towards the Hall that I recognised who it was.

'Father! Father's come home!' I heard Margery shouting down the corridor, and then heard my aunt hissing at her to be quiet, 'And walk!'

Slowly, as if the day was too hot for us to possibly move any faster, though in fact it was sharp with April glitter, we sauntered together down the stairs and into the yard.

Father hugged Margery and kissed her and told her how beautiful she was getting, and she laughed and twirled for him. He bowed slightly to his sister, who just bent her head and tilted her mouth in the polite simper she had taught me to make. And then Father turned to me, as I stood waiting and watching. He said nothing,

27

nothing at all, but clutched me quickly to him till I could feel the warm air of his breath on my hair. As I lifted up my arms to hug him properly he stood away again at arm's length.

'I could swear you've grown!'

'Not at all,' said Aunt Carew. 'I have taught him to stand upright as he should, proud and tall, instead of slouching round like a farmer carrying hay on his shoulders.'

'Are you back with us for ever now?' Margery asked, standing on tiptoe with her hands behind her back, as she used to do when she was little and wanting a special treat. '*Please!* Say you are!'

'Of course he isn't,' Aunt Carew said. 'My husband will need him back in court. He has work to do. Your father is staying here overnight to rest, and then tomorrow he and William are leaving for London.'

'For London?' I gasped, staring at my father.

'Don't gape, boy.' Aunt Carew lifted her hands in despair. 'You look like a fish. Of course you're going to London. Haven't I told you? You're ready now for life!'

London

'Please don't go!' my sister Margery shouted the next morning. She was following me down the track from our house with mud on her skirt and her hair loose and tousled over her shoulders. 'Don't leave me here alone!'

'I have plans for you too, ma'mselle!' my aunt said, striding after her. She dug her bony fingers into Margery's shoulders. 'Put your coif back on, and come inside at once.'

I looked back, just once. I saw Margery being hauled into the house by my aunt, and Nurse Joan clucking and flapping behind her. I saw Ned turn away from us, his cap in his hand, and trudge to the stables. I saw the old crumbling walls of my home, and beyond it, the sea, stretching blue and deep and far, far away into the line where it became shimmering sky, and then I turned back and kicked my pony into a trot till I caught up with Father.

'Why do I have to go to London?' I asked him.

He shook his head. 'You keep asking me that and I've told you, Lord Carew asked me to bring you to see him. That's all I know.'

'But why? What does he want?' I asked anxiously.

'He's my employer, he doesn't give me reasons!

29

That's what it's like at court. I have no idea what plans he has for you.'

'But have I got to stay?'

'I don't know. Probably.'

He retreated into his silence, and I gazed around me, too miserable to enjoy the ride with him. The thought of leaving my home and Margery behind was unbearable. We'd never been separated before. We were closer than ever these days. I still didn't know what had happened to Brother John. Perhaps I would never see him again. And as we left the last glimpse of the sea behind, I thought of Matthew, still lost somewhere under the waves. I felt as if I was abandoning him now, for ever.

We rode on through green, rolling hills covered in trees. The birds sang different songs now, I noticed. I had left the gulls and the curlews behind.

'Is it like this in London?' I asked. 'Green, and trees everywhere?'

Father gave a short laugh. 'Not at all. You'll find it interesting, William. It's an adventure for you. Think of it that way.'

'Do you like it, Father?'

'No,' he said shortly. 'I can't say I do. But that's not the point. I have an important job, and that matters to me.'

'I wish we didn't have to do things that Uncle Carew tells us to do,' I muttered, but if Father heard me he didn't say anything. I had no idea then, that the nearer you got to the king and his court, the less you could call your life your own.

'Father, do you know where Brother John is?'

He shook his head. 'My sister tells me she has provided for him. I think he will be tutoring in another house somewhere.' I heard the trail of doubt in his voice, and knew he was only guessing.

'He didn't even say goodbye to me. He wouldn't leave without saying goodbye.'

'Then perhaps he has only gone away for a few days. He'll be back soon, and Margery will tell him where you've gone.'

'If he does come back, I'll write to him,' I said. 'In Latin.'

We spent that night at the house of my father's closest friend, Lord de Crecy, although His Lordship wasn't there. He was at the king's palace in Greenwich, where he was a counsellor.

'He is a very dear friend,' my father told me. 'If anything ever happens to me, you should go to him for help.'

'Why should anything happen to you?' I asked, puzzled, and suddenly afraid. 'What kind of thing?'

But Father refused to say anything else. I slept badly, aching from spending so long in the saddle and in the cold fresh air, and fretting over everything. I was quite glad to be setting off again next morning. We spent a few more nights in manor houses on the way, and people always asked Father what it was like to attend court, and what he thought of the king.

'I don't see much of him,' he said. 'I'm not a courtier, after all, I'm in the service of one.' He never wanted people to think he was important, and that he attended one of the highest courtiers of all, and had his own study in the Palace of Westminster.

31

'But you do see His Majesty sometimes?' he was asked by the lady of one of the houses. She looked as if she would eat him, she was so keen to hear his news.

'Oh yes. He's a splendid king. Magnificent.'

'But he has a fierce temper, we've heard? Everybody's afraid of him!'

And Father just nodded. 'He has few favourites.'

'Favourites?' I asked, joining in. 'What does that mean?'

My father frowned. 'He takes a liking to people sometimes, and embarrasses them with fine presents. He's very generous.'

'And then chops their heads off!' the lady sniggered.

'So I hear,' my father said, rising abruptly from his chair. He bowed politely to the lady and went to his room.

And that was all he would say. Even though I asked him to tell me more about King Henry, he would just say things like, 'He's a fine tennis player,' or 'His banquets are wonderful.' He would never talk about the king himself, which was a great disappointment to me. For most of the time we trotted along in silence. I went over Latin verbs in my head. I knew some of the poetry that Brother John had taught me by heart, and it was a kind of comfort to think them to myself. I could hear his warm, kind voice and imagine his bright-eyed smile, and his chuckle of delight when he was pleased with me. And I had his rosary, snug in my pocket. *Where was he?*

'I have no sight nor hands, many ribs, a mouth in my middle,' I said aloud, remembering one of his riddles. 'I move on one foot, I am swift as the wind. What am I?'

Disappointingly, my father said nothing.

'How far now?' I asked him, after nearly a week of riding. My poor old pony was as tired as I was.

'Very soon,' Father said. 'Listen!'

He halted his horse, and so did I, and we heard London on the wind. We heard the mad ding-dong of hundreds of church bells, and the thunder of carriage wheels, and the sound of distant shouting. We climbed a hill and looked down, and the din of the city rose up to us: hammering, bleating, chiming, babbling.

'Is it always as noisy as this?' I asked.

'Oh yes. Sometimes when you're in the middle of it all you can't hear your own voice. But at night, the city sleeps. Then it's quiet.'

I looked down at the spires and turrets and the cram of buildings with black smoke hanging over the roofs, the twisting river bustling with boats and the swarm of people like maggots on a carcass, and my stomach churned with misery.

'Let's go back now,' I begged, and even as I said it, I heard Matthew's voice in my head, 'Onward, ever onward.' So I followed Father down the slope, and soon we came to hovels and sheds where people were selling all kinds of things; wooden spoons and strings of onions, dried herbs and cooking pots, grubby bits of clothing. Ragged children ran up to us, tugging at the reins of the horses and the hems of our clothes. Dirty hands stretched up, pleading for money, for food, for anything. Now I could *smell* London too. It was the smell of sweat and dirt and rot.

We rode on into the dark, cramped alleys of leaning houses. Smoke and cooking fumes billowed round us, choking us with a stink of hot grease and damp wood.

I felt stifled, as if the air had been snatched away from me.

'I don't like it,' I said. 'Father, I can't stay here. I can't breathe. Can I go home soon?' I looked round, panicking. I wouldn't be able to run in the fields, or fish by the stream, or let my pony gallop into the wind. I would never ever hear the sea. 'Please, don't make me stay here. Can we go home now?'

'You're not a child any more,' my father said, and that was all.

'You are to meet the king today'

My father lodged just inside the city walls, at the top of a tall thatched house with tiny, latticed windows. It looked out onto a large yard, but the sounds of hundreds of horses trotting by on the cobbled road beyond kept me awake till well after dark and woke me again at first light, along with the church bells and the cries of the watchman shouting the hour. I didn't want to know what time it was. I wanted to sleep and to wake up at home again. I had a headache from the stench of dung and other foul smells rising from the streets. I felt sick and miserable, and I couldn't touch any of the cold meats and cheeses that had been laid out for me by the goodwife of the house.

My father made me kneel and say our morning prayers with him, and it was comforting because it reminded me of the time before Matthew died, when we always prayed together in our little chapel. Matthew used to pull faces at me behind his splayed fingers, and I would be squirming with hidden giggles. But as soon as the goodwife knocked at the door and said that Lord Carew and another gentleman were below, I began to feel nervous again. I could hear someone snorting like a horse as they climbed the narrow stairs. I'd never met my uncle before, and I was surprised to see how thin he was, and grey, not at all plump and colourful like my aunt. He was all of a quiver, with dry, crackling hands that he stroked together all the time, one palm flat against the other as if there was always an unseen speck of dust to be wiped away. His eyes were sharp and bright as a bird's, and he flicked his head from side to side, noticing everything in the room, and not liking any of it.

He had brought another man with him; a tailor, whose face was pitted with smallpox scars. He had a basket of heavy, fancy clothes with him, and he darted round me sizing me up with his hands and his eyes, then sorted through the basket and brought out an embroidered doublet of green velvet.

'This should fit you well, young sir,' he said to me. 'And it's a good colour. His Majesty is very fond of green.'

'His Majesty?' I swung round to look at my father, but the tailor tutted and pulled me back so he could lace the sleeves on. The doublet was heavy on me, and had long slashes in the sleeves, so my linen shirt gleamed through them as I moved. Over that he fitted on an even-fancier jerkin with puffed sleeves. Then came the baggy upper hose, which was pleated and panelled round my knees, and last of all my nether hose. What a time it took to dress me! I had never worn such a fancy doublet and hose in my life. I wondered what Margery would have thought of me in them. Well, she would have giggled, I know that much. At last, after much snorting and sweating, the tailor had finished lacing me up. At my uncle's command I turned awkwardly to be admired.

'A little stitch or two on the shoulder, and he'll be perfect!' The tailor clapped his hands as if I'd just done one of Aunt Carew's dances for him. 'What do you think, My Lord?'

'He looks well enough in them.'

'Thank you, Uncle Carew.' I bowed my head slightly, as Aunt Carew had taught me.

'Make sure you earn them. These clothes have cost me as much as your father's salary for the year.'

My father bowed and thanked him. I flushed. I was hot enough already, and now I was embarrassed too.

'How will I earn them?' I asked my uncle.

'By pleasing the king.'

I stared round at my father again. He looked as tense as I felt.

'Yes,' he said. 'Your uncle has just told me that you are to meet the king today.'

'I've mentioned you to His Majesty,' my uncle said, wiping his palms together. 'In fact, I have made him a gift of a leather quiver in order that I may present you to him. He has accepted my gift. Now it's up to you. If he speaks to you, think first before you answer. Put your hat on – ah yes, I like that feather. Your hair looks good cut that way. It's the same colour as King Henry's. He'll like that.'

'I've heard the king's as bald as an egg now under that floppy hat of his,' the tailor muttered, pins like hedgehog bristles between his teeth as he altered the doublet to fit me. But he said it too low for my uncle to hear him.

Uncle Carew was talking softly to my father, but when the tailor had finished with me and I was dressed up in all the rich clothes again, he walked round and round me as if I was a maypole, murmuring instructions to me.

'Hat off. Bow, boy. Lower, lower. Nose towards your knee. Up. Straight. Remember to remain standing in His Majesty's presence. Do you hear me?'

'Yes, Uncle Carew.'

'What is my proper address? Again!'

'Yes, My Lord.'

'If I were the king?'

I took off my hat and bowed. My nose squashed against my knee. When I came up again, my head was spinning. 'Yes, Your Majesty.'

At last he and the tailor left us alone. I was more nervous than ever by then, fidgety as a mouse in a bed of straw. My head fizzed with questions, but my father seemed as anxious as I was and couldn't answer any of them.

'It's just an idea of your aunt Carew's,' he kept saying. He twisted his ring, rubbing the engraved seal on it as if it were a good-luck charm. 'Remember, Lord Carew has no family of his own – no son to present to the king. Families are very powerful here. If he can get you a situation in court, it would be very important for him.'

'What kind of situation?'

'I'm not sure,' my father frowned. 'Lord Carew hasn't told me. You'll find out, if you get it.'

While we were waiting for the time to go down to the river and take a wherry along the Thames to the Palace of Westminster, my father talked to me in Latin, in case the king wanted to hear me. I answered mechanically, and when he switched to Greek and then to French I followed without even thinking about it. But I couldn't concentrate on lessons that morning. Who would have done, when they were about to meet the king?

I was distracted by a rumbling in the yard below, and went to the little casement window and pushed it open. Beyond the yard people were gathering on a bald bit of common land, all shouting lustily. They were pushing and jostling with no manners or care for each other, as if something exciting was going to happen. Some dogs were brought through, bright-eyed and dribbling, snapping at each other, closely held by four men. Then a gate near the yard opened and a large flop-bellied bear loped out, with two men hanging onto the chain around his neck. They fastened the chain to a ring on a post, and the bear looked about curiously at the crowd, as if he was hoping someone would step out and give him some breakfast.

'There's going to be a baiting,' my father said. 'I'm afraid they often hold them here. Why don't you watch, William? It will help to pass the time.'

'His blood's up,' a woman in the crowd shouted. 'You'll see some sport now!'

A great shout went up as the bear suddenly lunged at one of the men, scoring his face with stripes of blood. The man screamed, people yelled, but the bear couldn't get near enough to attack the man again because of its chain. The four dogs strained on their leashes, snarling and yelping, cowering with their ears flattened in fright, their teeth grinning and wet. The huge bear dropped down onto all fours, watching them, backing off as they came grizzling towards him.

39

'Go for them! Go for them!' my father shouted.

'I don't want to watch,' I said. 'It's horrible.'

He looked down at me. 'Oh yes, it's horrible, all right,' he said. 'But you get used to it. I want him to rise up again like a man, not cower like a beast! Don't you?'

But I was frightened of the bear, even from up at the top of the house. When we were little, Margery and I used to pretend there were bears in our garden, but I had never actually seen one before. I hated the way the dogs taunted him like that, making him roll and sway on his great black paws. I hated the screams and the roars and the yells of the people and the animals. I hated London, with its sweating crowds, its foul air and its noisy streets. With all my heart I longed to be back home again with my sister, riding in the long grass around our ancient manor house. I closed my eyes, willing myself there, and it was as if I could smell the yellow gorse and the meadow flowers, and hear the skylark spilling its song. I remembered right back to the time when my mother was still alive, when Margery and I were both little and Matthew would have been out riding or hunting with my father. Margery was hiding from me, and my mother was sitting sewing on the grass, laughing at my frustration because I couldn't find my sister, and shaking her head when I asked her to give me a clue.

'Margery, Margery, where can you be?' I shouted, stamping my foot in annoyance. It was a game we played over and over again, like a rhyming nursery song. She always found somewhere different to hide. She answered at long last, 'I'm hiding under the willow tree.'

'Margery, Margery, why are you there?'

'I'm scared of the dragon,' she would say.

'I'm scared of the bear,' I finished, and she crawled out of her hiding place and laughed up at me. My mother hugged us both then, and said there was nothing for us to be afraid of in our lives, nothing at all.

A year later my mother died. She had been to stay with some friends, and some visitors from London had arrived and brought the city sweating sickness with them. My mother never even came home again. I was five, Margery was six and Matthew was eight. I can remember the house of grief we lived in then, and how my father cried and cried, and how frightened I was.

The roars of the crowd grew louder, and suddenly I was back in the awful present. The great bear lunged at another man and suddenly there was a spill of crimson blood on the earth. My father tensed beside me and shouted, 'Kill him! Set the dogs on him!' I didn't know my gentle father then; I didn't understand why he wanted the bear to die. The dogs were unleashed with a great snarling and whining, and the people yelling at them like a rising storm. I couldn't help watching now; surely the bear would rally and give us a good fight?

'Fight! Fight back!' I shouted, and my father laughed and put his hand across my shoulder. It felt good then, to be with him again, to be watching this together. Now I felt sorry for the bear, I didn't want to see him die. But I didn't want to leave my father's side.

I could see a boy and girl squirming their way to the front, just common ragged children, a brother and sister laughing together, and I thought of Margery again. I wanted her to be with us too. I turned my face up to my father, and he looked down at me.

'Whatever it is that Lord Carew is asking of you, do it, William. Do it, for my sake.'

And I felt a warm rush like a river inside me, because my father had asked me to do something for him. I wanted him to be as proud of me as he was of Matthew. I would do it, whatever it was.

'I will, Father,' I said. 'I promise.'

The golden sun of His Majesty

When it was time, we had to walk down a slippery catwalk over the mud to the wherry. The river was grey and moody, bustling with crisscrossing boats piled with fruit and fish. As we moved forward to step onto the wherry I froze in terror; we were to float on that water, that grey churning restless water, and though my sense told me it was only a river, my terrified mind told me it was the sea, and that at any moment huge waves would rear their heads like monsters from the deep and drag me down the way they had dragged Matthew and me down. I tried to turn away, but there was no going back, and no staying there; I was pushed from behind, I was being shouted at by the wherrymen. I had to step into the boat and cling onto the sides with my knucklebones white and bulging and my eyes shut tight. Flies danced over our heads, the smell of salt was stinging and strong. I wanted to be sick.

When we reached Westminster steps I was the first off the boat, and then I remembered why we had come and was low with nerves again. I looked up at my father but he just nodded to me to go on, and my knees nearly gave way with fright. I floated, rather than walked, up the steps away from the river, and into the Great Hall of Westminster Palace.

I had never been in such a huge, noisy, colourful place before. There was a roar of sound as we went in; a terrible echoing din that made me want to cover my ears. Hundreds of voices spiralled round: laughter and gossip, high chattering of children, music from trumpets and tabors, and the whining and yapping of dogs. Crowds of courtiers strolled around in their bright satins and velvets, nodding their fine feathered hats at each other. The ladies wore gowns the colours of apples and raspberries, lavender and mint, forget-me-nots and dog roses. Everyone smelled of the spiced pomanders they carried. Servants in green livery held up branches of candles, and the golden light danced and flickered on the wood-panelled walls.

I gazed round and up, and noticed that painted angels with folded wings were carved into the vaulted ceiling. I felt calmer when I looked up at them. Maybe my guardian angel was among them, protecting me. I pulled my rosary beads out of my purse and touched the little crucifix to my lips for luck.

'What are you doing? Not saying your prayers to the rosary? The king doesn't allow it!' my father gasped, closing his hand quickly over mine. I scrunched the beads into my fist, and tried to cram them back into the purse on my belt, but his fingers worked into my palm and took the traitor beads away from me. My hands were shaking, and I felt sick and dizzy with fear. 'I'll run out and throw it in the river,' he whispered, bending down to me so his breath was hot in my ear, but before he could move away there was a sudden deafening blaring of trumpets and beating of drums. My father clutched my shoulder.

Everyone fell silent and turned to look to the far end of the hall.

In walked His Majesty King Henry the eighth of England. Like all the men, I took off my hat and bowed. All the ladies dropped deep, low curtsies, and rose like the waves in a windswept meadow of flowers. King Henry stood for a moment to let us all gaze on his glory. His jewels flashed in the candlelight, his golden clothes shimmered as if they were made of the sun. He was the tallest man in the room, the biggest, proudest, fiercest man in Europe.

And I was there, standing in his court.

My uncle Carew sidled up to us through the crowds of courtiers, nodded at my father and then pecked his face towards me.

'Come on, boy. Follow me, do as you're told, look pleased to be here!'

I clutched my father's arm in panic. It was too soon, much too soon, but my father loosened my grip and patted me on the shoulder. I put on the simper that my aunt had taught me, and followed Lord Carew through the crowd to the front dais, right up to where King Henry was now sitting on a massive carved golden chair. I felt as if my legs had lost their bones and my shoes were filled with pads of wool instead of feet. My stomach was quaking with fright. I had no idea what was expected of me. But at least I had been taught courtly manners by my aunt. I knew how to bow and ingratiate myself, how to look interested, how to say clever things to make people smile.

Lord Carew bowed deeply, and I did the same.

'Your Majesty, allow me to introduce my nephew, William Carew,' my uncle said.

I gasped. *But I'm not a Carew, I'm William Montague!* I wanted to say, but didn't dare. My tongue was stuck to the roof of my mouth, my lips were dry. My uncle cleared his throat. 'He is lately of Montague Hall, Your Majesty,' he added.

The king nodded. He studied me closely, and I felt myself sweating with embarrassment. Then he smiled.

'A fine-looking boy,' he said. 'Come closer, William Carew. I believe your golden-red hair is the same colour as my own!' He laughed with a deep, pleasant chuckle, and all the people round him laughed too.

I bowed very deeply so I could have a little think about this. What would Aunt Carew have expected me to say? When I came up again I said, 'The golden sun of His Majesty touches the lowest of his subjects and causes them to glow in his presence.'

He liked that. He loved to be flattered; everyone knew that. He put his head to one side and beamed at me so his fat cheeks bulged and his sparkling eyes disappeared into his head like currants in a pudding. I felt a warm glow of pleasure, and stopped trembling at last. My uncle Carew patted his hands together in silent applause.

Four other boys were led up by their fathers to meet the king. They were all highborn nobles like my uncle, Lord Peter Carew. One of the boys was introduced as Lord Percy Howard. He came from one of the most powerful families in the country. Even I knew that. He was older than me, and very sure of himself. He already had a pale fluff of hair on his chin, reminding me of a newly hatched duckling. He was tall and thin-faced with a swaggering walk and an unpleasantly curling lip. He had heard what I said to the king, and sneered at me, but I didn't care. I was dizzy with pride. When he came up from his bow of introduction he sleeked aside his own lank hair, which was the colour of candle wax, and made a long speech to the king in perfect Latin. It was a little too fast for me to understand, and even the king frowned slightly as he tried to catch it. Then His Majesty clapped his hands together.

'Aha! *Tu regere imperio populos, Romane, memento* ... Virgil, my favourite poet! You are a scholar, young Howard. Who will translate?'

I gave him a bright smile and opened my mouth to speak, but Lord Percy chimed in immediately with, 'You, Roman, remember to rule the peoples with your power ... ' What a gabble he made of it too. A turkey-cock would have made a better speech. I could have quoted a beautiful Virgil poem to the king's glory, and I would have said it slowly and meaningfully, too. I glanced at my uncle, wondering whether I should recite it as it should be done, but he shook his head, his lips pursed, his eyes glinting. It was too late. I had lost my chance.

One of the other boys piped up in Greek, and Percy turned to the boy, finished his speech off for him and bowed. Flop, the waxy strands fell across his face, the thin fingers brushed them back, and flop they went again. The other boys bowed and spoke, smiled, and stepped back as King Henry nodded curtly at them and flapped his hand as if he was shaking flies away.

Then he sat back with his arms folded. He looked at

47

me, and looked at Percy Howard, and I realised then that this was some kind of a contest, that the competitors had been narrowed down and that it was now between the two of us. Lord Percy's face had turned white. Whatever it was that we were there for, I realised, he hadn't expected any competition. He drew in his breath sharply and slid a cold glance at me. And because His Majesty had smiled at me, I suddenly wanted to win; whatever the job was, I wanted it to be mine.

'I have a yen for music,' King Henry said. 'Can either of you young men catch this tune for me?'

He began to sing, in a full, pleasant voice, and the ladies around him smiled and made their long gowns sway. A lutenist sitting with the musicians quietly plucked a few notes and then picked up the tune, and with a flourish, the king stopped singing and held out his hand towards us. I had never heard the tune before, but some starling inside me picked it up and sang it in my head note for note, and some nightingale filled my throat with sweetness, and I sang words that I hardly understood, in praise of His Majesty the King of England.

The secret thought

My dear sister, Margery, I wrote. My fine goose quill scratched across the paper. *You will never guess what has happened to me. I am in the service of His Majesty the King! I am Prince Edward's page!*

I paused, still too dazed to really believe it was true. I could remember the day we heard that Prince Edward had been born, and how the whole country had celebrated because King Henry's third wife, Queen Jane, had given him a son at last, an heir to the throne. The bells had rung wildly from every church, the guns had fired from every hill, the greens and lanes and towns and cities had streamed with cheering people. We had held a party for all the farmers and land workers and villagers. Ned Porritt had danced with my sister and made her blush. Matthew had helped himself to more wine than we were allowed, and was found as green as a marrow in the laundry basket.

I carried on writing.

The prince is eighteen months old now, and I'm living in his home, at the palace of Hampton Court. It is the most beautiful place I have ever seen. I think King Henry must be the richest man in the world to have so much gold and silver and jewels in every single thing he owns. Each room glitters like the sun. They say this is his favourite of all his palaces. I get lost every time I leave the prince's suite – there are so many rooms and corridors.

This is the first chance I've had to write to you; I have had permission from Mother Jack, the prince's wet nurse. She gave me the paper and the quill, and she says she doesn't need me for an hour or so, as the prince is having his afternoon rest.

I do miss home. But I love living in a palace. I love being Prince Edward's special servant, his page. He has so many servants and attendants: physicians, musicians, litter-bearers, jugglers, all puffed up like cockerels in their fancy doublets! (I suppose I must look like a cockerel too, in the doublet my uncle bought for me. I can't undo it myself, or lift it off my shoulders. I can't even bend down in it to do up the points on my shoes!) I love everything. And most of all—

But no, I couldn't tell her that bit. That was a secret thought. Much as I wanted to, it surely couldn't be spoken, not even in a letter.

In the adjoining room I could hear Mother Jack singing a lullaby to the little prince. He had many servants, but I thought I must be the most important, even more than Mother Jack. That's what he called her, in his jumbled nonsense speech. She was really Mistress Jackson. She was very strange, but I liked her. She had a little button of a nose, and grey, grey eyes like a pigeon's wing, and she loved to daydream and to tell gruesome stories. I had to take orders from her, and when she asked me to do something, I had to do it immediately. No loitering, no gossiping with the other servants. The only person I was allowed to think about was Prince Edward.

Before I had left London, Uncle Carew had made sure I understood how important my work was going to be.

'You are probably the most important boy in this country,' he told me.

I went hot with sweat at the thought of it.

'Apart from the prince himself,' he added. 'You have a magnificent future in front of you. Your aunt will be proud, if you behave exactly as you should.'

'I will, My Lord,' I said, and bowed. He had made me afraid again. I was always afraid of him.

'But beware: if you do anything wrong, you will be disgraced; your entire family will be disgraced. Including my wife, including me. Do you understand?' He was shouting now, pacing up and down his study, booming the words out to me so they echoed and rang. 'Never, never do anything to displease His Majesty. And never, never refer to the Pope as the head of the Church. His Majesty forbids it!' His voice rose to a fury, his mouth was a square, snapping hole; his eyes were black, fierce lights. I covered my ears. I wanted to turn and run, run back to Montague Hall; to be safe again with Margery and Nurse Joan.

'Go, William.' He dismissed me with a curt nod of his head. 'Do your work with pride.'

I would never dare to do anything to make him angry, that was for sure. But I had already made someone else angry, and that was Lord Percy Howard. He had really thought he would be chosen. So had everybody. He waited for me in a corridor, that day when the king chose me.

'That job is mine!' he hissed, and all the time he was

smiling so that if anyone saw him they would think we were joking or something. 'My uncle is the most powerful man in England. He promised me I would be Prince Edward's page! I have been groomed for it! What right have you to take it from me? Your father is nothing but a common scribe.'

I had no idea what to say to him. I tried to walk away but he grabbed hold of my wrist and grasped it so tightly that it made my eyes sting. He let go of me at last, just dropped my hand as if I was a soiled shirt to be washed by a servant.

'I'll be watching you,' he warned. 'I have friends and cousins everywhere, watching you. Everywhere. If you put one foot wrong, I'll know about it, be sure of that. If you displease His Majesty he'll probably shut you away for the rest of your days. If you're lucky.'

I wanted to punch his bony aristocratic nose, but I held my tongue and nodded to him as if I had just had the most pleasant conversation with him, and walked away. As soon as I was out of his sight my legs nearly collapsed from under me.

I read through my letter to Margery again. I wouldn't dare to write down any of that, in case it was intercepted by my uncle. I stood up and stretched my arms. It was mid-afternoon, and the entire palace was quiet, waiting for the prince to wake up and for the business of the day to begin again. Everything that any of the hundreds of people in the whole of that palace did, was for the baby prince. Nothing else mattered. Nobody else mattered. I walked round the room, watching my shadow as it followed me along the walls.

Round again, and round again. I went back to my letter, read it through, and carried on.

Hampton Court is on the banks of the River Thames, quite a long way from the city. I'm so glad to be out of London. I felt as if I was in a stinking prison when I was there. Mother Jack says the king is afraid to bring his little son into the city in case he catches a disease. Plague and sweating sickness are the worst, but there are plenty more. Mother Jack loves to tell me that people drop dead like flies in London. Like summer flies, she says. The streets are full of rotting corpses.

I believe her, Margery. The whole city reeks. Rotting corpses, yes, I'm sure of it. And horse dung everywhere, and the gutters running with slops.

But Hampton Court is washed and scrubbed three times a day!

The gardens stretch right down to the river, and peacocks strut about like little King Henrys on the lawns. I like the river here because it's clean and fresh, and it's teeming with fish. You should see them, leaping for flies! But I don't like the peacocks. Mother Jack says Queen Anne Boleyn hated them when she was here because of the way they screech. I'd rather have our fussy old hens any day. And there are monkeys here too! They're like little dogs, but they have flat faces, a bit like people! They chatter and squeal all the time. I don't like them much either, but they're quite funny.

Inside, the whole palace is painted with gold and rich colours, especially the prince's rooms. All the walls are covered with tapestries of hunting scenes and stories from the Bible, and they're all new and bright. They make ours look as scruffy as hairy dogs. Doors are hidden behind them, like ours, so servants can just slide in and out of sight when they're called for. Do you remember the day we hid and listened to Aunt Carew and Brother John talking?

Oh, Margery, where is Brother John now? Do you have any news of him? As soon as you hear anything, let me know, won't you? I hope he's with a kind family, and that the children enjoy his riddles!

I stretched my fingers. I thought about our little chapel at home, and Brother John lighting the candles before Mass. I loved the way the flames used to whisper, as if they were praying with us. I loved the painted wooden statues of the Holy Family and the saints. My favourite was Jesus, in his red robe. You could see his wounded heart. Margery's favourite was the Virgin Mary in her blue gown, with the chubby baby Jesus in her arms. And Matthew – Matthew loved the wall painting of Saint Nicholas in his boat, and the black sea rocking round him.

The royal chapel at Hampton Court was twenty times bigger than ours. No statues, no paintings. Its ceiling was as blue as the summer sky, and sprinkled with golden veins and hundreds of golden stars. Heaven must be like that, I thought, gazing up at it. I was terrified of being accused of not accepting King Henry's reforms. It was treason, my aunt and uncle had told me time and time again, especially for a courtier. So I said aloud the *Our Father* in English like everyone else, but in my mind I said it in Latin – it reminded me of home. And when I opened my eyes, the candles blazed with such a fury that I thought they must be the eyes of the devil himself, rising out of the fires of hell to find me.

I don't have time to be lonely or bored. I have to be with the prince all the time that he's awake. He can only just walk, and he's forever tripping over his long skirts, and jabbering funny little words that only he and Mother Jack can understand. Some afternoons I have lessons from the knights who visit the court. I'm learning to fence and joust: I can send an arrow singing through the air; I can hold a falcon on my wrist; I can hunt deer. Soon I will be taught to wrestle and to swim, and to play tennis! It's all part of my job, to learn to do these things so I can teach them to the prince when he is older. Sometimes Mother Jack brings him to watch me, especially during my archery lessons. Sir Andrew, my archery tutor, is my favourite knight. I think he is Mother Jack's too. He teaches me how to choose the best and sharpest arrow, how to hold my bow. He lays a clout of linen on a butt of earth and I have to aim for it again and again.

He shows me how to send my arrow like a pike to its prey. 'It swims! It swims!' he says, and Prince Edward claps his hands and shouts, 'Wims! Wims!' And that's what he calls me, Wims. Funny, isn't it?

He waddles up and down the lawns with Mother Jack holding the sashes on his long gown. She smiles at Sir Andrew, and he pretends not to notice. Up and down, up and down the prince goes, clutching at the leaves on the bushes he passes, stroking them. Or he sits on Mother Jack's knee watching me, crowing and clapping his little hands together. His two half-sisters, Lady Mary and Lady Elizabeth, hardly ever visit him. King Henry doesn't like them to, Mother Jack says. She says they must be lonely creatures, out of the king's mind most of the time. They live miles away in Hatfield, right in the middle of England. Prince Edward knows me best of all. He loves me best.

Mother Jack has plenty of errands for me: get this, say that, find Lord so-and-so. Everything the prince needs, I have to fetch, and no one else is allowed to do it. When she puts him to bed at night I stand by his cot, listening to the stories she tells him. They're frightening enough to curdle my own dreams, much scarier than Ned's. But the prince stares at her, listening to every terrifying word as if she's singing a lullaby. Gradually his eyes close and then I can tiptoe off to the room I sleep in with the other high servants, my head full of ghosts and magicians. I drop into bed at night like a sack of turnips and never wake up till the cock crows and my own servants come to dress me for the day.

I paused, with the quill poised in my fingers. I must have been writing for over an hour, and I still hadn't said what I really wanted to say. My secret.

Next to the prince, I wanted to add, I think I'm the king's favourite boy.

I whispered it into the pages, then signed my name and sealed it. In the adjoining room I could hear the prince chirping like a sparrow to Mother Jack. He was awake again; my time was no longer my own.

The king's favourite

There, I've said it now. I've brought the secret out into the open and let it dart away bright and free, like a dragonfly.

How did I know I was his favourite boy? Because he treated me like one. And I think I know why.

He sent for me one day when he was visiting the prince. I was already on a long-winded errand for Mother Jack, but I knew the king had to be obeyed instantly and came straight back to Prince Edward's apartments. The little boy was in his bed, and there was a ghostly sweating paleness about his face. He had been taken ill, suddenly. Mother Jack was crying, the room was full of people, the king was pacing up and down.

'I will try a new potion,' the court physician said, and King Henry turned on him, his face blazing red. 'You will not touch him! It's because of that foul potion you gave him this morning that he's sick now!'

The physician bowed. The boils on his neck were as red as rosehips, I noticed. 'Yes, Your Majesty. But I have another to try.'

'Out, out, out!' the king roared. 'All of you! Out!'

The servants backed away, dithering with fright. I was backing out too. I had never seen the king behaving like this before, and I just wanted to run and hide, but

His Majesty flicked his hands in an angry gesture for me to stay. I bowed deeply, and waited.

'What does my son need, woman?' the king asked Mother Jack, who had refused to leave her charge. His eyes were glittering.

'Sleep,' she whispered. 'All he needs is sleep, but he can't settle, he's too poorly.'

The king turned to me. 'You, page. Sing to him. Sing him to sleep.'

I shuffled my feet, and gulped. My throat was as dry as a desert. I remembered one of the Bible stories we used to read with Brother John, about the shepherd boy David singing to the mad King Saul. 'Imagine how frightened he must have been!' Brother John used to say.

'Get on with it!' King Henry shouted.

So I sang, and my voice was a poor shaking thing at first, like a baby sparrow that's just crunched out of its shell, but I kept going, I closed my eyes and kept going, and when I opened my eyes again the prince was asleep and Mother Jack was patting his covers round him, and King Henry was nodding and smiling.

'You did well, boy,' he said. 'What's your name again?'

Before I could speak to say William Montague, Mother Jack answered for me.

'William Carew,' she said. 'He's Lord Carew's nephew, Your Majesty.'

The next time the king came to visit Prince Edward I was playing with him in the paddock where the ponies were grazing. His Majesty stood watching me, making me as nervous as a mouse. Mother Jack and the prince's servants hovered round, and the groomsmen and stable masters and boys were standing by the king's horses, waiting for him to inspect them. Courtiers who had travelled with the king stood idly by like painted maypoles.

'Give him a ride!' King Henry called. His voice boomed around the stable walls, and I realised with a little skip of fright that he was talking to me. I lifted the squirming boy onto the back of a fat little pony, and there was an 'Ah!' of horror all around me as I did so. I had touched the royal person! I knew that the eyes of the entire household of Hampton Court were on me; the eyes of the whole country, it felt like. What if he fell off? I could see Mother Jack clutching the sides of her skirts, ready to run and catch him, and the head groom with his hands dithering out like white fishes. The prince's many servants shuffled together like a little velvet-coated army of protectors and the royal physician broke out into bubbles of sweat, padding his boils with a handkerchief. The royal jester, Will Somers, gave a little 'Hoopla!' of delight. 'Oh, fun! Fun!' he called. 'Don't drop the royal egg!'

I nudged the pony forward, so gently, just a few steps, so Prince Edward could feel the rolling movement under him. I clung onto him fast. His eyes were wide and bright, and he chuckled with joy. So did the king.

'That was well done, young William Carew,' he called as I lifted the prince down again and he toddled off into Mother Jack's arms. King Henry strolled up to me, towering above me. He had a sharp, sour smell about him that day from a sore on his leg. It made me want to move away, but I couldn't. His breath came heavy and wheezing, because he is so large.

'Do you enjoy riding?'

I bowed. 'I do, Your Majesty, though I will never be as fine a horseman as you.'

He laughed and walked away. My uncle Carew was there that day, and he stayed behind a moment to whisper behind his hand.

'You do well, William.'

'Thank you, Uncle. I'm glad it pleases you.'

'His Majesty told me that he is as fond of you already as if you were his own son,' he said. He stepped back. His stern eyes shone. 'Do not displease him. Ever.' And he strode away, leaving me glowing with pride. And yet, the more I thought about his last remark, the colder I felt.

Mother Jack swept past me, with the little prince in her arms. 'Stay in the sunshine,' she murmured.

I wondered, later, whether she had heard what my uncle had just said.

Next day, one of Prince Edward's footmen came bowing into the royal chamber. The prince was bobbing across the green tiles on his hobby horse, squealing noisily, and barging into me on purpose, so I didn't pay much attention to what the footman was saying. 'William Carew,' was all I heard.

'William Montague,' I muttered, jumping out of the prince's way.

'Oh, in that case the message can't be for you,' Mother Jack said, teasing. 'What a shame.'

I turned to the footman, and he raised his eyebrows. 'If you're William Carew, then His Majesty's head groomsman has asked permission to see you. If you're not him, then please tell me where I can find him, because it's a matter of great importance.'

I swallowed. 'I am William Carew,' I said. 'Sometimes,' I added quietly.

'Then His Majesty's head groomsman has asked to speak to you in the stables.'

He bowed to the prince, who had just fallen over and was howling, and backed out of the chamber.

'May I go?' I asked Mother Jack.

'Well, you'll burst with curiosity if you don't go, and I'm as keen as a cat to know what he wants with you,' she said. 'But you must wait till the prince has his afternoon sleep.'

Wait, wait, wait. That's all anyone did at Hampton Court. At last Prince Edward's eyelids dipped down, and I was given the nod to slip away.

The groomsman was standing with his back to me, talking to the Keeper of the Stables. It was obvious that they were talking about me, because their words froze like snowflakes on their lips as soon as they saw me. The keeper went away, shaking his head as if he was trying to solve a great mystery, and John, the groomsman, took up sweeping the straw across the yard, pretending he hadn't noticed me. At last he swung round to me and grinned, showing four brown stumps of teeth in his gums.

'See that black 'un there?' he said, pointing to one of the stalls. 'He's yours.'

'Mine?'

'Present from His Majesty.'

'Mine?' I couldn't believe it. 'Mine? From the king?'

'Seems like.' John shrugged his bony shoulders.

I led the beautiful young stallion out into the stable yard. One of the stable lads brought me brushes and I groomed the horse myself, the way Ned Porritt had taught me at home, sleeking and smoothing, murmuring all the time to the horse as he lifted his head and nodded and pawed the earth. I love the smell of horses, full of haystack warmth; and I love the striking of their hooves, and the whickering of their voices. I love everything about them.

'What shall I call you?' I whispered into his ear. He flicked his head away and lifted his hooves daintily. He was the colour of deep water, rippling with light, and he moved like a dancer. I suddenly decided to call him Green Willow. Green is the colour of magic, the colour of the fields of home. My sister's best gown is green. 'Green Willow' is the title of one my favourite songs; and best of all, green is the colour the king loves most.

I am so clever! I know how to please the king, I thought. I went back to the palace humming the tune of 'Green Willow', and Mother Jack said, 'I haven't heard that song for some time. There's a rumour that His Majesty wrote it himself, you know.'

'Did he?' I gasped. *Even better!*

'Oh yes, When Lady Anne Boleyn was teasing and tempting him and tearing his heart in two, the vixen, he sang it to her. Well?' She folded her arms and tapped her foot, making her little grey shoe dance like a vole in the dry herbs. 'Well?'

I pretended not to understand her. 'Very well, thank you,' I nodded.

'You imp, William Carew! What did the head groomsman want with you?'

I tried to tell it casually. 'Oh, just that...erm...' and then it burst out of me. 'His Majesty has given me a horse!' I jigged up and down on the spot. 'A beautiful black horse, just for me!'

Her mouth opened in a little 'Oh!' of surprise. 'A horse! My goodness, all he has ever given me is a piece of cloth to make a kerchief with! A horse! Mind you, His Majesty can be very generous when the mood takes him. One of Lady Elizabeth's pages got a dog. A nice dog, but it barked too much for my liking. Then he was thrown out for being lazy – the page that is. Beaten within an inch of his life, and thrown out of court. And he was a Neville mind, very important family. Disgraced. Oh, a horse!'

On his next visit, the king asked me how I like my horse. His followers were standing about, watching and listening. The jester, Will Somers, was standing with his arms folded. He wagged his head at me and bowed a deep, low bow.

'A boy may ride as high as a prince, but who would catch him when he falls?'

The courtiers around him tittered. I bowed back, but I had a feeling he was making fun of me. Well, it was his job, to make people laugh, but I didn't think he was at all funny. My favourite knight, Sir Andrew, was watching, smiling encouragement. My uncle Carew was there, as always, close enough to the king to whisper in his ear if anything was wrong. He never brought my father with him on these visits. He wasn't important enough, I realised. Lord Thomas Howard was there; and his nephew Percy, hanging his head sulkily, hating me.

So it was in front of all of these and many more, that King Henry called out, 'How do you like my gift?'

I gazed round at everyone, too embarrassed for a minute to think what to say. Percy Howard picked at the fluff on his chin.

'Does he not suit you, young William Carew?' the king asked, pretending to be upset by my silence. Whatever you do or say here in front of the king, there is always an audience of courtiers, curling their lips with scorn, slanting their eyes towards one another in shared mockery. Will Somers leaned forward and put his hands behind his ears, making them flap. But Sir Andrew's smile gave me courage to speak up.

I bowed my thanks. I remembered the speech I had prepared, a speech to delight the king. 'Your Majesty has been too kind. I hope he will do me the honour of letting me name my horse after his own song, "Green Willow".'

But King Henry's eyes clouded and went cold – glittering ice-cold. Sir Andrew flashed me a warning look. What had I done wrong? I had no idea. The whole court was breathless with expectation, watching the king.

'You are a child,' His Majesty murmured at last. 'But I don't like that for a name.'

I looked at him helplessly, wishing that I could take the words back. 'I'm sorry, Your Majesty,' I stammered. 'I'm sorry if I offended you. It's just – he is so beautiful. I wanted a beautiful name for a beautiful horse.'

'But not that one.' The king turned his back on me and walked away. His courtiers bowed and curtsied and made way for him, and his jester bobbed up to him, prancing about like a horse to try to bring a smile on his face.

'Get out!' the King roared. 'Get rid of this idiot! He's not funny any more. Whip him, and find me someone new. I could slay him with my own hand!'

Will Somers was grabbed by one of the knights and pulled out of the courtyard, and I closed my eyes in shame. I felt the shadow of cold clouds across me, and fear as well. Would he ask the soldiers to carry me away too?

'Think of a proud name for a proud horse.' King Henry's voice boomed from the other side of the courtyard. He still had his back to me.

'Tudor!' I grasped at the first word that came into my head. 'Black Tudor! If I may use the royal name? Nothing less would suit this magnificent prince of horses.'

There was a long, aching silence. Then the king turned.

'You may.' His Majesty smiled as though I had called him the very god that he thinks he is. He threw back his head and laughed, and all the court laughed too.

'Bring my fool back!' he called. 'I'm merry again.'

'A near thing, William,' my uncle hissed at me when the king walked away. '"Green Willow"? That song is never played here now. King Henry hates the memory of Queen Anne Boleyn. He had her beheaded, and her brother, and others who were close to her. Why on earth did you think he would want to be reminded of her?

In future, keep your wits about you and your mouth shut!'

And that was exactly what my aunt had told me, the day I left home. 'Think before you speak! It should be written in Latin above your bed. *Cogita antequam dicas.*'

But I could breathe again. I was back in the sunshine again. I could be proud.

Proud, yes. Proud.

Who wouldn't be proud to be the king's favourite?

Mother Jack gave me permission to exercise Black Tudor every day when the prince was sleeping, and I rode him round the huge estate, watched with envy by some of the other servants – envy, and hatred. I rode him every time I was free. But I wasn't really free. There was nowhere for me to go, nowhere outside the vast palace grounds, nowhere beyond the walls, nowhere outside the gates. I was always riding alone. Round and round I went. Round and round. It made me think of the bear I had seen, chained to a post in a yard, pacing round and round. Wherever I went I saw my lonely shadow stalking me. He was my only friend. What I really, truly wanted, was to go back home.

Matthew is found

Two letters came for me on the same day. The highest servant, the chamberlain himself, brought them into the prince's suite on a silver salver. He looked at me sternly as I stood in my place by the fire, arms behind my back, perfectly still and waiting for instructions. He handed the salver to Mother Jack and she took the letters. 'You will read them first,' he told her, glancing at me again, and left the room.

'They're for you, William. Two at once!' Mother Jack said. She could have read them, but she screwed up her grey eyes as if she was too tired to bother, and handed them to me with a nod that I could take myself off and read them on my own. I recognised the handwriting on both of them. One was from Margery, the other was from my father. There must be something very important to tell me, I thought. I had no idea why my father would write. I put his aside uneasily, and read my sister's first.

My dear little brother, Margery wrote. This made me smile. I was a year younger than she was and she was several inches taller than me too. She never let me forget it. *So much has happened! I've been trying to find a chance to write to you, but I knew that Aunt Carew would insist on reading the letter before it was sent.*

Today she has a bad cold, and she's gone to bed, sorry for herself and sneezing her head off, so at last I have some time to myself. (Here there was a drawing of Aunt Carew balanced like a turnip on a pile of cushions, with a nose throbbing with redness.)

I'm so happy to hear about your wonderful time at Hampton Court. You have all the luck! I'm so envious! It's very, very lonely here without you. And I have so much to tell you.

First, and most important, is that Matthew has been found. His body was washed up further along the coast. Oh, now I'm crying again. Some tin miners there found him and carried him into their hamlet. He is buried in the local churchyard. We only found out two weeks ago, when a pedlar came to our kitchens full of local news in exchange for soup. Cook told Stephen, and he said the drowned boy must be our Matthew, and he told Aunt Carew and she wrote to Father. He came home at once. The men who had found the drowned boy had kept his doublet, and sure enough, it was poor Matthew's.

I put the letter to one side for a minute. I couldn't carry on reading it; my eyes were so full and my hands were shaking. I paced round the room and let the hurting sobs come, and there was no one to turn to for comfort.

Father has put up a gravestone for him there where he's buried. Oh, and it was such a cold and windy place for our brother to be, Will! We prayed to thank God that his soul was finally at rest. But you should have been there. Of course I asked if you knew, and why you hadn't come, and Father said King Henry wouldn't allow it.

All the servants came to our little ceremony in the churchyard. We walked there all the way from our house (well, Aunt Carew didn't. She had to go in the rickety old carriage. Ned Porritt drove her, and wept like a little boy all the time. 'Master Matthew was my friend,' he said, and Aunt Carew snapped at him for that. 'You were his servant, not his friend,' she said, and that made poor Ned sob even more).

Father has asked a local woodcarver to make an effigy of Matthew from a drawing Brother John did. Do you remember? The carver said he can change the face so it looks as if he's sleeping. It's going to go in our chapel.

You asked about Brother John. Nobody knows where he's gone, but Nurse Joan said a letter came from Lord Carew the night before he left. Aunt Carew read it and went very pale, and went straight to Brother John's room. No one saw him again after that. Joan thinks he was simply turned out of the house with nowhere to go. I can hardly believe that even Aunt Carew could be so cruel, but wouldn't he have said goodbye to us all otherwise? I miss him so much, even his riddles. He was so happy all the time. I'm so glad I have the little statue he carved for me.

No more fun here, but you would laugh to see me learning to dance under Aunt Carew's instructions. She gets carried away, furious and impatient with me for being so clumsy, and she sweeps into the middle of the room like a barge in full sail. She is a sight to be seen, Will! If you were here watching I wouldn't be able to stop giggling! Her chin wobbles, her head is thrown back as if she's in some sort of trance. 'Like this, my dear,' she murmurs. 'Like a leaf in the wind!' Oh, but *she wobbles, Will! She thinks she's floating airily, but she just sways and wobbles, and all her clothes sway and wobble with her. Sometimes she asks Nurse Joan to come up and dance with me, and you know what she's like; she's so shy, she would rather hide under the table than be asked to dance in front of anyone. So she flusters and stumbles and goes redder than cherries. But what's it all for? Where can anyone dance round here? I don't want to dance anyway.* (Here there was a drawing of my Aunt Carew, full-sailed and wobbling, and Nurse Joan crouching under a table).

Oh, I wish you were here!

There, that's it. I wanted to write to you, and I'm really miserable, but it's made me feel a little better to be thinking about you as I write. I hope you're happy in your glorious palace. I wish I could see you soon soon soon.

Your loving sister,
Margery

I read the letter again and again. I think it made me lonelier than ever. I thought of my brother, brought up out of the sea by strangers, carried to shore by strangers, buried in the earth by strangers. And it made me angry because my father hadn't told me himself about Matthew. Why not? Why not? Didn't he think I cared? Didn't he think I was worth telling? No one in the world was closer to Matthew than I had been. Surely, surely my father knew that.

And now I knew what my father's letter would be about. I opened it, and sure enough it was a brief note telling me about Matthew.

I delayed writing to you because I first needed to ask permission from His Majesty for you to return to Montague Hall with me. I am sorry to say that permission was not granted. I am deeply saddened by these events. I have left it to your sister to give you the details.

But I knew, deep down, why Father hadn't told me himself about Matthew. It was because he blamed me for Matthew's death. And if there'd been a choice, that terrible time in the bay, he would have saved him, not me.

Clever

'His Majesty has sent two gifts,' Mother Jack announced one morning. She spoke lazily, as if nothing was really important, yawning into the back of her hand. 'One for his son and heir.' With a flourish she pulled a cloth away and revealed a large wooden painted horse with a mane and tail of golden thread, and a green velvet saddle. Prince Edward shrieked to be helped to climb on it straight away.

'What are you going to call it, Your Royal Highness?' I asked him, fitting his feet into the stirrups.

'Tooda,' he said. 'Like Wims.'

'Tudor,' Mother Jack laughed. 'Like yours, William. Oh, and for the one His Majesty calls his special son, there's a gift too.' She turned to me, and though she was smiling now, there was a flicker of worry in her grey eyes. 'Sir Morgan Kemp has it for you.'

It was a falcon. My very own kestrel, for when I hunted with Sir Morgan and the king's other knights. She was a beautiful tawny-gold and silver-grey. I called her Clever, because she was just that. She learned to obey my whistles of command almost instantly. She knew everything. She knew me, she knew the sky, she knew the earth and the wind. She knew the little creatures that snuggled in the grass. She could

72

hover overhead, and then plunge like an arrow down to her prey. She was as swift and keen as a knight's sword, cutting the sky. She could cleave the air. All these things made her name.

And as I watched her sure flight I thought about the sparrowhawks I used to see quartering the fields at home, lords of the sky. I longed for that freedom – to be able to lift my wings and soar, to rise high, high above the trees, and climb higher, higher still into the line of the sun, and float effortlessly over the walls of Hampton Court. And away.

But my kestrel Clever was no freer than I was. She could go no further than I would let her. She had to come down when I whistled, she had to come down and down until she was on my gloved wrist again. I put her hood on, I tightened her leather jesses on her legs and clutched them in my fist, and I carried her to her post. She was mine.

And as long as King Henry wanted me there in his palace, I was his. I belonged to him. I had to stay.

It was late June when the king came to Hampton Court again. It was the last time he would see Prince Edward for weeks because he was about to go on his summer progress round England. There were more than a thousand people travelling with him, and they arrived by river in a trail of decorated gilt barges for a farewell banquet. They surged up the steps into the palace, babbling and bowing and showing themselves off in all their glitter, carrying their smell of sweat and nosegays with them wherever they went. At night their servants slept in the corridors and in the corners and hearths of the three huge kitchens, even under the hanging fowl and the pig carcasses. Their pages crowded the floors of my sleeping quarters, their snores mingling like a choir of farm animals. I hated having so many people round me.

The banquet was on the king's last evening. Even more courtiers seemed to have arrived by then, and the din of all their talk made my head spin. I never knew where I should be, and I kept having to dodge round people to do my errands for Mother Jack.

Servants were running here and there like rabbits in a warren, laying out the trestle tables for the feasting, bringing baskets of logs for the fire, setting tankards and platters on the great oak boards. At last it was all prepared; the fanfares blared, the guests began to make their way in.

Margery would have loved to have been there. She would have wanted to be one of the painted eavesdroppers' heads that are carved on the ceiling of the great hall, gazing down, especially when the ladies of the court came in. Tapestries had been rolled down the walls, and they swayed and flapped with the movement of so many people, as if there was a wind coming up from the sea. And in came the ladies on the arms of their escorts. Their dresses reminded me of poppies and marigolds, red for the ladies-in-waiting, gold for the wives of lords, all threaded with jewels and shining silk. They had diamonds and rubies shimmering on their fingers and round their necks. It was as if all the stars had dropped out of the sky and showered down onto them.

The Lady Mary and the Lady Elizabeth came in surrounded by their own maids and servants. I'd never seen them before, and I knew Margery would want me to write to her with every detail of what they looked like and what they wore. Little Elizabeth was excited, bobbing up and down on the toes of her shoes like a spring-time lamb. She wore a daisy-white satin gown threaded with gold, and there were golden beads on her hood, bobbing with her like fireflies. But Mary was stiff and cold and still. She wore an ice-blue gown. Even the pearls round her neck looked cold to me. They were not the most important children there, and she knew it. Prince Edward was the only child who mattered to their father. I knew what that felt like too. I remembered how my father used to praise Matthew in front of visitors as if Margery and I didn't exist. I remembered how it used to hurt me.

I saw my tutors, Sir Andrew and Sir Morgan, wearing white satin like the other knights. Lord Carew looked like a peacock in shiny blue and green, darting his bird-like glances at me. I bowed my head to him, and his teeth parted in the slightest of smiles. He would know about my falcon. Everybody knew everything. I was disappointed to see that the waxy-haired Percy Howard was there too, close behind his uncle, the Duke of Norfolk. He seemed to haunt me.

I mustn't worry about him any more, I thought. *I'm the prince's page.* Yet the very sight of him made me cold inside, and the memory of the words he had said to me hovered like night moths in my head. *I'll be watching you. I have friends and cousins everywhere, watching you . . . If you put one foot wrong, I'll know about it, be sure of that.* He had no power; he was only a boy, not much older than me. But his uncle was the most powerful man in the land, next to King Henry. I decided to keep as far away from him as I could. Maybe he wouldn't even notice me in the crowd.

Fanfares sounded again, and the guests stood waiting.

'Pray silence for the king!'

Just as His Majesty came in, a serving boy tripped and fell headlong on the floor, bringing a clatter of serving knives with him. It spoiled King Henry's entrance, and he was furious.

'Get out! Get out!' he roared. 'Throw him out of the palace! Where's the steward?'

The boy was handled roughly from the hall, and a flustered steward went on his knees in front of the king, bowing till his head touched the ground.

'Did you hire the boy?'

'I did, Your Majesty.' The steward mumbled. 'He comes from a good family.'

'Not good enough. You will both be whipped. Get out.'

There was a hush in the room. I had seen this before, I had seen the king's temper swing like a bell. Kind, cruel; smile, frown; sing, shout; ding, dong. Mother Jack had told me you never knew when his mood would change. 'And the nearer you are to him, the worse it gets,' she'd shuddered. 'I wouldn't be one of his advisers for anything. Off with their head, as soon as they say a wrong word.'

Everyone watched to see what His Majesty would do next. If anyone spoke or moved or smiled until he did, they could be the next to be punished. The king turned away from the trembling steward, smiling as if nothing had happened, and his courtiers smiled with him. 'Ah!' went a breath of pleasure round the hall. His Majesty is happy again.

He signalled that he wanted a few moments alone with Prince Edward before the feasting began.

'Mother Jack, bring my son to my rooms,' he ordered. He stood in the doorway, magnificent and gleaming in his golden doublet and jerkin and ruby hose. He was huge anyway, but his shoulders were so wide in his padded doublet that they looked like eagles' wings. He filled the doorway. He was a big proud man, a giant bear of a man. Mother Jack had told me that he had once been the handsomest man in Europe, and he held himself as if he still was. He needed to have everyone's attention at all times, and he got it. So all eyes were on him as he looked round the hall – and again, and again – searching for someone. Little Elizabeth stepped forward and curtsied, but she wasn't the one he was looking for. He looked straight past her, and then his eyes met mine.

'Ah, William!' he laughed. 'William Carew! There you are. I want you to come too. Come and sing for my son.'

Across the stifling room, the lanky Percy narrowed his eyes and scowled like a gargoyle.

'I should be careful, if I were you'

There were so many people at Hampton Court that day that there had to be two sittings at the banquet, and I was at the first – the main one. As I went to my place a girl caught my eye and nodded slightly to me. I nodded back, and she came up to me, her face pink with smiles.

'Will Montague! It is, isn't it?'

Then I recognised her as Lady Catherine, who used to be Margery's friend, who came to play with us in the gardens at home. It felt like years and years ago.

'I knew it was you! But I heard the king calling you William Carew, and I thought I must have been mistaken. Are you really Prince Edward's page?'

I nodded, proud. 'But what are you doing here?'

'I'm a maid-in-waiting to Lady Elizabeth,' she said, just as proudly. 'But there are lots of us! I stay at the palace at Hatfield. It's huge! It's like a village.'

'What's she like?' I was thinking how much Margery would love to hear about this. She had always loved anything to do with Elizabeth and Mary.

'She's perfect!' Catherine said. 'She can already speak three languages and dance and make music, even though she's only six years old. People say she's brilliant. But poor child! She talks about His Majesty all the time. She was so excited about seeing him today.

He comes to see her at Hatfield sometimes, and he's very kind when he's there, but he really only has eyes for the little prince when he's around. Oh, I must go!'

A fanfare announced the entry of King Henry, and Catherine bobbed her way to her place. The king sat with the highborn aristocrats at the high table, and below him, lesser nobles, the lords- and ladies-in-waiting. Next came their pages and ladies' maids, and after us, lower servants. I tried to stay away from Percy, but he deliberately put himself next to me on the bench. *So, be friendly*, I thought. I know my manners, even if he doesn't. I gave him the courtly slow nod, and he returned it, but his eyes were ice-cold. I turned away from him to talk to the page on my other side. My stomach was dithering with worry.

Children were playing up and crying, dogs were barking and snapping at each other, bowls and goblets clattered on the tables, and the more wine people drank, the louder their talking and laughter became. It was impossible to have a conversation with anyone, even if I had wanted to. Men stood round the Hall holding branches of candles, hundreds of flickering lights, and they made the room so hot and stuffy that I could hardly breathe. I wished I could get rid of my heavy doublet. I ate more than I could manage, and still the food kept coming in processions; salmon and venison and roast beef and stuffed boar, porpoise and crab, each plate held high above the heads of the servants, who went down on their knees to present them first to King Henry.

Percy ate hardly anything. He took a tiny morsel of food from the serving platter and played with it with his thin fingers instead of putting it into his mouth. He disgusted me as much as the fat belching page on the other side of me who gorged himself until he was sick, and then kept on gorging. I kept my eyes down, wishing I could just rise from my place and go. Then I felt Percy's cold hand on my arm. His pale eyes looked inside me. He put his mouth to my ear.

'I hear that you and your father are Papists.'

I started.

'Do you still follow the Pope's teaching? Do you accept the Act of Supremacy?'

I didn't know what to say. I knew that to follow the Pope was a dangerous thing. To deny that King Henry was the Head of the Church in England was even worse.

'I go to the chapel with Prince Edward,' I said. It was true, but I still mumbled the Lord's Prayer in Latin my head.

'And at home?'

'I'm not at home, am I? I'm at court.'

Percy turned his head away, and I hoped he was satisfied with that, but he came back again, his mouth so close to my ear that I could feel his breath, and the tickle of his fluffy chin. It made me shudder.

'Your father is never seen in the chapel at Westminster. Isn't that strange?' he said. 'I find it very strange, and so does my uncle. You know him?'

I nodded. Of course I knew him. What did the Duke of Norfolk have to do with me or my father? Why was he interested in whether my father prayed in the chapel or not?

But Percy whined on into my ear, making the hairs

of my neck crinkle up. 'Sir Thomas Howard, the Duke of Norfolk – that's my uncle. He is at the right hand of King Henry, his friend and chief adviser. And he finds your father's behaviour strange. He is watching him. Yes, a humble clerk, but he is being watched. I should be careful, if I were you. And so should your uncle, Lord Peter Carew. Oh yes, the whole family is being watched.'

A fanfare drowned out his hissing whispers, and he pulled his head away from me. I felt as if I could breathe again. Another dish appeared. It was a swan stuffed with a goose and inside, a duck, and inside that, a pigeon, and at the centre, a tiny quail. Percy groaned, but the courtiers cheered and clapped as if they'd been starving for a week. Prince Edward squealed in fright at their sudden noise, and King Henry, laughing, held him up for Mother Jack to take to his room. As she walked to the door the little prince held out his arms to me, still sobbing. And then the king caught my eye and nodded to me to follow. It was unheard of that anyone should leave the hall before His Majesty.

I stood up, bowed deeply and hurried away, trying to force Percy's words out of my head, trying to fill up my mind with stories of elves and fairies that I would tell to the prince while he fell asleep in Mother Jack's arms. I was safe, for a time, from Percy Howard.

But I fretted all night about my father. I dreamed he was surrounded by hooded men with flashing knives in their hands. I dreamed of gallows on lonely hillsides and dark shapes swinging from them. I woke up sweating and scared. I had to warn him.

A bruise deep inside me

The king and his huge retinue set off the next day on their progress round the kingdom. It would take them weeks. I was glad to be seeing the back of Percy Howard and his uncle. I would be glad to see the back of everyone. Hampton Court was in a bustling, cheerful uproar as the court prepared to follow the king, and I sidled from group to group in search of my uncle Carew. I was desperate to find my father after what Percy had told me. My uncle swiped one hand across the other in annoyance when he saw me, as if he wanted to be done with me.

'My Lord, will my father be joining you when you travel with His Majesty?'

'Most certainly not!' he snapped. 'Your father remains in London tidying up my business.'

'Thank you, My Lord,' I bowed. That was all I needed to know. I could write to my father at his lodgings. He was alone, and surely no one would be watching him while the king was away.

The king and his followers left with much blaring of trumpets and beating of drums, waving of flags, ringing of bells, so that everyone on their route would know they were coming and would line the riverbank and the lane sides, cheering and hurrahing the huge procession. I watched them away, and then turned back to the quiet court and my duties. The little prince was exhausted and over-excited, Mother Jack told me. He needed rest that morning.

'Go to your studies for a bit,' she told me. She yawned like a cat. 'Isn't it peaceful now that's all over!'

Now at last I had time to myself. I could write to my father and warn him, but still I didn't. I chewed the end of my quill, chasing words in my head the way a cat chases birds, watching them fly away. I just didn't know where to start. I hadn't seen him since that day in Westminster Palace when Uncle Carew had presented me to King Henry. He had never written to ask me about my life at Hampton Court. He hadn't even told me about Matthew being found and buried. All that was like a bruise deep inside me, which hurt every time my thoughts wandered near it. And anyway, I told myself, how would I know for sure that my letter wouldn't be read first by one of those 'watchers' that Percy had whispered to me about? Was it true? Was I being watched in everything I did? I felt cold and lonely.

Maybe Percy was just trying to bully me because he was jealous of my horse and my falcon. He was only a boy, how could he know whether my family was in danger? I decided not to risk sending a letter. It was easier. And yet, I longed to see my father again. I longed to be home, longed for it to be the way it was before Matthew died. For everything to be the way it used to be.

And then, one day, something completely unexpected happened. I was in the long gallery near the Prince's chambers, playing football with him with a stuffed bag of royal rags. He tottered after it, tripping over his skirts, squealing with laughter every time I kicked the ball out of his way. Then a footman came down and murmured to Mother Jack that there was a visitor with a letter from Lord Carew, and she nodded to him to let the visitor come up. She scooped up the prince and handed him to a lady-in-waiting to take away, and told me to follow her to the receiving room. The visitor was ushered in.

It was my father.

He went straight to Mother Jack and handed her the letter, while I dithered behind her, scuffing the cloth ball about between my feet as if I was trying to polish the floor with it.

Mother Jack read the letter and wrinkled her nose in that rabbity way she has and tossed her head as if to say, *What do we care? I can manage without him. Take him!* And then she pressed a coin into my hand and said, 'Lord Carew says His Majesty has already agreed that you may be relieved of your duties for a short while. You may go. I'll send for you when I have to. Go well, and keep safe, young William!'

'Where?' I asked, catching my father's eye at last.

'Home.'

I wanted to hug him. I wanted to race down that long gallery whooping and cheering and skipping. Instead I bowed and went quietly to my room and ordered my servant to put together some clothes for me. He loaded them into Black Tudor's saddlebag, and followed me to the stable yard where my father was waiting. A stable boy led my horse out. Tudor stepped out proudly, as eager as if he was on display in front of the whole court. I stood watching my father, trying not to smile.

84

'That's a fine horse you have,' he said, surprised. 'A real beauty.'

I mounted slowly, keeping my face straight. I waited till he was mounted on his own horse, and trotting beside me away from Hampton Court, and then I told him.

'He's a present from the king!'

And then I couldn't help it, I laughed out loud, I was so full of pride and joy. I kicked Black Tudor on, so my father had to canter to keep up with me. It was like the old days again, racing into the wind over the meadows of home.

And there beside us, cantering with us, his head thrown back and his mouth open as if he was sipping the wind, urging us to go faster, faster, was Matthew.

Does my father see him too, I wondered? *Is he there for both of us?* And as soon as I thought that, Matthew had gone. But he had left my happiness with me. I imagined the orchard, with apples swelling on the trees, and the swallows darting and swooping round the barns, and the cry of the seagulls. Home, home, I was going home.

'Why are we going home?' I asked Father eventually, pulling up Tudor so I could trot beside him. 'How long will we be staying?'

He was out of breath with the race, and just shook his head. 'I don't know,' he said at last, wiping the gleam of sweat from his brow. 'I received an order from Lord Carew to return to Montague Hall with you. That's all I know. He has business for us there, and when it's completed, no doubt we'll receive a letter telling us to return to our duties.'

'Why do we have to do everything he says?' I asked angrily. Even though I was excited about going home, I hated to think we had been ordered to go there.

My father didn't even bother to reply to that. 'We have a long, long journey ahead of us,' he said. 'We'll ride hard, and rest at inns on the way. We can visit the home of my good friend de Crecy. He may be at Greenwich, or even away with His Majesty, but his wife will make us welcome there again.' He glanced at me, a little twitch of a smile on his lips. 'I heard from Lord Carew that the king is pleased with you. He must be to have given you this horse.'

'And a falcon.' I was jittery with pride then. I glanced at my father to see if he was proud of me, but he kept himself stern and tight.

'He's a generous man.'

'Yes, he is generous. But he's also fat, smelly and mad.' I laughed at the shocked expression on Father's face. He glanced nervously over his shoulder.

'It's all right, no one's following us, and no one can hear us.' I raised myself on my stirrups. 'Fat, smelly, mad and OLD!' I shouted. In the distance I could see two figures through the shimmering heat haze, sitting at the side of the road.

'He'd have you rotting in the Tower if he heard you were talking like that,' my father muttered. 'And there's plenty who would take great pleasure in telling him. The Howard boy, for a start.'

My smile turned to a ghost of itself on my lips. I gripped Tudor's reins tightly. 'You know about him?'

'I don't listen to gossip,' Father said. 'But people enjoy telling me how much the boy hates you. He's jealous, that's all. But he's dangerous. They're a dangerous family.'

'Father, Percy Howard tells me that we are being watched, both of us. Did you know that? Is it true?'

'I expect it is. Everyone is being watched these days.'

'But aren't you afraid of what might happen to you?'

For a long time my father was silent.

The two figures emerged from the heat haze – a boy and girl, dressed in brown, simple clothes. Their feet were bare. They were standing up now, weary as if they'd been walking for miles, and as we drew up to them I pulled a coin from my purse and tossed it down to them. I didn't even look at them. I had no idea what kind of coin it was. It was the one Mother Jack had given me, to spend on my travels. I did it to please my father. He didn't even seem to notice. He had closed up inside himself again, and when he spoke, it was as if I wasn't even there.

'When your mother died,' he said, 'I thought it was the worst thing that could happen to me. Only my faith, my belief in God and my prayers kept me going. And then, I lost Matthew, my fine, loving, lovely son, Matthew.'

'I slipped,' I blurted out. 'I couldn't help it. I grabbed at him, I didn't know what I was doing . . . ' I had never cried in front of Father for Matthew before. I hadn't been able to; I was so wrapped round with guilt. Now the tears streamed down my cheeks, burning tears that blurred the trees and the sky around me. I couldn't brush them away, I couldn't stop them. My father kept looking ahead of him, staring into the dark, hurting tunnel of his past.

'Without my faith, I would not have been able to carry on,' he said. 'My only comfort was in praying as I had prayed every day of my life. I cannot change now. But not Lord Peter Carew, nor Lord Thomas Howard, not even King Henry himself will change my belief that the Pope is the true father of the Holy Catholic Church. It is all that matters to me.'

Home

At last we could see Montague Hall, set in its own velvet green valley. I saw it as I'd never seen it before; grey crumbling stone, flaking timbers, sagging thatch, and I loved it more than ever. A gift from a king to his favourite. *Like me*, I thought proudly, stroking Black Tudor's mane.

My father pulled in his reins. 'What do you think, William? Is it as beautiful as Hampton Court?'

Skylarks were looping over our heads, filling the air with their rippling song. Scarlet poppies and golden marigolds dotted the lane side. Our cows lumbered towards us, mooing softly. The only other sounds were the river loose on its bed of pebbles, and the drowsy hum of insects. And the sea, the long sigh of the sea.

'Twice as beautiful.'

I kicked Black Tudor's side, and we galloped headlong to Montague Hall.

We were greeted by the servants, who stood in a motley, untidy row outside the doorway, grinning and waving to us. *What a country lot they are*, I thought, gazing down at them. The servants at court would have laughed to see them. I slid off Black Tudor's back and tossed the reins to Ned Porritt. He gawped at me, full of awe for the beautiful horse. I wasn't supposed to notice him, Aunt Carew had taught me that. A year ago we would have chased each other round the stableyard, whooping with excitement, shouting Black Tudor's name at the tops of our voices. But I just let my eyes smile, and walked on into the Hall. I would have run in, if Aunt Carew hadn't trained me not to. Fresh lovage had been strewn on the floor, and I breathed in the sharp, pungent smell, satisfied. It was the smell of home.

'Lady Carew is expecting you in her room,' Bailey, Father's whiskery servant, murmured. My father nodded wearily.

'I'm sure she is, but we've ridden a long way without eating today. We'd like to dine first.'

Bailey flapped his hands. He was upset about something, I could see that. 'Lady Carew has arranged for your meal to be taken to her room, Master Robert. She wishes to speak to you urgently.'

I looked round for my sister, but there was no sign of her. Nurse Joan was hovering anxiously by the door.

'Where's Margery?' I asked.

'Mistress Margery is in her own room,' Joan's kind face was creased with concern, and her freckled hands were worrying each other.

'Is she ill?' If Margery was well she would have come running down the lane to meet us, her skirt in her hands, her tawny hair bouncing under her coif. We would have heard her laughing before we saw her.

'A little.' Nurse Joan looked at my father's servant, and looked away again. Her dusty shoes toed the new rushes. 'You could say that, Master William, though my Lady Carew would say it's of her own doing.'

She pursed her lips. I knew that look of hers. *Don't ask me*, it meant. *I'm only a servant here.*

'Come on, William,' my father sighed. 'Let's get it done with.'

I followed Father up the dim stairs to my aunt's room. She was sitting by the window, catching the last light of day. She must have seen us coming. She must have seen me riding my beautiful Black Tudor. She hardly turned her head to look at us, but motioned to her maid to finish lighting the candles and to leave us alone. She made no mention of my horse, our long journey, our empty stomachs, anything like that.

'Your daughter,' she said to my father, 'is a wicked, ungrateful child.'

'Oh dear,' he sighed. 'What's she done now?'

'I'm talking about what she hasn't done, or won't do,' my aunt said angrily. 'And I've told her she'll be whipped for her disobedience, and that you will do it yourself.'

'Oh dear.' Another sigh, deep to his boots. Father lifted his hands slightly helplessly. He had never whipped anyone, not even Ned Porritt, and I know he'd deserved a beating sometimes.

'If you don't, I will.' She peered then at me, hovering by the door, desperate to edge out and run to Margery's room. 'Come here, William, let me look at you. Do you like court life? It seems to suit you. You've grown.'

I bowed, as I would to any highborn lady in King Henry's court.

'Madam,' I said. 'I owe everything to you.'

'Hmmph.' Her eyebrows arched up like a pair of wings.

'He's learning fencing and archery,' my father told her. 'And did you see that beautiful horse? A gift from the king himself.'

'And he gave me a falcon of my own,' I added quickly, bold with pride to hear my father say that.

Aunt Carew's eyebrows hunched themselves up again. 'Thank goodness you're in his favour. You're a good boy. I wish your sister would be as sensible. I expect you're completely fluent in Latin and Greek by now? And jousting, and archery? And practising music? The king loves music.' She turned back to the window, bored with me, and pulled the flap of deerskin across it. The room darkened, and the candles stroked the shadows with light. 'One day,' my aunt said with the cream of greed in her voice, 'the king might marry you to one of his queen's young maids-in-waiting.'

I felt my knees going weak at the thought. I could imagine Matthew spurting with giggles behind me. Marry? Not me! Not for years and years. *Anyway*, I reminded myself, *there isn't a queen*. They're all dead, his wives. Katherine of Aragon, Anne Boleyn and Jane Seymour. He was hardly like to marry again, now he had a son and heir. No more ladies-in-waiting at his court, except for visitors. So I was quite safe.

'Can I go and see Margery?' I asked.

My aunt shuddered and put her hand to her cheek, as if the very name of Margery gave her toothache. 'She's in her room.' She turned to my father. 'I will not have it! I have given up my life to look after your children, Robert, and they give me no thanks, no obedience.'

'I'm sorry you think that, Elizabeth,' Father said. 'William has just thanked you, and so do I.'

'Hmm,' she sniffed. 'Thank you is easy to say. And you're no better, with your ridiculous Papist beliefs. You must do what the king does now. You will lose everything if you don't, I'm warning you. Really, brother, you're no better than a peasant. You have a peasant's mentality!' She looked at me again and dismissed me with a haughty sweep of her hand. 'Oh, stop fidgeting, William, you're like a dog with fleas. Go up to your room. I want to talk to your father.'

I was glad to leave. In spite of the fire, that room was icy.

My old servant, Stephen, was waiting in the corridor, half-asleep. 'Your room is ready, Master Willim, sir.' He didn't know what to call me any more now I lived in one of King Henry's palaces. He counted his tasks out on his bony fingers. 'Fire lit, bed made, candles ready, change of clothes, tub by the fire if you want a bath.' A smile creaked across his face. 'Would you like your meal brought up?'

'I'll have it with Margery. I'll go to her room now.'

Stephen frowned. 'She won't see anyone.'

'She'll see me,' I said cheerfully. I wanted to tell her about meeting Lady Catherine at Hampton Court. It would cheer her up, surely, to hear about her old friend. In spite of my court training I bounced along the corridor to her room, making the tattered hangings sway, and pushed at Margery's door. For the first time ever, I found it locked. I knocked loudly. 'Margery, it's me! Let me in!'

No answer. I pressed my ear to the lock. I could hear the sound of rustling skirts behind me, and then came Nurse Joan's voice. 'She's locked in, Master Willim.

We can't open the door. Your aunt ordered her to be locked in.'

I turned angrily to Stephen. 'Stephen, go to my aunt. Tell her I must see Margery at once.'

He hesitated; his shoulders drooping like a kicked dog's. I would have to rephrase it for him.

'Please ask my aunt for her gracious permission to enter my sister's chamber.'

He shuffled off. I could hear him muttering the words to himself so he wouldn't forget them. I banged on the door again. 'Come on, Margery, speak to me. Why are you locked in your room? What have you done now, you ninny?'

All I could hear was the sound of sobbing. Behind me, Nurse Joan's soothing voice crooned to Margery to stay calm. My father, surely, would persuade Aunt Carew to have Margery's door opened for me. He was master of the house, after all. Sure enough, I heard a skirt swishing along the corridor, and my aunt's maid came up with Stephen loping at her side.

'I may open the door for you. My Lady Carew is preparing to dine with your father, Master Willim,' she said. 'And when she has finished, she wants this room locked again. Unless you've managed to talk some sense into your sister.' She spoke loudly, so her voice echoed down the corridor. Maybe my aunt was listening for her to get the message right. But the maid's eyes were soft and pleading. All the servants loved Margery.

'Bring me some food,' I said. 'I'll eat it with her. And bring something sweet. Strawberry pudding. She'll like that.'

Stephen nodded and shuffled slowly away as if he had the whole night to spare. His bones have been put in the wrong place, I always used to think. His knees were like elbows, and his arms hung stiff and awkward at his sides as if they didn't have any joints in at all. I used to think he was as old as the house.

'A hideous old man'

Margery's room was almost in darkness. In the hearth a miserable fire licked damp logs. I felt my way to the bed and touched the heavy curtains that hung around it.

'Margery, Margery, where can you be?' I said softly, trying our old hiding rhyme. There was no answer from the curtains.

Nurse Joan lit a candle and carried it across to me. I drew the bed curtains back, and I could see that my sister's face was ashen, her cheeks red and blotchy, her eyes raw. She looked as if she'd been crying for days. She moaned and rolled away to hide her face. I pulled her shoulder to make her turn back to me.

'Tell me,' I said. 'And then we'll eat. I've sent for some food.'

'I can't eat!' She started sobbing again. 'I never want to eat again. I want to die. Let me die.'

'It's the aunt, isn't it? What's she done to you?'

Margery hunched herself up so she was sitting with her arms locked around her knees. Her hair hung like ragged strings round her face. She looked about six instead of thirteen. 'She wants me to get married.'

I giggled. 'Oh, that! She wants me to get married too. To someone who doesn't even exist. Don't take any notice of her.'

'But she means it. To a hideous old man from King Henry's castle in France! France!' Her voice was strangled in her throat. 'She went to visit him last year, don't you remember? Lord Richard Oakland of Carlisle! He minds the king's castle in Calais, or something. She wouldn't stop talking about him when she came home. He must be at least as old as she is. I won't, I won't, I won't marry him!' She moaned and hugged her knees. 'But I have to. It's all arranged. She's taking me over there tomorrow. Tomorrow, William! I'll be married off to a man of about *forty*! Just because he's rich; just because he's a lord; just because he's in charge of the king's castle. Calais! It's over the sea. It might as well be underneath it. I hope I drown on the way, that's all.'

She gasped in horror at what she'd just said, and started crying again. Nurse Joan clucked soothingly and sat on the edge of the bed. She took Margery's hand in her own and held it tight. I stood up and walked away, over to the fire, and stared at the wriggling flames. Not one of us said anything else. There was nothing to say. After all, Margery was right. If our aunt had decided to take Margery to France, it was beyond undoing. You might as well ask a bolting horse to stand still, as ask Aunt Carew to change her mind.

'I'll talk to Father,' I promised. But it was hopeless, I knew that already.

The next morning my father and my aunt and I ate our breakfast in complete silence. Margery wasn't there, and I wasn't allowed to go to her room again. I wished I wasn't there either. I almost wished I was back at Hampton Court. But I remembered my promise to Margery.

'Please, Father. Please, Aunt,' I began. 'I have something important to say.'

My aunt folded her hands under her chin as if she couldn't believe such a thing was possible.

'It doesn't seem fair to make Margery live in France, when she doesn't want to go,' I said. There was total silence. 'And she doesn't want to marry Lord Richard. She doesn't want to get married at all. Not yet.'

'Really?' said my aunt. She unfolded her hands and carried on with her breakfast as if I had never spoken. I looked at my father helplessly.

'It is your uncle's idea,' he said quietly. I sighed. Uncle Carew again, organising our lives for us.

'And he has had permission from King Henry himself to arrange this marriage. For a Carew to be marrying the king's right-hand man in France is a very important match. Very important.'

'But she isn't a Carew...' I began, and then I remembered how my uncle had introduced me to King Henry as William Carew. I would never have become Prince Edward's page if I had been introduced as a Montague. Lord Carew was building up his connections through our family, seeing as he didn't have any of his own. We would be like the Howards, like the Seymours, if he had his way. We would be among the most important families in the country. Aunt Carew looked at me, and her eyes were glinting and bright, with a kind of greedy excitement. She was ambitious. She wanted to be as important as the Seymours, and only Margery and I could do it for her. I understood it all now. I felt a shiver going through me. I knew there was nothing more I could say.

'I went to the chapel,' my father said to break the silence. 'And the door was locked. Do you have the key?' I saw that his hands were clenched so tight that the knuckles bulged through the skin. He twisted his ring round and round. 'This is my house, sister. Remember that.'

Sighing and shaking her head at him, Aunt Carew slid her hand into her girdle and brought out the key. 'Don't expect me to go there with you. I can't bear to see those statues all over the place,' she said, shuddering. 'We don't need wooden dolls to pray to. And lock the door when you come out. No one else must enter it.'

Father took the key and walked out of the room in silence, and I hurried after him, pretending not to hear her hen-like squawk of protest. The chapel was at the side of the house, down a long, dingy corridor where the stones were crumbling with age. It was where we used to begin every morning of my life until Aunt Carew came to live with us. It was very, very ancient, my father told me once. Older even than the house, though it had been strengthened and added to over the years. There had always been a chapel on that spot, since the time England had a king called Harold Harefoot, he said, and that always used to make me giggle and glance down at my own feet. Did he mean hairyfoot, I used to wonder?

'Why does she lock it?' I asked.

'In case we have visitors. She and her husband are reformists. She'd like people to think that I am too.'

'Nobody ever comes here. It's too far from London. That's what she always complains about. She says we live beyond the back of beyond.'

'But if they did. She suspects my views about the king and the Pope. She's frightened that someone will betray me, perhaps.'

'Mother Jack told me that King Henry executes people who think like you do.' I said, scared at his words.

'Mother Jack is right,' Father said grimly. 'I have seen executions. The king encourages his subjects to go and watch, as if it's a public sport. Most people actually enjoy going.' He closed his eyes, and shuddered, as if he was remembering a horrible dream. 'I have heard the crowds jeering and taunting as men are lifted to swing from ropes. I have seen women thrown on fires and heard them scream till they could scream no more. I have watched noblemen, friends of the king, being beheaded on Tower Hill, and heard their heads thud into baskets. I have seen the heads of courtiers thrust onto spikes along London Bridge for everyone to gawp at, and the sky around them black with ravens until the flesh is all gone. King Henry does this to people who he thinks might be traitors.' His voice was thin and bitter, and I didn't recognise it, I didn't know him. I was afraid.

'Please, Father! Please, please don't say it then. Don't tell anyone you follow the Pope. Not ever.'

He put both his hands on my shoulders and looked down at me, the way he always used to do before Matthew died. For the moment, it was almost as if he was noticing me again.

'William, you don't have to come in with me.'

At Hampton Court, I did what everyone else did. I wanted to please the king. But today I was home.

I wanted to please my father. I followed him into the chapel. It was dusty and damp, with spiders' webs looping from the ceiling beams to the floor, like gossamer chain mail. I helped to pull off the shrouds that Aunt Carew had thrown over the carved wooden statues of the saints and the child Jesus. She had put them on their sides and turned their faces to the wall. She'd had the statue of the Virgin Mary beheaded, perhaps to remind anyone who found it that this could happen to them, or perhaps to convince any soldier sent by the king that nobody in the house prayed to images.

'I shall have her mended,' my father murmured. He picked up the broken statue as gently as if it were a wounded child. 'I can't leave her like this.'

There was a light tap at the door, and we both started. I felt a rush of guilt and fear. My father motioned to me to stand behind the door, so I wouldn't be seen. I did as I was told, but my heart was thudding like drums. Surely it would be heard.

'Come in.' My father's eyes fixed mine. *Be brave, be strong*, they said to me. *Run for safety*, my head told me. The latch was lifted, and I tensed myself. The door opened slowly, and Nurse Joan came in, looking as weak as I was with nervousness.

'Sir, I've come to tell you that my Lady Carew and Mistress Margery are almost ready to leave for Calais,' she announced, twisting a handkerchief round in her hands.

'Already?' I gasped. I stepped out of my hiding place behind the door.

She nodded. 'And I am to go with them, and I have to tell you that I'm as limp as a rag with fear, and I would have run away from this place till they'd gone, if it wasn't for Mistress Margery. I've never left her since the day she was born, and I'm not going to leave her now.' She wiped the handkerchief across her face. 'But Master Robert, sir, I need to tell you something else.' She glanced behind her, and my father came forward and closed the door, drawing her closer in.

'Oh, sir, I'm frightened to tell you.' She put her hand across her mouth.

'What is it, Joan?'

'I have news for you,' she whispered. 'News of your cousin, the priest.'

'Brother John?' My father sat down on the bench. 'Not bad news, Joan?'

She nodded, clasping and unclasping her hands. Hidden in her skirts was a string of wooden rosary beads. I watched her hand fumbling for them, touching them for comfort. 'He's been back here, more than a week ago,' she whispered. 'But my Lady Carew sent him away again.'

'She sent him away? But he's our cousin! He's homeless.'

'I heard her telling him she wanted none of his Papist ways in her house, and she sent him away. He had no shoes on his feet, sir, no covering on his head, and she sent him away without giving him so much as a crust of bread to eat.'

My father started up. 'How long ago was this? A week, did you say? He might still be in the neighbourhood.'

'He is, sir.' She looked round again, as if she expected Aunt Carew to come gliding through the door

102

like a vengeful ghost. 'As soon as I was able to, I ran after him, and I found him on the lane, just sitting, waiting for a passer-by to throw a coin to him, no doubt. He was completely exhausted. He's been living that way, sleeping rough and begging, since Master Willim first went to the court, sir, all those months and months. He's used up all his strength. He came back to beg her to give him shelter in the house he was born in, so he could die here. And she turned him away.'

'Did you give him some food, Joan? I hope you did.'

'I took him to the shepherd's hut. The shepherd took the fever and died not long ago, and no one will use his hut again till next lambing time. When night came, I took him food and warm clothes. He may still be there, I don't know. But I just wanted you to know before we left. And we must leave now, and my lady will be wanting to know why I'm not with them.'

'Thank you, Joan,' my father said. He took both her hands in his, and kissed them as if she were a lady from the court. 'You are a good, kind woman. Look after my little girl, won't you? Look after her. She's precious to me.'

'I will.' She bobbed a curtsy to him. Her eyes swam with tears.

'Goodbye, Nurse Joan,' I put my arms round her and hugged her, and she pressed me to her warm, soft body as if I was still a little boy and she was still my own nurse. Then I turned and ran out of the chapel. I could hear my father following me, hear the whisper of rushes as Nurse Joan hurried behind us both, but I was first in the courtyard. The old wooden carriage was already there, and Aunt Carew and my sister were both in it. I climbed in and hugged my sister. Her face was white and tense. I jumped out again without being able to say a word, and let my father lean across to hug her. I said nothing at all to my aunt Carew, did not even look at her. Then Nurse Joan arrived, panting and red-faced, with a warm cloak for Margery and a sheepskin rug for my aunt's knees, and my father made way for her.

Aunt Carew huddled into the rug, pretending to shiver. 'Thank heavens I'm leaving this place! I won't be coming back here, Robert. Don't ever expect me to do anything else for this family. I'm not proud of being a Montague, never have been. Walter Montague was disgraced, and he deserved it. But I *am* proud of being a Carew.' She sighed happily. 'I wear that name like a jewel. A sparkling diamond!'

'I'm grateful for everything you've done for us,' my father said. His voice was like a thin wind, and I wondered whether he had ever liked his sister. I wouldn't blame him if he hadn't.

'And so you should be,' she nodded. 'Because of my husband's generosity you have an important job in court. Don't let your treasonous ways rob you of it, because I'll do nothing to help you if you do, and neither will he. And you can thank my husband for getting this plain creature a very important match to a very wealthy husband,' she went on. 'Be sure it's because I am married to a Carew. Who else would have her? What other husband would want a wife who can't even dance? Be sure my husband has paid a very handsome dowry to get her into that noble family.'

My father touched my sister's pale cheek.

104

'And the boy is well on his way to becoming a nobleman, either in this king's court or the next. None of this would have happened without my husband and me. Ask me no more favours, because you'll get none.'

She leaned back against her cushions, as if the very thought of it all exhausted her, and then jerked herself upright again. 'But remember this: you owe it to both of us to forget your Popish ways. You are rooted in the past, brother, and it will be the death of you. I beg you, for your own sake, for the sake of your children – burn your Latin Bible and prayer books. Renounce the Pope.'

The coach jerked away, and we could still hear her voice jolting over the stones. 'Leave Montague Hall, brother. If you persist in the old faith your life is in danger.'

I ran after the coach, waving and waving till the dust was choking and blinding me, and Margery's face was just a white, miserable blur, and her hand, lifted, motionless, was just a memory.

Brother John comes home

The shepherd's hut was a mile or so from the house, on a windy hill leading up to the moors. We went on foot, and I was carrying a basket of food from the kitchen – new bread, ham and cheese, a handful of cherries from the orchard. I was so anxious to see Brother John again that I ran ahead of my father and burst into the hut without knocking. I was taken aback to see what looked to be an old man in the hut, as frail and as thin as the yard brush. His hair was white and matted, his feet swollen and his skin worn leathery with weather. Surely Joan had been mistaken. It couldn't be Brother John.

He was on his knees, whispering prayers, and his mind must have been in some place far away, because he didn't even see or hear us at first. When he noticed us he peered at my father as if he might be something magicked up by a wizard.

'John!' my father said, and the monk's eyes lit up, and all of a sudden the sun was shining in his wintry face. He crossed himself, and my father helped him to his feet and put his arms round him.

'John, John, I'm sorry to see you like this,' Father said. His voice was husky.

His cousin chuckled. 'But I'm pleased to see you! So pleased. What a happy day!' He looked at me, 'And,

William, is this really my William? Ah, but I'm honoured! Joan told me you are the page to the future king of England, no less!' He bent his head in a bow, and I couldn't tell whether he was mocking me or not. Perhaps he was expecting me to return his bow in the courtly way and say, 'The pleasure is all mine, sir,' but I was too shocked. He was a tattered old man, and he smelled like a stinking fish, and my father had been embracing him as if nothing had changed. I thrust the basket of food towards him, and he hobbled to me and took it from me with a groan of pleasure.

'With thanks to God,' he said, and tucked into the food as noisily as one of the stable dogs. I felt sick at the sight of it. He nodded towards the cherries, inviting me to share them with him, but I shook my head. I wanted to go outside, where the air was fresher, but it had begun to rain. Drops slid through the holes in the thatch and pooled on the floor, turning the earth to mud.

'You can't stay here,' my father said, looking round the hut.

'This is the best home I've had for months,' Brother John said. 'You're not going to turn me out, are you?'

'You're coming home with us, to the Hall. Right now, if you're strong enough. If you're not, I'll send William back for the horses and we'll ride you home. But you can't stay here. It's no place for you.'

'You put yourself in danger, Robert. To harbour a priest who openly refuses to swear the Oath of Supremacy is to invite the king's punishment. Great, grave danger.'

But my father motioned to me to take his cousin's arm in mine. He took the other, and slowly, painfully, chuckling with every step, Brother John hobbled home with us. As we approached the gateway the rain stopped, and we stood for a moment to look at the Hall with the fresh sun turning the stone to pale gold. Brother John sighed deeply.

'I love this old place. If I die here, I will die happy. Thank you, William. Thank you, Cousin Robert, for bringing me back home.'

It was during that same week that Bailey brought news to my father that the woodcarver who had been working on Matthew's carving had died.

'It was nearly finished,' Bailey said. 'But for the face. And the man's wife wants to know, sir, if you'll still pay her for the work that was done, as she's a widow now.'

'Of course I will,' Father said.

'And have the work brought here,' said Brother John. He looked at my father. 'Will you let me finish it? A sad, sad task, but I can do it. It will be an act of love for all of you.'

So Ned and Bailey went to fetch the carving on a handcart. They carried it into the chapel with a piece of sacking wrapped round it, and laid it on a raised bench. Brother John found his old chisels and blades, and laid out his drawing of Matthew's face beside it. I couldn't look at it. Not yet. But he spent every morning patiently working the wood into a likeness of my brother.

I think it was doing this that made him well again. All the servants loved him, and he loved them, even shambling Stephen and slow, steady Ned Porritt. He had the kind of smile that creased his face into a hundred lines, like a crazed plate. Sometimes I felt guilty for enjoying myself so much with him, when poor Margery was gone for ever to be married to an ugly old man in France. We heard nothing from her. I knew from servants' tales that the sea between England and France could be as rough as wild horses, even in the calm of summer. What if her boat had gone down, and Margery with it? Would we ever know? I made myself go and stand on the cliff looking down across the summer-calm sea, though I would never go down into the bay where my brother had drowned.

'Help her, Matthew,' I whispered. 'Help her to be safe.'

When Brother John was getting better we spent hours walking in the grounds and lanes around the house, and it was slow progress, because he had to admire the mulberry tree, smell the flowers and listen to the birds, and watch the fishes leap in the lake as if he was doing it all for the first time. Or maybe the last time. Who would know what went on in his mind?

'*Deo gratias!* Thanks be to God!' he said, flinging out his arms as though he wanted to embrace everything he could see. 'How I love life! Don't you, William? Watch the bee nuzzling into the roses there! Doesn't he love life? Watch the swallows tumbling in the sky! Don't they love life? Nothing is more precious. Every day I thank God for giving me health and happiness and for keeping me alive! One day I'll meet Him, and thank Him in person,' he chuckled. 'But not yet.'

'Did you think you were going to die?' I asked. 'When Aunt Carew turned you away and you were out on the moors with no food or dry clothes? Did you think, *That's it; I've had it now*? Were you afraid?'

I wanted to think that my father and I had saved his life. And I wanted to punish Aunt Carew in my thoughts. How could anyone be cruel to someone like Brother John?

'Afraid? No, I was never afraid,' he said. 'You can only die once, after all. It might be the plague that takes you away, and you could be one of hundreds, oh, thousands, to die of it that week. Or it could be the sweat, or hunger, or the gallows, or a bolting horse, but it only happens once. So why be afraid? And, remember, leaving this life takes you to the next, to the Kingdom of Heaven, William!'

He talked to me in Latin, and wouldn't let me reply in English. If I did, he would look at me with a blank smile on his face, as if he hadn't understood a word of it. Before I went to court I used to get in a complete tangle with my Latin, angry with myself. I couldn't say what I really wanted to say. I couldn't even put all of my thoughts into English. Now I could do it almost without thinking, but I still didn't like it.

'Oh, what's the point of this?' I shouted at last, in English. I picked up a stone and hurled it into the lake, and we both had to jump back because of the huge splash it made.

Brother John put both his hands on my shoulders, serious for a moment.

'You must speak Latin, William. It's the language of the world. One day you may be a traveller, if you stay with the king and the court. You're a clever boy. You can pick up languages easily. If you can talk to people, you can understand their minds. If you understand people, you'll love them. Nothing is more important than to understand people and to love them.'

It took me a good few minutes to translate all that.

'I couldn't possibly love everyone.' I was thinking of Aunt Carew and Percy Howard. 'Is there anyone you don't like?'

'No one.'

'Not even Aunt Carew? Not even King Henry?'

He looked sideways at me. 'Do you hate King Henry?'

'No,' I admitted. 'He's kind to me, and he laughs and sings a lot, but I think that's because he's with Prince Edward whenever I see him. He's always happy then. Everybody around him seems to love him.'

'Do they?'

I thought for a minute, remembering all the bowing and smiling that went on in court, everybody hanging onto everything the king said, as if every word he spoke was made of pure gold.

'They act as if they do,' I said.

Brother John put his head to one side. 'Well, that's different.'

I knew he was right. They acted as if they loved him because they were afraid of what he might do to them if they didn't. 'I know they're afraid of him too. He has terrible rages, and he had Queen Anne put to death! His own wife! And he closed down all your monasteries, and he threw everyone out. He turned out thousands and thousands of poor and sick people, and left them to beg and starve on the streets. Don't you hate him for that?'

'What good does it do to hate him?' Brother John picked up a pebble and tossed it into the lake. 'Watch the ripples. Ripples of love, ripples of hate, they all spread out from there, you can't stop them. Which would you rather spread, if you were that pebble?'

We turned to go back to the Hall, and heard the sound of horses cantering up the lane. We watched them from across the meadow, shielding our eyes against the sun. Two horsemen arrived at the Hall door, dressed in the rich velvets of noblemen. I groaned. *It must be something to do with Aunt Carew*, I thought. No one important ever came to Montague Hall except by her invitation, and even then they hardly ever accepted, because it was so far from London. And because it was so far, if they did come, they stayed for days and days. We had to feed them and entertain them. Margery was made to dress up and sing and play music for them. I had to fish and hunt with them.

But Aunt Carew was in France. Why would anyone come when she was away?

A few servants scurried out to meet the visitors, followed by my father. Now we could see their servants going into the stables with Ned, leading their sweating horses into the cool.

'Was your father expecting visitors?' Brother John asked.

'No,' I said. I felt bitterly disappointed. I didn't want to share our summer together with anyone. 'I hope they won't stay long.'

Brother John shaded his eyes with his hand. 'One of them is a boy, not much older than you. A friend for you, William. Better than spending your time with two dusty old men! You go and greet them. I'll walk on.'

He hurried away from me, and was soon lost from sight among the trailing willow trees. I went slowly up to the house. My heart was heavy. The riders had dismounted. The older one talking to my father; they obviously knew each other. The younger one turned, scowling as I approached. He pulled off his riding glove and swept his lank, yellow hair away from his eyes. Percy. Of all people – Percy Howard.

The sweat

I walked towards them as slowly as I could, knowing I couldn't avoid them, though I was sulking inside my head. Why were they here?

It was Percy himself who told me, in that languid, drawling voice of his, as though talking was really too much effort. My father and his had gone ahead into the house, and I could hear the same news in their voices. Percy hardly looked at me.

'My father and I have come as messengers,' he said. 'In case you haven't heard, in this far-flung little place of yours. There is a serious outbreak of sweating sickness in London. His Majesty wants us all to stay away from London, and from him, until it has passed. And you, of course, are to keep away from Hampton Court. The little prince is to be isolated from contamination until the summer is over.'

He dawdled away from me, and I stared after him. Why had he and his father come all the way to Montague to tell us this? Why hadn't one of the king's messengers been sent from Hampton Court? And part of me sang with joy because I would be spending more time at home, weeks maybe. And part of me groaned with despair. Were Percy and his father going to stay with us all summer? Of course they couldn't go back to

114

London while the Sweat raged there. But surely, surely, there was somewhere else for them to stay?

Brother John didn't appear at the evening meal, which was as grand an affair as our kitchen servants could get together without Aunt Carew's instructions: herbed trout from our river, venison baked in port wine, plums and raisins soaked in brandy spirit, creams and cheeses from our own dairy. Percy sneered and picked his way through it, but Lord Howard was gracious enough to compliment my father on the tenderness of the venison, and to ask if he had shot the deer himself.

'I would like to hunt with you tomorrow,' he said.

Of course. Visitors always did.

My father bowed and said he would be delighted, and refused to catch my eye when I tried to remind him that we had planned to ride to the market to buy some new leather boots for Brother John. I stopped short of mentioning his name; I had more sense than that, but I saw Percy's eyebrows meet in a scornful smile as I hesitated, as if he had caught me out; and I thought again, why have they come here? Why them, and not a messenger? I didn't understand that. Percy hated me, and my father was well below Lord Howard's rank in court. They would know each other by sight because of Uncle Carew, but they were certainly not friends. Had they come to mock our humble way of life? Or had they come to snoop and spy? Percy's whispered words at the king's banquet crept through me like trickles of ice sliding through water. *I will be watching you.*

*

Later that evening, when we left the hall where we had been dining, I saw Percy slip into the shadows of a side corridor instead of going upstairs to his room. I followed him. What was he looking for, I wondered? But I knew, deep in my heart I knew. I went quietly after him, watching how he opened doors, peered into rooms without entering, closed the doors again. Finally he came to the oldest part of the Hall. Damp and musty as it was, it was hardly a place for visitors. But it led to the chapel. I knew for certain now what he was looking for, and why he had come. I called his name, and he turned sharply, guilty as a prowling cat. He smiled his vinegar smile.

'Are you lost?' I asked pleasantly, though my heart was in my throat and beating as wildly as a trapped bird.

'What's this room?' he asked, nodding towards the chapel door. His knuckles brushed it.

'Locked,' I said firmly. 'You are quite lost, Percy. Follow me.'

I stepped back and picked up a branch of candles, then led him past the chapel to a door at the other end of the corridor. I wanted to push him inside, but had to bow and fuss and wave my hand to show him I wanted him to go in first. I was just too late. Behind me down the corridor, the door to the chapel opened. Brother John peered out, revealing for a brief second the inside of the chapel, the holy paintings, the carved statues that my father loved so much and that Brother John had mended. You could just see the edge of his robe. He closed the door abruptly, silently, and perhaps, I thought, perhaps, Percy hadn't even noticed. But perhaps he had. He raised one eyebrow in that annoying way he has, so it disappeared under the pale hair, and closed his eyes as though he was enjoying a wonderful, private joke.

I'm glad to say that I beat him at chess that night.

The following morning Lord Thomas Howard said with great courtesy to my father: 'My son tells me your chapel is locked. This is most unusual.'

My father nodded. 'It was at the wish of my sister. She is a staunch reformist. She would like to have it refurbished.'

Lord Howard nodded. 'And in the meantime, where do you pray?'

'In the chapel,' my father smiled. 'I have my own key.'

'And I believe your cousin, John, is living here?'

My father glanced at me. I squeezed my fists so tightly that the nails bit into my palms.

'He is an ordained priest?' Lord Howard went on. 'Can he celebrate Mass?'

'He can,' my father said quietly. We knew, we both knew, what was coming.

'Then my son and I would be delighted to join you in the chapel this morning.' Lord Howard was jovial, but firm. There was no way of putting him off; he was a guest in our house. But if Brother John insisted on saying the creed in Latin, as he did every morning of his life, then he would be seen to be performing an act of treason. I knew that Brother John would never betray his Faith. He would never celebrate the reformed Mass, no matter who was there, no matter what the danger was.

And it was as we feared. Lord Howard and Percy came into the chapel, glanced at the statues but said nothing. *Perhaps*, I thought wildly, *they are of the same thinking as Brother John and my father, perhaps privately they don't accept the king's ruling*. But then I remembered again what Percy had hissed down my ear at the banquet. We were being watched.

Never have I prayed so fervently. Never have I wished the Mass to end more quickly. But the moment came, just as it must, when Brother John ended the gospel and said: '*Credo in Unum Deum*.'

'I believe in one God,' Lord Howard and Percy said loudly.

'*Patrem omnipotentem*.'

'The Father Almighty.'

'*Factorem coeli et terrae*.'

'Maker of heaven and earth.'

And so it went on, line after line of our most beloved prayer, tossing backwards and forwards in Latin and English round the chapel, the voices growing louder and louder, my father's voice with Brother John's, the two Howard voices together, and I was silent, too terrified to say a single word. At last the Creed was finished, the preparation for the sanctification of the bread and wine began, the loud voices dropped to a murmur. I could see the perspiration on my father's brow; I could hear the shiver in his voice.

And afterwards, nothing was said about it. Nothing at all. Maybe, maybe, everything would be all right. We were as polite to the Howards as they were to us. We were perfect hosts. But it reminded me of being back at court, talking in whispers, watching the shadows,

118

minding your tongue. I didn't want my home to be like this too. I wished they would go away. There was no more sign of Brother John. He wasn't in his room; he was nowhere to be found. The chapel door stayed locked. I was worried that he might disappear again and stay away for good now, and let the dusty lanes swallow him up.

At last, at long last, the visit was over. Lord Howard told my father that sadly he and Percy must leave and catch up with the king on the last stage of His Majesty's summer progress. How glad I was. I was sick of playing chess, even though most of the time I won. But on his last night, Percy beat me so easily and quickly that I knew he had been teasing me the way I teased Prince Edward.

Before the game began he nursed the bishop in his hand and said, very slowly, 'I met a family once who kept a hangman in their house. Can you believe it? Their very own hangman!' He turned the piece round carefully, as if he was looking for faults in the wood. Then he replaced it on the board next to the knight and moved his first pawn. 'A dangerous guest, wouldn't you think?' His moves were fast and clever. I knew there was no way I could win. In half the moves it would have taken me, he had my king in checkmate.

Next morning, as he and his father were leaving, Percy leaned down from his horse, smiling at me. 'You play your game well, William. But I play another game just as well. And I always win.'

Two letters

Now I felt as if the blue summer had turned to grey winter; as if even though the gardens were full of flowers, they had ice on their petals. Brother John was found again hiding in the shepherd's hut, and Father begged him to come back to the Hall.

'You belong there,' he insisted. 'Whatever happens. You're a Montague too, remember.'

'I'll only stay till my work is finished,' Brother John said, shaking his head. 'Every second I spend in the Hall brings danger. But Matthew is almost complete.' He strode ahead of us, his rosary swinging from his belt. 'Come to the chapel this evening,' he called over his shoulder. 'I'll have him ready for you.'

Father was already in the chapel when I arrived that evening. He was standing with Brother John in front of the life-size carving of my brother. The candles were lit, and the light shone on Matthew's face. He almost looked real, lying there on the plinth Brother John had made for him. He looked asleep, and he looked calm.

'Hello, Mattie,' I whispered, and the candles around him fluttered as if he was breathing back to me: 'Hello, Will.'

It felt to me, then, that he had come back home.

*

The weather turned, it was grey and rainy, and for days the sea lay hidden under a fret. I watched out every day for riders looming out of the mist, and one day, one did come, but he was a comical red-faced figure. He brought us the best thing I could have hoped for – a letter, at last, from Margery.

He arrived late one afternoon, spattered in mud and full of wild tales. Ned ran to take his muddy horse into the stables.

'I 'ave 'ad a terrible monster of a journey,' he told us in his broken English. 'The sea between France and England was like a field of wild ponies, *mon Dieu*! My entire stomach went overboard to feed the fish. And then...' he gazed round dramatically, and fixed Ned with his bulging eyes, 'I am set upon by four – no – five men. They 'ad 'oods over their faces, and knives in their 'ands. Like this, they went – flash, flash – and I fight them off. And in the night, a black pig 'e come at me out of the forest and try to eat me. And then, my 'orse 'e stumble when we cross the ford, and *poof!* I go head over my heels into the river!'

'But the letter,' my father reminded him.

'Ah yes, I still 'ave 'im. Safe as a baby in my pouch! *Voila!*' He brought it out with a flourish, like a court magician. Brother John smiled gleefully through all this, and I was clenching my fists in my mouth to stop myself from laughing out loud. My father was so grateful to the muddy messenger that he gave him a straw pallet in the kitchen instead of the stables, and told him to rest himself before he set off back for Calais. We ran to the window to read the letter in the last of the daylight. I jumped up, trying to snatch it out of my father's hands,

121

but he laughed and held it high above my head. In that brief moment, I thought, the gap between us was closing at last. But if he was happy that day, I realised, it was nothing to do with me. It was because Margery had written home.

And after all that, after everything that poor messenger had gone through, even if half of it was true, it was just the briefest of letters.

My dear Father and Brother, I don't know whether you are still at Montague Hall, but my Aunt Carew has given me permission to write to you there. I think about you often. I am married now. This castle is very grand and my husband, the Lord Lieutenant, is very important. He looks after it for King Henry. We have many visitors; we always seem to be having a banquet or a ball. I am Lady Richard of Carlisle and Calais, if you please, with many beautiful gowns to wear and more servants than I know what to do with. Your loving Margery. And then, in hurried scrawl, *I miss home.*

'I think she's happy,' my father said. 'It's not a cry for help, is it?' He turned the letter over, looking for more. He was as disappointed as I was.

Margery's letters to me when I was at Hampton Court were usually pages long, full of poems and little drawings and secret, wicked comments about Aunt Carew. This scratched message was hardly worth the messenger's sweat and seasickness. I knew Aunt Carew had dictated it, except perhaps for the last scribbled words. I imagined her standing over Margery as she nibbled the end of her goose-feather pen, snatching the letter from her as soon as she'd finished, frowning over her tiny flourishing handwriting, which was like the trails birds make in the snow. But it was a letter, at least, and that was better than nothing, and I heard her voice in my head as I was reading it.

'I wish she'd told us a bit more,' I complained.

'Your Aunt Carew was never one for writing long letters,' Brother John said. 'So I wouldn't expect her to encourage Margery to.' He smiled knowingly, and tried to cheer me up with stories about what a hopeless letter-writer Aunt Carew had been when she was little, breaking her quill, ripping the parchment, dripping ink everywhere, over her face and her gown, the table, anywhere she turned.

'I thought she was good at everything,' I said.

'She was good at nothing,' Brother John chuckled. 'She couldn't walk across the room to meet visitors without tripping over her skirts. She couldn't climb on her pony without falling straight off again.'

'She fell badly, once. She never got her courage back. That's why she never rides anywhere, even now.' My father gestured to us to follow him back into the house, away from the bothering midges. 'She prefers to have her bones thrown about in that rattling carriage of hers than to fall off her horse. She has a deep fear inside her.'

I understood that fear. It was like my deep fear of the sea, ever since Matthew had drowned. I thought of the way Aunt Carew shouted at us and beat us to do things right, to do our best, to be better than anyone else, and in a very small corner of my heart I forgave her, just a tiny bit, because she had been good at nothing and because she knew what it was to be afraid. But I didn't visit that corner of my heart very often. It was full of cobwebs and dust.

Next day brought the sunshine back, and another letter. This one came from Hampton Court, from Mother Jack. It smelled of the rose petal oil she used on Prince Edward's skin.

We need you here, William, it said. My throat tightened with disappointment. *The sweating sickness is over, and His Majesty returns from his progress. He will want to break his journey here. I have heard from my sister that he has had a very bad time. It has rained for a week solid; the fields are awash, the tents blown down, and all his courtiers and servants up to their thighs in mud. His Majesty travels home in a bad mood, and will want to see his son very soon. You must come back, William.*

So, my wonderful summer was over; my walks in the grounds with Brother John, riding out with my father, reading in turns to each other in the evenings. At least I had the pleasure of knowing that Percy Howard would have been sleeping in a sodden flapping tent and splashing his spindly legs with mud. But the sun here was no use to me any more. I had to go back to court; back to work, back to my cage.

'I must go too, now the sweating sickness is over,' my father said. 'Lord Carew will be travelling back with the king, and he'll be sending for me any day. I've been very lucky to have been able to stay here so long. But you must stay, John,' he told his cousin. 'This is your home again now.'

'And mine is Hampton Court,' I sighed. 'It's so different there.'

'Aha, I have a riddle for you!' Brother John's eyes lit up. 'I carry my home wherever I go. I live off the land, though my progress is slow.'

124

'Easy,' I grinned. 'A snail.'

'And have you ever looked closely at a snail, and seen how perfect and beautiful its home is? Your home goes everywhere with you, William, as long as you don't break the shell. It's in your heart. We could do a drawing of Montague Hall today, and you can keep looking at it so you never forget it. We must make our last day very special. Morning prayers in the chapel, then a ride, with hunks of bread and cheese in our packs? William, I will be sad to see you go, very sad. But one day soon, please God, we will meet again.'

That was the plan. But it was never to be.

The king's visitors

I woke up early with the sound of birdsong rippling into my room, and I went straight to the little chapel. Brother John was already there, lighting the candles with a long taper. My father joined us and he and I kneeled together by the carving of Matthew. We attended Mass and gently sang the responses to Brother John's verses. I loved Mass as much as Father did, I think. It was part of my life. Sunlight poured through the yellow and green linens over the window slits, and the smoke of the incense and the candles clouded into it and turned amber.

As we prayed, I dimly heard a distant clattering sound of hooves in the lane, but my hearing must have been better than Brother John's or my father's, or else they were not disturbed by it. They kept their heads bowed, their whispered prayers shushing calmly over urgent sounds that were coming nearer, sounds that eventually alarmed me so much that my face was beading with sweat.

'Father!' I whispered, but they both ignored me. Surely I wasn't imagining the sounds now; raised voices, marching feet, nearer, coming nearer, and still Brother John's soft voice hummed on.

'*Agnus Dei, qui tollis peccata mundi, miserere nobis.*'

Lamb of God, you who takest away the sins of the world, have mercy upon us.

Suddenly the door to the chapel was flung open.

My father's steward, Bailey, heaving gulps of air into his chest, stood like a wounded bear in the doorway, eyes bulging, arms flailing, swaying backwards and forwards on the balls of his feet. 'Soldiers have come!' he gasped.

My father nodded. He showed no fear or surprise, except in a clenching of the muscle at the side of his jaw. He stood up, grasped my arm, and hauled me down the corridor. Brother John followed, clasping the precious golden chalice in both his hands. My father rushed us into a room at the far end of the corridor, opened the door of a passage concealed in the painted panel, and tried to push Brother John inside. The priest stood back, staring from one to the other of us.

'Go on, go on!' Father urged. 'You too, Will. Get in!' He shoved me through, and Brother John tumbled in after me. The door was swung to; I heard my father and Bailey panting as they lifted a heavy table and pushed it against the door.

We were in total darkness. It was stiflingly hot and smelled of damp and the sweat of fear. I could hear Brother John's breath rattling in his throat with fright. Blind and terrified, I groped my way on all fours the whole length of the passage, which seemed now to be over the kitchens. I could smell our breakfast fish cooking; I could hear the clattering of pots, men's raised voices, but I couldn't make out the words. Brother John didn't follow me. I could hear him whispering, and knew that he was praying.

We seemed to be there for hours; perhaps we were. I had cramp in my legs and my head was throbbing

127

violently, and I felt faint and sick with the heat. I was straining for sounds, any sounds. Where were the soldiers now? Had they gone? I had no idea.

And at last, when I thought I couldn't bear it any longer and I was screaming inside my head for something, anything, to happen, there came the muffled scraping of heavy furniture being dragged, and the cupboard door was pulled open. Blinding daylight scorched my eyes, and then a dark shape blocked the opening. The shape crouched into the cupboard, grabbed Brother John and hauled him out. Then the door was slammed shut and I was in darkness again.

I still daren't move. I still had no idea what was happening out there. I stretched myself out on the floor to ease my cramped legs, and must have fallen asleep. At last the door was opened again. I sat up, screwing my eyes against the soft light of a candle, and heard my father calling my name. I crawled out, and he put his arms out to help me to stand up.

'Have they gone?' I asked. I was sobbing with relief at being outside that tomb.

'Yes, they've gone.' My father's voice was breaking to pieces. 'They've taken Brother John. They have spared us. They told me their orders from the king were to take the priest, as a lesson to us. He will hang, William. He will hang.'

The first time I saw a hanging, I must have been about ten years old. It's like a party, full of shouting and jeering, caps being tossed into the air, mugs of ale being passed round. If the crowd hates the victim, even if all he's done is to cut a purse from a rich-man's belt, they howl at him. If they like him, even if he's a murderer, they howl at the hangman. I remember watching the hangman, wondering what his face was like under his black hood, wondering if he'd ever had to hang someone he knew. I used to dream about him at night, coming for me out of the darkness, the slits of his eyes glinting through his mask. I remember once an old woman next to me whooping and cackling as the man to be hanged was dragged to the scaffold. 'Oh, what a villain!' she chortled. 'See his sweet face! Full of wickedness!'

And that villain was a priest, I remember, like Brother John. He prayed his Latin prayers in front of the scaffold. The crowd went absolutely silent, listening for what would be said.

'Do you accept that King Henry is the head of the Church in England?' an official asked him.

'I do not,' the priest said, clear and calm.

'Do you reject the teaching of the Pope in Rome?'

'I do not.'

And that set the crowd roaring and jeering again, and I couldn't take my eyes off him, that little priest with the gentle forgiving face, and yet every bit of my body was jingling with nerves and excitement and fear and thrill and horror, all those things, as the board under his feet was pulled away and he twitched and bobbed and dangled like a puppet on a string. And then he was still, so still, and would be still for ever.

My father was right, and I knew it. Brother John would hang. But we had been spared. Why? And for how long?

'Edward loves you'

It was a relief to get away from Montague Hall after that awful day. I kept thinking about Brother John. I could hardly think about anything else. He was my favourite person in the world, next to my father. I missed his jokes and his riddles and his happiness. I even missed our difficult conversations in Latin. Night after night I dreamed about the hooded hangman coming to drag him to the scaffold, and I woke up screaming and sweating. There was no one I could talk to about it. If I'd told Mother Jack she would have filled up my head with even more frightening stories.

I was afraid, too, of going back to the king's court. He knew about Brother John. He had had him killed, but he had spared us. Why had he spared us? Did it mean he had forgiven us, or was he just biding his time? I had no idea, and every second that I spent in Hampton Court I was afraid. I couldn't trust anyone any more; I felt sure I was being watched, everywhere I went, everything I did. I listened for whispers. I looked into shadows for the hangman.

But I had my work to do, and the prince and his funny little ways helped me through my nightmares. He had learned lots more words while I had been away, and he chattered all the time. He was shy of me at first, and then when he remembered me he followed me everywhere, towing Mother Jack along behind him too, as if they were river boats and I was a royal barge.

'He's missed you,' Mother Jack said. 'He wouldn't even ride on his little pony without you helping him. But I couldn't send for you because of the Sweat. Nobody was allowed to come here in case they brought it with them. Nobody left the place, either. We have to keep the little prince out of harm's way. Oh, the scrubbing that's gone on here – every wall, every floor. Tell me about your big world outside, William. I'm starved of gossip.'

But I had no stories to tell her. And now I had come back, I wasn't allowed to leave the grounds again. I felt as if I was in prison.

I dreaded the thought of ever seeing the king again, but in October it was Prince Edward's second birthday. The king invited a thousand guests to Hampton Court. In they flooded, bringing all their noise with them. There were banquets and pageants for the whole week. Musicians from all over London were called in. Everyone dressed up, flirted, simpered, laughed. The king's tumblers jested and skipped and kept my prince amused. I didn't smile once, but nobody noticed or cared. I knew my uncle Carew was watching me, I knew Lord Howard kept his eyes on me, but I just got on with my work. I didn't want King Henry to notice me at all. All I could think about was that he had caused thousands of his own subjects to be killed. He didn't care whether they lived or died, as long as they obeyed him. I had known that and had hardly grasped it, I had

been so proud to be his son's page. But now he had had
Brother John hanged. He had ordered his men to come
to my father's house and snatch him away from us.
Now I understood how cruel he was. I understood why
people were so afraid of him. I never wanted to see him
again, and yet I couldn't get away from him. He
dominated my life. He owned me.

One rainy afternoon Mother Jack told me to take Prince
Edward to watch his father playing tennis. His other
servants bowed as we passed them, then followed on
behind us in case they were needed for anything. I held
the little boy up to the grilled window so he could see
the game without being harmed by the ball. I watched
the fat, gross man who thought he was chosen by God,
lumbering and sweating as he played, and I saw how
weak he really was. He still had a stinking wound on his
leg that never seemed to heal in spite of all the
physicians he called in. He limped rather than
swaggered these days. The nobleman who was playing
tennis with him was kind to him, I could see that; he
rolled the ball gently against the wall rather than
slamming it, so His Majesty never had to reach out or
run, but still King Henry sweated and heaved, until it
was clear that he was in too much pain to carry on. He
kneeled down, hugging his bad leg. The wound in it
gaped open, blood and yellow pus oozed from it.
Servants rushed to help him and he swept them away,
furious. He limped out, reeking of sweat and the sour
wound. His nobles clustered round him, bowing deeply,
murmuring concern. He bellowed at them for fussing
over him.

Then he saw me with Prince Edward. I kept my eyes lowered, but His Majesty called out, 'William Carew!' and I bowed to him unwillingly. He limped towards me and put his wet hand on my shoulder.

'Edward loves you, young William,' he said. 'You're like a brother to him. Sometimes I wish you *were* his brother.' All the courtiers standing round us laughed and clapped, and so did Prince Edward. I blushed and bowed my thanks. I was the king's favourite, after all. There wasn't much I could do about that. But for how long? I clenched my fists together tight, tight. I wanted to scream out loud: 'Let me go! Let me go!' I wanted to be anywhere in the world except at Hampton Court.

At last the whole glittering court took to their barges and sailed back to London. The palace sank into a swoon of exhaustion. But at least I had the freedom to ride Black Tudor again in the afternoons, and to take my falcon and release her into the sky. Lucky, lucky Clever, to be able to stretch her wings as far as they would go.

During one of my archery lessons my tutor, Sir Andrew, was called away. It was a blue, bright, sharp day in late November, a day that was full of surprise sunshine before the deep winter set in. Prince Edward was chattering, waving his teething stick of coral in the air as if he was painting the clouds, and Mother Jack was singing to him in her dreamy way; *I had a little nut tree*. They were both muffled up in furs against the cold.

I put down my bow and arrow and waited for Sir Andrew to come back. I watched the drift of the last golden leaves from the great trees, curling and uncurling like lazy dancers on their way to the ground, and I thought; *I wish this moment could last forever.* I was actually happy.

'Say goodbye to Prince Edward, William,' Mother Jack called. 'He's going for his rest now.'

'Bye, Wims,' I heard the prince call.

Mother Jack laughed lightly and walked away. How I wish now that I'd touched Prince Edward's little hands and smiled at him and wished him well.

I crouched down by the linen clout, idly collecting up my arrows, daydreaming, and suddenly heard the sound of someone hurrying across the grass. I jumped up guiltily, thinking it would be someone coming to tell me off for laziness and disrespect. It was Sir Andrew. His face was tense and white with worry.

'William, your father needs to see you straight away,' he whispered, catching his breath.

'My father? Is he here?'

'No, he's sent a messenger to fetch you. A boat is waiting at the steps.'

I looked up at him, puzzled. What could be so urgent that my father would send for me? Did he have bad news of my sister?

'I've brought you a cloak. It'll be very cold on the river when the sun goes down,' Sir Andrew said. 'I'll walk you down to the landing steps.' He glanced round to see if anyone was watching us, then he looked at me gravely. His eyes were sharp with concern. 'I must warn you, there are serious problems at Westminster. There is danger everywhere.'

'Danger? What do you mean?'

But Sir Andrew was looking away from me. We were within earshot of the oarsmen; maybe he had already said too much. He handed me onto the boat, where my father's messenger was waiting, and then walked briskly away as if he had never spoken to me.

A palace of whispers

By the time I arrived at the Palace of Westminster I was tired and aching with cold; dizzy for food. Courtiers were moving idly about in their usual languorous way, jesting, bowing to one another, smiling and whispering. The air was brittle with tension. I felt anxious and afraid. The closer you came to King Henry, the more afraid you were. It was like being in a garden of brightly coloured chirruping birds – one clap of the hands would send them squalling and fluttering away in fright. There were footsteps ahead of me and behind me, the swish of skirts on dry rushes, flickering candlelight, shadows cast by the great fires, tapestries swaying. It was always like this – someone there, someone not there. It was a palace of whispers, a palace of shadows, and that day it seemed to be a palace of nightmares.

The messenger ushered me quickly to the room my father used as an office. My father was there on his own, pacing up and down, up and down, his hands behind his back. When he saw me he stopped and stared at me as if he didn't know me. His face was ashen.

'William! William!' he said. His voice was a strangled sound in his throat.

He went over to the casement window and I followed him. I took off my cloak and laid it over a chair, and bowed for his blessing. He put both his hands on my shoulders and when I looked up at him I saw that his eyes were bright, too bright.

'I wish I hadn't sent for you,' he said breathlessly. 'It was the wrong thing to do.'

'What's happened?' I asked. 'Is it Margery?'

'Margery? No, she's safe where she is, thank God. But I should not have called you here.' His hands were trembling; I could feel them through my heavy doublet. 'I should have taken the chance and come for you myself. We could have gone to my friend de Crecy's house. We would have been safe there for a while. Perhaps. Perhaps. It's too late now.'

'But what's happened?' I had never seen my father like this, not when Matthew died, not when Brother John was taken away. I had never seen cold fear like this in him before.

'We haven't much time left. I wanted to see you, and to warn you myself. I was afraid to send a message that could be used against you. But you must hear what I have to say and then go.' He dropped his voice to an urgent whisper. 'I think my life is in danger. Ssh, and listen. You know that I cannot accept King Henry as head of the Church. It is against all my beliefs. I have refused to swear to the Act of Supremacy. This means I am accused of treason. Many have turned away from the old ways to please him, but I can't. I won't. My faith is everything to me.'

'Nor will I.' I said firmly. 'But why is he doing this?'

'At first it was because he wanted to marry Anne Boleyn. Years ago, when you were a little boy. Now there are rumours that he's thinking of marrying a

Lutheran from a Duchy in Germany. Lady Anne of Cleves. This is up to him.'

'Then it's nothing to do with you,' I said, relieved. My father was just a secretary, after all. His rank was well below any of the officials like Cromwell who dealt with such things as weddings and foreign affairs.

'Your uncle Carew wants to speak to me later today about this. All I can think is that His Majesty knows that I hid Brother John in my house, and that I have refused to swear to the Act of Supremacy. Now it's my turn to be punished.' His voice broke, and he breathed in sharply, squeezing his eyelids together.

I thought of that stifling passage behind the kitchens; I thought of Brother John whispering his prayers. I thought of the soldiers dragging him away. To be hanged.

'Lord Howard has told him,' I shouted. 'Percy Howard!'

'Ssh, William. For God's sake keep your voice down. I think Lord Carew sent the Howards to our house. He wanted them to find me praying in chapel. He wanted them to betray me.'

I stared at him, mystified. 'But why?'

'So he can disown me. You and your sister are known as Carews now, but I am still a Montague. If he disowns me, he can't be blamed for what I do. I might be hanged, but he will be rid of me, and safe. That's what I think.'

He took his Montague signet ring off his finger, twisting it slightly over his knuckle, and held it out to me. 'Take it. Keep it, William.'

I shook my head, scared by his serious expression, but he pressed it into my palm and curled my fist around it.

'Keep it safe. Take it to my dear friend Lord de Crecy at Greenwich. He doesn't know you, but by this seal he will know our family. Go on your knees to him to beg him to help me. It's my only chance. He may now be of the same belief as the king, as most people are if they want to keep their heads, but he's my friend. He may feel moved to listen to you at least. Surely he'll help us, and speak to the king to pardon me.'

'But I can't go on my own! Come with me, please! We could leave now!'

'I can't. They'll stop me at the gates. I should never have sent for you, I've put you in danger too. But I wanted to see you. To say goodbye.' He paused for a long moment. 'Do this for me, William. Leave this palace now, and trust no one.'

I still couldn't move, couldn't believe what he was saying to me. Only the urgency in his voice told me that what he was saying must be true, that he had lost favour with my uncle and that his life was in danger. And mine too.

'But I still don't understand,' I whispered. 'Why pick on you?'

My father put his hands across his face as if he could wipe away the weariness of so many sleepless nights. 'I don't understand either,' he whispered. 'I don't understand why a man can't worship God in the way he's always done. And just by saying that, I am guilty of treason. I can be hanged for that, or tortured. Remember Daniel in the Bible? Remember how he was put in the lions' den because he refused to pray to anyone except to his God? This is what happens in our country, only men are not thrown to the lions any more. Monks and nuns have been thrown onto the streets, priests are sent to the gallows, like our dear Brother John. Churchmen are incarcerated. Terrible, monstrous things are done to them. Our king is a tyrant, William.'

He opened the casement window and peered out, as if he was searching for someone, then he came back in to me.

'Why don't we go home?' I said again. 'We could leave the court, both of us! We could try, at least. Don't give up.'

My father's face was ice-grey. 'There's more to tell you. It is rumoured that our chapel is burned to the ground, our house destroyed, the servants dismissed. We will have no home any more. Now do you understand how serious this is?'

I nodded. Tears were streaming down my cheeks, the hot blinding tears of despair. I felt as if everything I loved most in the world was being taken away from me. My home. My chapel. Matthew's statue. Father. Margery. Gone, all gone. 'Let me stay with you.'

He shook his head. He turned slightly, hearing as I did the sound of brisk feet marching along the corridor. Soldiers walked like that, not courtiers. 'If you stay here you are in as much danger as I am. Go.' His voice was hollow. 'Trust no one. Do this much for me, William.'

He pushed me towards the window, but at that moment the door began to open, and Father slid me behind the hanging and stood directly in front of me.

Someone came quietly into the room. He stood rubbing the palms of his hands together, and I knew it was my uncle Carew.

'Aha. You are here, Robert.'

My father bowed stiffly. 'My Lord Carew.'

I could hear my uncle pacing towards us, and my heart was jerking in my chest. I thought I was going to faint with terror. Then he stopped. For a waiting moment that lasted for ever neither of them spoke, then my uncle cleared his throat with a little yelping sound.

'Robert, you will have heard that with great regret my wife and I have closed down Montague Hall.'

My father answered quietly. 'I have my Lord, but I don't understand why.'

'Oh, I think you do.' My uncle was pacing round the room again now. I heard more footsteps. Someone else had come in, but I daren't look. I was willing Father to say the right words, whatever they were, the words that would save his life.

'I am told by reliable witnesses that you have acted against His Majesty's decrees,' my uncle went on smoothly. 'You never attend chapel here. You continue your Papist worshipping, in spite of my insistence that you cease. Even, I hear, that you kept a seditious priest in your house. Is this true?' His voice rose. I imagined his taut, angry face, the cold glitter of his eyes.

My father spoke, calmly, quietly. 'I have acted according to my conscience, Lord Carew.'

'Your conscience? Your conscience should tell you that you must be loyal to your king! Do you realise how dangerous this practice is? Do you realise you could be hanged for this?'

141

My father kept his silence. My throat was throbbing with fear. I had no idea what to do.

Then the other man spoke, and I knew at once who it was. It was the Duke of Norfolk. His brother had visited our house, eaten our food, and ridden with my father. His nephew Percy had played chess with me every night. Now I knew what he meant when he had told me the story about the family who had kept a hangman in their house. Because of Brother John, my father and I would hang.

'Robert Montague,' he said. 'I hear you have refused to agree to the Act of Supremacy. Would you care to tell me why?'

There was a moment's silence. Then my father said, very quietly, but quite clearly: 'I do not accept that King Henry is head of the Catholic Church in England. The Pope in Rome is the head of the Holy Catholic Church.'

There was a deep sigh from the Duke. 'Then, Robert Montague, you are accused of high treason. His Majesty the King spared you once. Your priest was hanged as a lesson to you, and yet you have not learned anything, it seems. His Majesty is disappointed in you. He desires you to be detained in his prison at Newgate until such time as you repent.' There was an acid smile in his voice. 'You know what they do to those who refuse to sign the oath of allegiance to His Majesty? They are stretched on the rack, maybe. Or turned on the wheel.' He was slimy with pleasure.

My uncle cut in quickly. 'A few months in Newgate should jolt you out of this foolishness. If you live.'

'Or else you can die a traitor's death, by the hangman and by the sword,' the Duke of Norfolk added. 'Take him!' he barked.

The door swung open again. Soldiers came in, and marched towards where I was squashed behind the hanging. Then my father's weight lifted away from me as he stepped forward. There were footsteps leaving the room, and then, silence. Long, long silence, when I hardly breathed or moved.

At last I felt sure there was no one in the room. Yet I didn't dare to step out. Terrified, I hoisted myself up inch by inch onto the window ledge and somehow squeezed through the little casement opening. I rolled backwards through it and tumbled down into the shrubbery below. I froze there, not moving, not breathing. I crouched for ages longer, until I could tell for sure that Uncle Carew wasn't standing at the other side of the window, looking out. My limbs were trembling. I had to run, yet still I couldn't. I was paralysed with fear. I gasped for breath, as if the air had turned as thick as mud.

From across the lawns a voice called out to me, 'William! I can see you!'

I jerked my head round, terrified. It was Lady Catherine, Margery's friend. She ran across to me, her skirts lifted in her hands, just as she used to run across the long grass at home.

'Are you playing hide-and-seek?' she laughed. 'Margery, Margery, where can she be?'

I jumped to my feet. She held out her arms to catch me and I pushed past her, sobbing aloud. She put her hand to her face, surprise and alarm flitting across her eyes, and I ran away from her as I had never run before. I daren't turn my head, I daren't think, I daren't look to the right or left of me. Courtiers were strolling across the darkening lawns as if it was just another evening, laughing and joking and teasing one another. They didn't see me; I was just a page running an errand for a knight. They didn't see that I was white with fear, or hear my breath tumbling in my throat. My father had been taken to Newgate prison, and all they could do was laugh and flirt with one another. My father was being tried for treason. My father might die. Like a hunted deer I ran to the gates of the palace. I lifted up my hand to show the guards the signet ring, so they would think I had an urgent message to deliver.

And then I was out in the street; homeless. I had only one thought in my head. To save my father's life.

Another world

Immediately I was surrounded by beggars. They stank of sweat and filth and disease, but I had no pomander to keep the smell away. The creatures were clutching at me, thrusting out their grimy paws for coins. A woman held out her baby towards me, letting it bawl miserably in my face. Its skin oozed with running sores.

'Let me through!' I shouted, but they took no notice. I still had to force my way through their stench of sickness and dirt. A legless beggar child clung to my doublet, and I shook him off roughly. What could I do for him? I had no money. My father was going to die. I was as wretched as any of them. 'Leave me alone!' I broke away from them and ran down a side street. They didn't follow me but stayed in a howling bunch at the gates, like a pack of beaten dogs, hungry for the next courtier to come out.

The further I ran, the filthier and dingier the streets became. They were so narrow that I could almost touch the leaning houses on each side of me. My feet were skidding in mud and horse dung. The smell of sickness was everywhere, mingling with the reek of wet chimney smoke. Pigs and rats rooted among piles of rotting food, hens shrieked round my feet. And everywhere I went, people stared at me, a page in velvet and silk, a member of the royal household running alone and scared in their streets. If a filthy street boy had run into the king's presence chamber he wouldn't have caused more of a stir than I did then. I paused to get my breath, and immediately a gang of men moved towards me, arms outstretched as if they were baiting a bear. A toothless woman cackled from her doorway.

I turned round and charged down another side street, then another, through a maze of suffocating alleys, each one darker than the first. The houses leaned dangerously towards one another like rows of drunken lords about to tumble into sleep. I had no breath left in my body. My legs were spent. I staggered against a wall, and collapsed into the doorway of a shop. The rush lights were lit; the tiny latticed windows were filled with bottles of coloured liquids. I could just see an old man in a dark green apothecary's gown inside, carefully weighing out powders. I could hear him counting to himself. His wand of golden willow lay on the ledge next to him.

At least I won't die yet if I shelter here, I thought. *If the cold chills my bones to sticks, this old man should have something to make me better.*

I curled up against the door, hugging my knees, and thought about my chances. I might die of starvation. When the beggars or thieves find me they'll tear me to pieces looking for a purse. And I've no money with me anyway; I might as well be a pauper. How would I get to Greenwich? How would I find Lord de Crecy? And my father was locked in Newgate, left to rot with the rats and mice. What would happen to him? I thought of the stories of terrible tortures that Mother Jack had regaled me with; girls crushed under boards that were piled with stones, men stretched on racks, or screwed into metal frames that twisted their bones until they cracked. My father. My father.

And if he didn't agree even then to say that King Henry was head of the Church, he could be tied to a stake and burned alive, or hanged until he was nearly dead, and then his insides cut out of him while he was still alive. All these things happened, I knew that well.

At that moment I thought my heart would break. I felt so alone, so afraid. I whispered prayers, my prayers, the Latin prayers of my childhood. Over and over again like a chant. I held my father's ring up to the light from the apothecary's shop. I could see the family crest engraved into it – our ancient family, beloved of a Plantagenet king, all brought to ruin by Percy Howard. I slipped the ring onto my finger but it was too big; I would soon lose it if I kept it there. I tucked it into my purse. All I could hope was that some cut-purse didn't sneak up behind me and snip it away from my belt. I huddled into the doorway as darkness grew and the night breathed a cold, sharp wind around me. The noises of the city died away, except for the barking of dogs. Eventually I was aware of the shop door opening, and a lantern casting a flickering light across my face. I looked up to see the old man coming out backwards, pulling the door closed to lock it. He almost stumbled over me.

'Good heavens, what's this?' He bent towards me, screwing up his eyes to look at me. 'A young courtier, by your fine clothes. On my doorstep? Young sir, sire, get yourself up! It's not safe for you here at night! It's not safe for anyone. Are you lost?'

I struggled to my feet. 'I'm all right,' I said stiffly. 'A bit tired. I needed a rest.'

The old man shook his head. The wispy hair straggling down from his cap fluffed out like the down on a duckling's back. 'Rest in a draughty doorway, when you might have a real bed in a king's palace! Is that where you belong? Let me take you to your gates. Which family are you from? They'll have set up a hue and cry for you if you're lost.'

He held out his hand, but I was too afraid to follow him. 'Trust no one,' my father had warned. This old man might deliver me right into the hands of the king's soldiers. I backed away from him, covering my face with my hand as he held up the lantern. I darted back down the street, slipping again in the slime, and came into an open square. Maybe I was safer here, where there were people. Merchants and street hawkers were making their way home for the night, dark shapes in the gloom. I was shivering with cold and hunger and fear, and I thought briefly of the court, the trestle tables bending with the weight of food, the king lounging with his new favourite lady by his side. He would be singing one of his songs, maybe, and the musicians would be fumbling at their harp and viols, keen to join in with his tune. The ladies would be dancing in the glow of the great fire, their rich gowns swishing like waves on the shore. Did anyone miss me? Why should they? The king did not even miss his dead queen. He had a son. That was all he cared about in the whole world. But did his son miss me?

Why should he? I thought miserably? *He's only a baby. He can't even say my name properly.* Mother Jack would wonder where I had gone, but servants and courtiers often disappeared when the king turned against them. Nobody asked questions; they might be the next one to lose their head.

The only person in England who would miss me was my father.

The thought of my father gave me the strength to carry on. I had to do something to help him. No one else would. I kept on running, away from the palace, away from the squalor of the streets, until I was too tired to lift my feet off the ground. That night I slept under the stars, and a cold night it was, and I swear the stars were shivering as much as I was. I kept thinking of my bed at Hampton Court, with its thick heavy curtains to keep away the draught, and the warm comforting glow of the fire in the hearth. I would probably never see the inside of a palace again in my life. Already it seemed like another world. I was still terrified in case any of the soldiers who had taken my father away would come in search of me next. I had been seen coming to the palace and running away from it, I could be quite sure of that. Someone would talk. They had only to ask for a boy in courtly clothes, and my way would be pointed out to them. *A hue and cry*, the apothecary had said. If they wanted to, they would find me in no time and drag me off to Newgate jail. And then what? Stretch me on a rack? Burn me? Hang me? They could do anything, if the king had decided that I wasn't his favourite any more.

A dead boy's clothes

The crowing of cockerels woke me, but I have no idea how I managed to sleep. I was stiff and cold, and my clothes were damp. I stretched myself and screwed up my eyes against the sharp sunlight. It must be about six of the clock, and my father had already spent a night in a filthy prison. What had they done to him by now? And when they caught me, what would they do to me? If only I still had my cloak, I could wrap it round myself and hide my rich courtier's clothes. And it would have kept me warm too, last night. But I had left it in my father's room, and there was no going back for it now, or ever.

I stumbled on again until I came to a cluster of thatched cottages. A man with a long red beard like a squirrel's tail was whittling spoons; shaving curling strips of wood away as if he was peeling an apple. He grinned at me, showing black stumps of teeth. A baby in a long, loose gown was crawling in the dirt, picking up grain that had been scattered for hens. A woman was laying out her washing on a patch of grass, helped by a girl of about my sister's age. She looked like Margery, but she was thin and plainly dressed. Her hair was tawny-brown, knotted like sheep's wool under her coif, and she had a white, heart-shaped face.

A boy of my age was strapping bales of cloth onto a cart. He was whistling cheerfully, but as soon as he saw me he stopped and nodded, staring and awkward. The woman and girl looked up, saw me, and curtsied. The baby cried and the girl picked him up so he was tucked under her arm. She ran into one of the cottages. An old woman in a faded brown kirtle came out with a drop-spindle of brown thread bouncing from her hands. She neither bowed nor curtsied, but stared at me, chewing something endlessly in her toothless gums, peering at me as if she could only just make me out.

'A young lord!' she said at last. 'What an honour!' Her blue eyes were clouded with mistrust. 'Or someone very wealthy indeed!' she chuckled over her shoulder to the shadowy depths of the cottage.

'I need bread and ale,' I told them helplessly.

'You'd better give him some, Meg,' the old woman called inside the cottage.

I turned to the boy. 'And I need your clothes.'

The boy clasped his arms across his chest. 'My clothes, sire?'

'Now. I must have them.' I held out my arms for someone to undo the buttons and laces of my doublet. There was no way I could do it by myself. The boy was still standing, staring at me. His sister came out of the cottage and stood beside him, a jug of ale and a hunk of coarse rye bread in her hands, waiting for me to take them.

'Don't stare at me!' I shouted. I couldn't hide my frustration any longer, but I sounded like my Aunt Carew, and felt sorry for that. There was a time when I would never have spoken to country people like that,

151

as if they were lower than I was. I softened my voice. 'I'm not robbing you. Here, see, you can have mine in exchange.'

'Yours? In exchange for mine?'

I could have shaken him. Was that all he could do; stand and stare with his mouth open and his eyes bulging, repeating everything I said? Couldn't he see how desperate I was?

He turned to the younger woman, half-grinning, and she came flapping forward and put her arm across his shoulders. I flinched to see it, thinking she was going to hit him. That's what my aunt would do, at the slightest hint of disobedience. But her fingers tightened, and she drew him closer to her side. She stared at me, her eyes nearly out of her head. The old woman chortled.

'Are you mocking us, sire?' she asked scornfully. 'How could a poor boy dress himself in the colours of the rich? Meg, give his lordship the food and drink he's asked for, and then perhaps he'll be on his way, and we'll get on with our work.'

The girl blushed right into her hair and came to me with the ale and bread, and for the moment I dropped my arms down and took the food and drink from her. I turned away and ate and drank noisily.

'The child's hungry' the old woman said. 'Take your time, or you'll choke on that!' She hobbled towards me, still bobbing her thread, and peered at me again. 'Oh, fine clothes, they are,' she nodded. 'Too fine for you, Nicholas. You wouldn't be in them five minutes before you were robbed of them, or put in jail as a robber and murderer yourself. You can't have them!'

'I don't want them,' the boy said. 'I wouldn't be right in them.'

'Or dragged away by the king's men,' she added slowly. 'That's it, I do believe, that's it. That's why you're so keen to get out of your finery, am I right, young sir? Perhaps you could tell us, in exchange for the food we've put in your belly, because I don't expect you intend to pay us, why you want Nick's rough brown stuff so specially, and why you want him to wear your fancy colours?'

I said nothing to the old woman, but looked helplessly down at my clothes and then back at the boy. Maybe I had to order them the way my aunt ordered the servants, after all. All I knew was that I had to get rid of the court clothes.

'Take your shirt off. Now!' I demanded. 'Take these clothes off my back.' I wrenched again at the laces, trying uselessly to fling off my doublet. A pair of jackdaws came squabbling round me for the breadcrumbs I'd shaken off, and I swung my arms angrily to make them flap away.

'Shall I tell you what I see in your eyes, young sir?' the old woman said. 'Fear. My guess is you're running away. Would it be from the king's soldiers? Am I right? Ssh!' She put her hand across her mouth. 'My lips are sealed. Whatever you've done, it's no business of mine. But you don't swap clothes with our young Nicholas here. Our boy is never going to dress up like a courtier and swing from the gallows for it. Oh no! If you want common clothes that badly, come with me and I'll get you some. Come on, follow me.'

She moved away, and then looked back, her eyes

wicked with suppressed laughter, 'Mind you, I do like a hanging!'

I started to follow the old woman. The boy Nicholas was loping along behind me, like a dog after its master. I turned to glare at him, but he returned me a friendly, honest stare. I decided that if he wasn't mocking me he might as well follow, because I trusted him more than the old dame. She hobbled and rocked as she walked, kicking hens out of the way, and paused at last outside a mean shack.

'In there,' she jerked her head towards the open doorway of the shack. 'Happened last night, poor soul. But his clothes are no use to him now, and if you don't have them, some other beggar will.'

I hesitated and then peered in. In the dim light I could just make out the shape of a child lying on the earth floor. He was alone, and in that still and awful silence I knew that he was dead. I drew my head back out again.

'He's the last of his family to go,' the woman said. 'A pox, they had. Wiped them out in a week, one by one. Cart'll be round to collect them soon, and I tell you, his clothes are more use to you than they are to him. Have them, go on.'

I shook my head. 'I can't. I don't think I can do it.'

'Oh, the misery of being highborn!' she scoffed. 'What you mean is, sir, you don't think you can get your own doublet and hose off! Nick, strip off that child in the cottage and cover him up with a blanket to keep his poor dead body warm. God rest his soul, for it isn't with him any more. It's with the angels, and that's a much better place to be. And you, sire, if you don't mind my grubby hands, lift your arms and I'll turn you into a ragbag!'

She tucked her drop-spindle and thread into her girdle and unlaced my sleeves and slid them off. Then she unlaced the rest of my doublet round my waist and lifted it away from my hose. She slid my fine hose down to my feet, tapping my ankles to lift first one foot, then the other so she could slip off my leather boots and the hose. Finally she threw my feathered cap on the ground, untied my fine linen shirt and tugged it up over my head. I stood for a bitter, shameful moment naked in the biting wind, till Nick ran out of the shack with a bundle of rough brown rags in his hands and held them out to me. I scrambled into them myself this time, as the shirt was as loose as a night smock and easy to pull over my head. I pulled up the coarse hose and flung on the jerkin, then stepped back into my own boots. I had no wish to go barefoot like the dead boy.

'Transformed!' The old woman shrieked. 'Doesn't he look as plain as you and me, Nick, except his face is clean as new washing and his hair's as soft as silk! I could quite take to him now he's one of us. Good day to you, sire!' she swept me a mocking curtsey. 'Rough your nice hair up, sire, and put on this hat, and no one will know you from any common child in London, Heaven help you.' She crammed my hair into the dead boy's brown wool cap and stood back to admire me.

'Grandmam, what will you do with his clothes now?' Nick called anxiously. 'You won't make me wear them?'

'Oh, I got plans for this fine cloth!' she said. 'Our Meg's as quick a seamstress as anyone I know. Next market day, there'll be pretty little velvet purses and silk handkerchiefs for sale, and maybe a French hood or two, and they'll be snapped up by the fashionable merchants' wives at the market, you'll see.'

I bent down and picked up my knife and my purse and shoved them quickly into my new belt. The old woman watched me keenly.

'Got money in there, have you?' she asked. 'Because if you have, you can pay for these new fashionable garments I've given you.'

I shook my head. 'No money,' I said. 'Just a trinket of my father's – to remember him by...' I tried to say, but my voice shook and I turned away, lost now for what to do next. She snorted and wandered back towards her cottage, and the boy stood with his thumbs stuck in his belt, watching me.

'I have to go to Greenwich,' I said awkwardly. 'How do I get there from here?'

'Down river,' Nick said, jerking his thumb. 'But it'll cost you.'

'Then I'll walk,' I said.

'I'll come with you if you like.'

I stopped and stared at him.

'You're dressed like a poor boy, but you don't stand nor speak nor act like a poor boy,' he said. 'You'll get yourself in trouble in no time.'

I turned away and began to walk off. 'I can manage.'

'Let me come too. I can help you, if you want.'

I turned round, sure that he was making fun of me. 'You mean, like a servant?' I asked.

Nick's eyes shone. 'Me! A rich boy's servant! That would be a laugh!'

'Then I don't know what you want,' I said.

He shrugged. 'Nothing. It'd be like an adventure, that's all.'

'I can't pay you, if that's what you mean.'

'I know you can't pay me. I don't want pay. I just want to come with you.'

I gazed round me, not knowing what to say. I was loose in the city, like a sheep that's got away from its flock and lost its way. I had no idea what to do or where to go; my servants did everything for me.

'If you *are* in trouble,' he said, 'and the king's soldiers or the constables are after you, then you should lie low for a day. And if you're with another boy, they'll be put off the scent, won't they? Come back to my cottage,' he said. 'Don't mind Grandmam, she talks rough and acts rougher but her heart's big and kind. Everybody round here knows her. She's Widow Susan. She's looked after us since my mother died last year. She births the babies and washes the corpses, she mends the sick and she minds the poor – and there isn't a living soul she doesn't shout at! Stay with us till you find your way again.'

I nodded dumbly, not chancing myself to speak. I would rather sleep in their cottage than under the frosty stars again, that was sure. Nick was right; I needed to hide from the king's soldiers, if they were out looking for me. And it would give me time to work out how to get to Greenwich and Lord de Crecy, the man who would save my father.

The straw dragon

I spent the rest of the day watching Nick as he collected bits of fallen wood from the edge of a nearby forest and chopped it up for firewood.

'I'm allowed to take this much, and no more,' he told me. 'Just enough to fill my cart, which is why I press it down as flat as I can.' He scooped up a load and spread it out, grunting with the effort. 'It's hard work, this. Makes you nice and warm though, I'll say that for it. Have a go.'

I shook my head and put my hands behind my back. At home, it was Ned Porritt's job to chop wood, when he wasn't seeing to the horses. I used to try to help him when I was much smaller, and he would bend over me, cross-eyed with concern if I got a splinter in my hand. But Aunt Carew had forbidden me ever to do the work of servants. Nick didn't seem to mind that I didn't help him. He chattered away to me non-stop, pausing every now and again to wipe the sweat from his face with the hem of his shirt. At last he had finished with chopping. He piled the firewood up onto a cart and took it round to the neighbouring cottages. The women there gave him cheeses or apples in exchange for an armful of kindling.

'Grandmam will be glad of these,' he said. 'She'll

store some of them up in the loft, if we don't eat them all before we get home. Here, have some of this.' He bit into an apple, sucking back the drool of juice on his lips, and offered it to me. I shook my head. I didn't want to be here, doing any of this. I wanted to be on my way to Lord de Crecy's. But it was nearly dark already. I had no idea what to do, or where to go, so I trailed after Nick, and when one of the cottage women shouted at me to help her carry her load of wood in, I turned away, my face burning, and ignored her.

'He's sick,' Nick explained cheerfully. 'Grandmam's looking after him.'

The woman peered at me. 'Doesn't look too sick to me,' she muttered. 'Looks well-fed enough, anyway.'

'It's his head that's sick,' Nick said. 'He's pining.'

We didn't go back to Nick's cottage until evening, and my feet were sore with trudging after him, and my head was sore with his prattling. I wanted to be on my way to Greenwich straight away now, but he kept saying, 'Tomorrow, tomorrow. You're learning to be a common boy, and I'm thinking how to help, sire.'

I had to believe him. I was too afraid now to go anywhere on my own. If the king's men had gone to Hampton Court, they would know I was missing. There would be a search on for me, I was sure of that. I might still be recognised even in my poor boy's clothes. Maybe it was better, after all, to lie low for a day as Nick suggested. But it was a long day, and the afternoon had brought sharp rain that soon dribbled through the thin shirt I was wearing, and dripped through my cap and over my face. I was glad when Nick's cart was empty of firewood at last.

'Done!' he said, wiping his dirty hands on his shirt. 'Come home with me for a bowl of Grandmam's stew, and welcome, sire.'

Nick's cottage was dark and draughty, till he got a good fire going in the middle of the room. The house filled with choking smoke at first, sparks flew and sputtered and then settled down, and the room filled with the sweet smell of burning apple wood and pine cones.

'Cover the windows now,' Grandmam Susan called out. 'Keep that wet wind outside where it belongs.'

The flaps of rags were pulled down, and then it was a cosy enough place and made me think of the hall at home, though it was so much smaller and didn't have the big woollen hangings to keep the draughts away. Gradually shapes loomed out of the shadows. The flickering light from the fire showed the contents of the room clearly now. At one end the milk cow munched thoughtfully, and around her in the straw and perched up on the beams a half-dozen scraggy hens crooned to themselves. At our end there was a table and three stools, a box chair, a chest, and a straw mattress pushed against the dresser by the wall. A wooden ladder led up to the sleeping area, which was like an open-ended shelf jutting out over the cow's half of the room. The woman who had been laying out the washing that morning with Meg wasn't their mother, as I'd thought at first. Nick told me she was called Sarah Downey, and lived nearby in one of the other cottages. She sat by the fire with us, feeding Nick's baby brother, Arthur. He gave quick, satisfied gasps as he sucked, and she hummed quietly to him. She never took her eyes off me, yet she wasn't

160

looking at me, not properly. She looked as if she was dreaming awake.

Widow Susan placed a big cooking pot on some stones in the middle of the fire, and after a time the liquid inside it began to bubble. She threw in some bones that had a few knobs of meat on them and a handful of vegetables that she and Meg had been chopping. 'Onion next,' she muttered. 'Some parsley and a bit of tasty lovage for flavour. Some oats to thicken, and we'll eat well tonight.' She grinned across at me, showing her wet, bare gums. 'You don't eat as well as this where you've come from, I'll be bound!'

'When we've been hunting, we have plenty of meat,' I told her, shocked that she should think I was used to such poor food. 'Venison, in plenty. And there's always good roast beef, and plenty of carp and salmon...' My voice tailed off. I saw that she was laughing at me.

'What else?' Meg asked dreamily. 'How I should like to eat like that!'

Her grandmother chortled again. 'They have so much to eat, their bellies can't take it. That's what I've heard from a kitchen boy I met from one of the big mansions. They eat so much it makes them vomit.'

'Sometimes,' I said. I felt uncomfortable now. 'Some people do.'

She clicked her tongue. 'While most of England starves!' She spat into the fire. 'Shame on them. Shame on all them lords and ladies. I hate them all.'

'Go on,' Meg smiled at me. 'Do they eat sweet things too?'

I nodded. 'Apricots and figs and honey cakes, and sometimes sugar shapes. Sometimes a whole meal is

161

made of sugar shapes, made to look like swans or castles or ships, piled with cherries and apricots.'

'Mmm,' she sighed.

'You should taste my pease pudding and wet suckets, then you'd know good food,' the grandmother muttered. 'You'll want nothing better than that. Our king would grow fat on that, and not want anything else.'

'He's fat already,' Nick giggled. 'When he steps into his barge, they say it rocks like a cradle. It will tip up one day.'

I was shocked. We would never even whisper such a thing in court. 'That's treason,' I told him.

'It's true though!' Nick giggled again, and Meg laughed with him, and then the old grandmother put in her coarse belly laugh too. Sarah Downey looked from one to another of them, and back at me. I was still uncomfortable. I glanced round, half expecting to see people in the shadows – dangerous, listening lords of the court. I ducked my head and allowed myself a quick smile.

We were sitting on the stools, pulled up so close round the fire that my legs and face felt scorching hot. Behind Widow Susan I could see an old dresser looming into shape out of the shadows. There was another black cooking pot on it, and some wooden bowls and cups, a few spoons. Piled up next to it was an interesting heap of objects and on top of them all a strange, staring head with large holes for eyes. I couldn't make it out properly in the restless flickering of the firelight, but it intrigued me. My eyes kept flicking back to it.

'What's that?' I asked at last.

Nick jumped up and picked up the head. 'It's my dragon,' he said. 'I made him myself, out of rushes and straw, and I'll wear him myself for the mummers' play at Christmas. What d'you think of him?'

He took off his cap and pulled the straw dragon's head on over his face, and then he picked up the bundle of rushes and shook it out. It became a full-length cape of green and sand and amber colours, crinkling and rustling like the reeds on a river bed. He slipped it over his shirt and began to dance, thrusting his head and arms out and hissing in a scary way. Meg clapped, and her grandmother chuckled.

'There now, a bit of cheer for the young lord. Fetch your good man, Sarah Downey, and Buttons the fletcher at the corner house. I've good ale for them if they'll come and play for us.'

Sarah passed the baby to Meg and ran out. A few minutes later she came back in with the man I'd seen carving wooden spoons outside the cottage next door. He grinned at me again and I ducked my head. I wasn't used to that, grinning so you showed all your teeth, like a ploughboy in the fields. No one did that in court. I was used to simpering. Another man with tight hair like blackberries stooped in carrying a fiddle and his wife followed him. Now the little room was crowded.

Meg passed round jugs of ale, and Nick put his dragon's head back on. Jack Downey pulled a carved wooden flute from his belt, and half of it disappeared into the red bush of his beard as he put it to his mouth and began to play a jig on it. I knew the tune, 'The Merry Haymaker'. In our old Montague Hall we used to dance to it at harvest time, when all the peasants

163

would be brought home for a feast and the music played all night. The rafters would be hung with sweet-smelling apples, and they would bob and swing with the dancing. Long ago, before our world went grey.

The fletcher picked up his fiddle and held it against his chest, bowing it briskly so it let out a yowl like a cat. Then he turned towards Jack and danced his fingers along the neck of the fiddle, making it sing the same tune as the wooden flute, and then changed his tune to a harmony. They smiled with their eyes at each other as they played because they knew all the old tunes and loved to make music together. 'The Seven Joys of Mary', they played, and I knew the dance for it would be 'Stripping the Willow'. *Clap! Clap! Clap!* went the women, and the fletcher's wife began to dance, and caught Meg's hands to make her dance too. Their skirts swirled, sweeping the grasses on the floor into dusty piles, puthering the smoke from the fire into dancing ghosts.

I even found myself shifting my feet from side to side in time to the music. I was back in the Hall. Matthew was whooping and clapping and laughing with all the farmworkers, my mother and father were swinging round together. My sister's eyes were bright with fun and pleasure as she watched and jigged from foot to foot, and Ned Porritt was standing proud next to his father, pumping a pair of bagpipes under his arm.

But my dream dissolved, and I was standing cold and lonely among strangers. I longed for it all to be over. All I wanted was to be on my way to Greenwich to tell Lord de Crecy about my father.

'He surely will die'

At last the food was ready. My stomach was growling for it by then. The music had finished, and Button the fletcher and his wife Kate had left. As soon as Nick's little brother was asleep, Sarah Downey lowered him into a wooden crate and draped a linen cloth over him. Without saying anything to anyone, she opened the door and went out to her own cottage, and her husband Jack put down his empty mug and followed her. Wind and rain spat nastily into the room as they went.

Meg ladled the broth into wooden bowls. The grandmother mumbled some kind of blessing over the bread and broke it. Nick poured more ale into the wooden cups and handed them round. And I felt as if I had never eaten and drunk so well.

Widow Susan was watching me all the time I was eating. The firelight showed her face creased and deeply lined, like a piece of bark, and her eyes were watery with the smoke. She asked me my name, and I gave her the first but not the second. She tapped the ground with her foot. 'Let me tell you something, young William. We keep no secrets here. We trust one another.'

Trust. That was a strange word to hear. I hardly knew what it meant. 'Trust no one' could have been written in Latin on any nobleman's coat of arms.

'And let me ask you something,' she went on. 'You have a purse hanging on your belt, but you say you have no money in it. Is it empty then, like a dead pig's bladder?'

Nick spurted his ale with laughter. It dribbled down his chin and he dabbed at it with the back of his hand.

I shook my head. 'It's not money. It's more precious than that.' I was bleary with sleepiness and ale or I would never have said so much.

'Then let me tell you something else now. If it's more precious than money, it's not safe hanging from your belt. A boy dressed like you are now doesn't carry a good leather purse like that on his person. It belongs to a court popinjay, not a street sparrow. It'll be cut away in no time, I warn you.' She sliced the air with her fingers.

'Is it something you could wear around your neck?' Meg asked. 'I could make you a strong braid for it. You could wear it under your shirt and no one would know it was there.' Her voice was sweet, her eyes soft with caring. She reminded me so much of my sister Margery, only prettier. Much prettier.

'Nicholas, give the gentleman more ale,' his grandmother said suddenly. 'He needs to sleep well tonight.'

Nick grinned and poured more ale into my goblet, and like a fool I supped it back. I longed for sleep. I would gladly have curled up in a box like baby Arthur and let the purring of the fire sing me into my dreams.

But the old lady wasn't ready to let me go to sleep just yet. She took off her coif and let her grey hair down, shaking it loose over her shoulders, drawing her fingers lazily through the thick strands. She hummed to herself while I took two or three long draughts of ale, then she yawned deeply and carelessly. 'Perhaps you should let Meg have a look at it, whatever it is, then she can see what she can do.'

I kept still, my fingers clutching the neck of my purse.

'You don't want thieves snatching it as soon as you step out of here,' she whispered, opening her eyes briefly and closing them again.

'And I can make you a braid at first light,' Meg said. She had a dimple when she smiled, I noticed. It came and vanished, came again and vanished in a fascinating way, like rain on a pool. Margery used to sit with the end of a quill probing into her cheek, trying to give herself a dimple, but it never worked. I think it was Meg's dimple that finally made me give in. I pulled open the purse and drew out the ring.

'This is all it is,' I said. 'Just a simple ring. It was my father's, you see.' Father's, grandfather's, great-grandfather's and all those who went before him to the time when it belonged to the Plantagenet king, Edward the second.

But I wasn't going to tell them that.

'Is he dead?' Widow Susan asked abruptly.

'No. I – I don't think so.' And falteringly I told them about the last time I had seen my father, and that he had been dragged off to prison until he signed the Oath of Supremacy.

'And this ring is to remember him by,' Widow Susan said. 'Because he surely will die, child. You must know that. Let me have a look at it.'

I stared into the fire. My eyes were stinging now. 'I must show it to my Lord de Crecy at Greenwich Palace,

167

and he'll save my father's life.' I clutched the ring tight. My voice was breaking. 'But I don't know how to get there, or anything.'

'Show it me first.' She held out her hand, and reluctantly I stood up and went round to her. She took the ring out of my palm and held it out to the flames. I thought she was going to drop it in and I tried to snatch it back, but she snapped her fist over it. 'I want to see it, boy.'

Meg and Nick crowded round to have a look. A log shifted in the fire, the baby shuddered in his sleep. I sank down onto my heels while Widow Susan turned the ring over and over, screwing up her eyes. 'Bit thin, bit old. There's a device on it, but it's worn away. And a crest!' she said.

'It's two gryphons,' I said. 'It's the family coat of arms.'

'Old family, are you?'

I nodded, swallowing hard. 'Very old.'

The old woman looked up at me, her eyes shining like little coins in the dark pockets of her skin. 'An old, old family,' she muttered. 'And how did your family get this ring, did you say?'

But no, I wasn't going to tell her that King Edward had given it to one of my ancestors. How could I trust her with a secret like that? 'It's my father's signet ring. It belonged to his father, and my grandfather, and so on.'

'A powerful family, did you say?'

Did I? I had no idea what I'd said. The warm ale was slurring my speech and blurring my wits. 'Not any more,' I said. 'All we have now is our name.'

'Which is?' Her eyes were dark and deep now as she stared into mine, and I knew she was reading me as she had read my ring.

'Montague.' There. She had pulled it out of me.

'Not one I know. But a very venerable name, I'm sure,' the old woman nodded. 'And this ring is like to be hundreds of years old. Just as you say. Of course,' she added, 'we come from a very ancient family ourselves.'

'Do we, Grandmam?' Meg's eyes were round with wonder.

'Course we do! Our family has been on this earth for hundreds of years, same as his. Everybody's has, since we're all descended from Adam! Only difference is, we're common people and he's a noble. The peasants work the land and the rich folks own it, and it's always been that way and always will. Makes no difference to me. It's the way things are in this world. But our family name is as old as his, make no mistake about it. And we're all born naked, and we all finish up dead!' She hooted with laughter and put the ring back into my hand. 'You guard it well,' she said. 'I hope this Lordy Crazy can work miracles for you. Nick will help you to find your way to him. God be with you tonight, if He spares you.' She slapped her thighs and heaved herself up. 'I'm going out for a piss.'

The cold stream of air from the open door nearly flattened the fire. Meg dampened down the flames and tucked the cloth more tightly round the sleeping baby. Nick dragged a humped straw mattress across the floor so it was near the fire, and spread a blanket across it for his grandmother. The old woman came back in and fastened the door, twitching a heavy woollen cloth across it. She handed Nick a smoking tallow candle and Meg and I followed him up the creaking ladder to the loft. The straw was scratchy through the blanket, and sharp with the smell of the wormwood they had used against fleas. I was afraid of rolling over the edge of the shelf onto the floor below. I lay awake, mumbling prayers for my father, listening to the coughs and snores from down below and the wind crooning round the cottage, and at last, at long last, I fell asleep.

On the way to Greenwich

I woke up with a start, trying to remember where I was. I could dimly remember the conversation of last night, the old woman's greedy eyes, her hand stretching out for my ring. Panicking, I groped under the straw mattress I'd been sharing with Nick. The purse was quite safe, with the ring snug inside it, and my dagger was secure in its sheath in my belt. There was no sign of Nick or Meg. I could hear the old woman chortling down below about something. The little child Arthur screamed for food and fell silent again. Then I heard the ladder creaking. Nick stuck his head over the top, grinning cheerfully.

'How you nobles do sleep!' he said. 'Half the day is gone already!'

'I would like to eat.' I felt bewildered and afraid. I didn't know what to do, or where to go, or how to behave in this strange tiny house.

'Grandmam says if you come quick, there's some porridge left. And if you don't, the pigs will have it.'

'How shall I get washed?' I didn't like being washed, but I felt sticky and dirty and itchy with fleabites after my night on the straw.

He wrinkled his nose, as if the idea of getting washed at all was very strange. 'You can draw up water from the well, but you'll have to bring it indoors in a pail. It's bitter cold out there this morning.' And he disappeared again.

I decided against washing. I crawled off the mattress and remembered I had no other clothes to wear anyway. I fastened my belt round my waist and patted my dagger and purse into place. The animals had been shooed outside, thank goodness, and Meg was sweeping their droppings after them. Her grandmother strewed a few fresh rushes behind her. The fire burned brightly in the middle of the room, and cold sunlight streamed through the open doorway, turning the smoke golden.

'Draw up a stool and eat,' Widow Susan called to me. 'And then you'll be on your way.'

I sat down by the fire and waited to be served, but she bustled away and picked up her drop spindle, bobbing it at her side while she drew the dark thread up and down, up and down. Her hands were gnarled and cracked like splintered twigs. She waddled outside, calling, 'Good Morrow,' to passing neighbours, as busy and bright-eyed as one of her hens. Sarah Downey slipped in like a silent cat, toed the last of the rushes into place and picked up the infant, who had started screaming. She put him to her breast and held him tucked firmly in place with one arm, while she picked up a pail of scraps with the other and carried it out to feed the animals. Meg was milking the cow, singing dreamily to herself. She half-turned her head as if she knew I was watching her, and smiled and nodded to me, which made me turn away, but I don't know why. I watched them all coming and going, busy with their work, and realised that no one was going to serve me with food. I poured myself some ale, fetched a wooden bowl and spoon and scraped the last of the porridge from the pot. As I sat down to eat, the grandmother Susan turned round from the doorway and grinned her gummy smile.

'When you've finished, there's a pail of water to draw from the well, and the pot to be cleaned,' she said. 'You'll find a bunch of horsetail to scrape it out with.'

I blushed with anger. Surely she didn't expect me to do it?

'And then Nick has a plan for you.'

I ate my porridge quickly and put my dirty bowl on the hearth next to the empty porridge pot, then hurried outside to where Nick was loading his handcart with his straw baskets for the market.

'What plan?' I asked.

'To get to Greenwich,' he said. 'I'm going to take you down to the wherry now. The tide should be right, if we're quick.'

'And look, I've made you this, to keep you safe.' Meg came out of the cottage behind me, holding out a slim plaited cord. 'Give me your ring, sir.'

I wouldn't do that. The cold daylight had cleared my head of any such foolishness. Instead I took the cord from her and turned away so my back was to Meg and Nick. I slid my ring from my purse and threaded it onto the cord.

'Will you let me, sir?' She was teasing me with her laughter, but all the same I let her help me. I clutched the ring the whole time, while she stood on her toes and looped the knotted cord around my neck. Then she

173

tucked it inside my shirt. Her fingers were icy cold, making my flesh tingle, but her breath was like warm feathers on my cheek. All the time the grandmother was watching us from the doorway of the cottage, her fingers twitching on the dark wool, her drop spindle bobbing like a wooden doll.

'There now, you're quite safe,' Meg smiled, stepping away from me. I remembered my courtly manners at last and I bowed to her as if she was a maid-in-waiting, half-mocking. She giggled and put her hand to her mouth in embarrassment. 'You and Nick should hurry now.'

I hardly had time to thank them before Nick sped off. I did my best to keep up with him, and he kept stopping and hopping impatiently from one foot to another, waving me on. At last we arrived at the river. Boatmen crowded round the wharf steps, waiting to ferry people across the river.

'Which one should I take?' I asked, gazing along the row of boats moored up to the bank. 'And how will I pay?'

'I'm going to ask one of the wherrymen to take us. If one of them remembers my father, we'll be all right. If not, we'll walk. Just wait here a bit.'

'I don't need you to come with me,' I said. 'I want to do this on my own.'

He took his hat off, turned it round in his hands gazing at it as if it had words written all over it if only he could read, then put it back on his head. 'Fact is, sir, you do need me. You may be dressed like a common lad, but you don't talk like one. You see them beggars over there? They've got a language all their own, that's how they talk to each other. I know their language because my family was begging just like them after my father went away. I know that language like you know that Latin language, and I can tell you which one is more important when you're out on the streets of London.'

I looked away, miserable. I knew he was right. Brother John had told me that Latin would take me anywhere in the world, but he never thought that I'd be homeless and fatherless in my own country. He must have known the language of beggars too, he had lived with them for long enough, but he never thought to teach it to me.

'Next thing,' Nick went on, 'you don't walk like a common lad. You've got this sort of rolling swagger like I only ever see rich people do, like you've never got anything to spend your time doing. Look around you. Everyone's walking fast, got to do this, got to do that, else they'll go hungry. You've got to learn to walk quick, then you won't be noticed. You won't last a minute, not without me to watch out for you. I tell you, you've got eyes that aren't bright enough, and feet that aren't fast enough, and ears that aren't sharp enough. You do need me, sir, or you'll be cut up like a rabbit for the stew pot in no time.'

My eyes were smarting. I wanted to block my ears so I couldn't hear his prattling voice any more. Why did my father have to be sent to prison? Why did my sister go to Calais? I was alone in the world, and none of it was my fault.

He went on relentlessly, Nick the chattering starling. 'And when you get to that Greenwich place, what then? What if someone sees you who knows your face or your voice? Are you going to go marching up to those gates all on your own? How are you going to find that Lordy Crazy? You do need me, sir. You need Nicholas Drew.'

I choked back the sobs of misery that were rising in my guts, and nodded blindly. I squatted on the wharf steps and left it to Nick to find a boat for us. It helped to calm my nerves, to watch the water. Nick worked his way along a line of bargemen and wherrymen preparing to go downriver, babbling cheerfully as he went, till he found one who knew his father. I could hear his voice all the way. The last bargeman said he would let us on for nothing, as the boat wasn't full. There were some rich folk on board already, but I didn't recognise any of them. I kept my head bent down just in case and my telltale red hair stuffed well inside my cap. Nick chatted to the oarsmen till they grew tired of him. Then he crouched down next to me, whistling brightly.

'Was your father really a wherryman?' I asked him.

'Used to be. Then he went away to sea and I thought I would never see him again, and he came back full of such wondrous tales that I wanted to sail away with him. He went to lands that were so hot that the people who live there have no clothes on, and lands that were so cold that the sea around them got blocked up with ice for weeks and weeks on end, and the ships were stuck there like nails in a coffin. Imagine that, sir, like when the Thames freezes up, only it's a sea, like this.' He held his arms out wide. 'And there's nothing but miles and miles of ice all around you – oh, and it creaks and groans, my father says, like it was alive sometimes.'

His eyes were gleaming with the mystery of it. He folded his arms round his chest, hugging himself.

'One day, one day, I'm going to be a sailor like my father. I'm going to sail round the world. I want to have adventures! I want to see everything there is to see; the monsters in the sea and the giants on the land.' His mouth puckered. 'But I wish I knew where he is now, sir. I wish I knew I would really see him again. There are things he doesn't know. Lots of things.'

He went so quiet and still then, as though he'd dropped into a deep well inside himself, that I thought he might be offended if I asked him any questions. Then he suddenly roused himself and said, 'For a start, he doesn't know that my mother's had a baby, does he? He went away eight months before Arthur was born. Arthur's nearly two years old now and doesn't even know he's got a father. And my father doesn't know that our Christian and our Henry took a sickness and died in the same week, just before last Christmas.' His voice shook. 'My little brothers. They died, and he doesn't even know that. And he doesn't know that we were turned out of our house because we had no money left.

'Mother was sick, so sick, she wouldn't talk or eat after my brothers died. I had to go begging and Meg had to look after Mother and Arthur, and we had nowhere to sleep but hedges. And then Mother died. And he doesn't know that. And then we came to Grandmam Susan's house, and she let us stay with her. And Sarah Downey, she didn't know us at all, but Grandmam asked her to feed baby Arthur like she would feed her own, and she does. She's strange, and she doesn't talk much. She frightens me sometimes, the way she stares. But she looks after Arthur, so she's not a bad woman, is she?'

177

I shook my head, not trusting myself to say anything at all.

'But my father doesn't know any of that. He doesn't know where we live now, sir. That's what I dream every night. I dream that my father comes back home from the sea, and he doesn't know where to find us.'

Then Nick fell into a deep, gloomy silence, and I didn't know where to go to bring him out of it. I had never thought much before about the misery of other people, especially not common folk. Nick was nothing to do with me; his life was nothing to do with mine. The poor were lowborn, and that was that. They had to put up with whatever happened to them. But all the same, I knew how much he worried about his father. I could understand that. And I knew what it felt like when your mother had died, and your brother too. I knew about those huge, dark, empty spaces that would never, ever be filled again. Just at that moment I knew that Nick and I weren't all that different, after all.

Because he wasn't talking, and because it hurt my brain to try and reason why God let such awful things happen to people, I concentrated on the other conversations that were going on in the barge. The young noblemen were laughing and gossiping. It was all noblemen ever did, I remembered. They were courtiers, I found out. After a time they began to talk about Prince Edward, my little prince. My ears were scorching with straining to listen to them; my heart was pounding uncomfortably. I shifted on my bench and leaned forward, and realised then that they were even talking about me.

'He just ran away!' one of the young men said. 'No permission asked for! Not a word of explanation, no goodbye, nothing.'

'Perhaps he's dead,' one of the others suggested.

'It's to be hoped he is. If he's not, and he's found, the king won't spare his life, that's for sure. You should have seen his rage when he heard about it! They say the boy was his favourite – must have been, because he wasn't an aristocrat, you know. Not a Carew by birth. Just a Montague.'

I felt Nick start beside me. I leaned forward, my hands covering my face.

'He came from some godforsaken old manor house miles away. King Henry took a liking to him, you know what he's like, and gave him the job that should have been Percy Howard's in the first place. Percy was out of his mind with fury. He was sure to be the prince's page, everybody thought so. I mean, he's the Duke of Norfolk's nephew!'

'Well, when the boy's found he'll be flogged in public.'

'Hanged for treason, more like.'

'What about the nurse? I heard she was punished for letting him go?'

'Aye, Mother Jack was beaten and locked away, but the little prince pined for her and King Henry had her released. But he's to have a dry nurse anyway, Sibell Penn, now he's two, so Mother Jack will be lucky if she can stay at Hampton Court. But do you know Sir Andrew? One of His Majesty's archers? Well, Sir Andrew was flogged, of course. He was the last to see the boy; he was having an archery practice with him. He refused to

179

say where the boy had gone, poor fool. No, there's no doubt about it – if the Montague boy hasn't drowned or been stabbed by robbers on the highway, he's in for an even worse death when he's discovered.'

They tittered at the thought, and then their gossip moved on to other things. Nervously I gripped Father's ring through my shirt. I felt that my world had truly gone dark, as dark as midnight.

Greenwich Palace

I was sick with dread at the thought of arriving at Greenwich now. I wanted to cover my face and stay on the boat, but as soon as the nobles disembarked, Nick tugged my sleeve and hauled me off.

'Now this is a grand place!' he said, his arms on his hips, staring round at the green hills and banks, and then with a sigh of wonder pointing out the beautiful palace beyond the bare trees. 'Wonderful, that is! I always wanted to see that! Grandmam told me that King Henry was born here. And the witch-queen set off from here on her wedding day, and it was a wonderful sight to see, because she was as beautiful as anyone could ever be, and dressed all in gold, and the river was like a scarf of jewels with all those painted boats and banners and streamers – and there were fireworks whizzing into the sky, and music, music everywhere! Did you know that, Master Will?' He turned to me, his eyes shining. 'And then, Grandmam says, no more than three years later that same beautiful lady set off again from here. Only this time, she was going to the Tower of London to have her head sliced off. Did you know that too?'

'Of course,' I said. 'Everybody knows.'

'Couldn't have thought much of her, then, could he? He's always getting people's heads chopped off,

Grandmam says.' Then he dropped his voice to a whisper. 'I heard those noblemen talking on the barge. That boy Montague they were on about, it's you, isn't it?'

I nodded miserably.

'The prince's page!'

'Don't tell anyone,' I muttered.

He blew out his cheeks, indignant. 'Course I won't! But weren't you scared, when you served at King Henry's palace? I would have been.'

Nick was right. I'd always been scared, right from the minute I saw King Henry, even when he was being kind to me. What if *he* was there at Greenwich Palace now? Why hadn't I thought of that? And if he was there, his court would be there. All the Howards, and prowling Percy and his father and the terrifying Duke of Norfolk himself. What if someone recognised me and dragged me into the king's presence? I could imagine his rage when he saw me; I could hear his bellowing anger like a great bull in a barn.

And I knew what Nick would say next. He'd heard what the nobles had said, about my favourite knight, Sir Andrew. Flogged for helping me, and Mother Jack. My throat was tight with grief at the thought of it. But that was how King Henry took his revenge. I knew how cruel he was; everybody knew, but I never thought it would come so close to me. Brother John, Father, Sir Andrew, Mother Jack. Would I be the next? And what about Nick, if he was found with me? It wasn't safe for him to be anywhere near me, least of all to be going to one of the palaces of King Henry with me. If I was captured, he would be too. I turned away, miserable and scared. The wherrymen were preparing to leave the steps.

'You'd better go,' I muttered.

'I'm not going to leave you, if that's what you mean,' he said, shocked at the idea. He dodged round me so he was looking into my face again. 'Master Will, we're not leaving now, either of us. We've come all this way, haven't we, safe and sound! We can't give up now. You must hide in those trees down there, and I'll go to the gates and ask if your Lordy Crazy's there. If we can go to him safely, I'll signal to you, like this.' He put his hands round his mouth and made the sweet fluting whistle of an oystercatcher. 'Don't move from here if you don't hear that whistle, cos I might come and fetch you, or even bring him to you if that's safer. I'll work it out.'

I nodded dumbly, too relieved to speak properly for a bit. But I was glad of his common sense. He had to be the one to go up to the gates and ask for Lord de Crecy. And if his lordship agreed to see me, I had my speech ready in my head. I would show him the Montague ring. I would go on my knees and beg him to help my father. Surely he would listen to me.

We watched the young noblemen from the barge strolling slowly up the steps to the palace. Halfway up, two of them pretended to have a fencing match, while the other one whistled and cheered and capered round them. I suppose they were drunk. They thrust their imaginary swords towards each other, they twirled and bowed, they held a hand behind the back or daintily out at the side; they lunged and parried and feinted. *I used to do all that*, I thought miserably. How foolish they looked. A little crowd gathered round them, laughing and clapping.

'If they were real swords one of them would be dead by now,' I muttered. I wished they would get on with it, so I could do what I had to do and then get away from Greenwich as fast as I could.

At last they finished their sporting and ambled on towards the red-brick palace. I hid in the shelter of the trees while Nick scuttled off. I felt sick with nerves, and hardly knew what to do with myself. I found a stick and tried to whittle a shape into it with my knife, but my hands were shaking so much that I stabbed my thumb. I kept squeezing the place where I'd cut myself, and sucking the blood. It tasted like rusty nails. The dry leaves fretted above my head, the branches scratched each other, the rooks croaked as they came down to roost, but there was no sweet whistling sound. The waiting seemed to last for ever. *Nick's gone*, I thought. *He's realised that it's too dangerous for him to stay with me, and he's gone.* And then I thought, *What if he gives me up to the guard at the gates? He might be hoping for a reward. They might come looking for me any minute, and he might be miles away clutching a gold coin.*

I shrank back into the shadows. What could I do now? Nothing, nothing but wait and pray.

At last, I heard the sound of feet padding quickly over the grass, and Nick was back at my side; alone.

'Is he coming?' I asked.

'He can't.' He bent over, panting, his hands on his knees.

'Can't?' I groaned. 'Won't, you mean. Why won't he come?'

'Because he's been clapped in the palace dungeon,

that's why. And he isn't likely to be let out till he's led to the gallows.'

I was as cold as stone then. 'Are you sure, Nick? Are you sure you asked for the right person?'

'Lordy Crazy, like you said. The yeoman at the gate said his lordship refused to sign that oaf of a premise you talked about.'

'Oath of Supremacy,' I muttered.

'That's right. He refused to say the king is the head of the Church. So it's more money for the hangman.' Nick squatted down next to me. His voice was husky with sympathy. 'You've lost your chance now, haven't you? I'm sorry for you, believe me. But we'd better be walking home. Take us about two hours at my pace and four at yours, so we'd better set off now while there's some daylight left.'

He was right. There was no point staying there, anyway. The sooner we left, the better. There was nothing else we could do. I trudged behind Nick, and I could feel the signet ring knocking against my chest with every step I took. When we got away from Greenwich and the track was quiet of horsemen and beggars, I untied the cord and slipped the ring onto my thumb, where it just fitted me. I felt closer to my father then, not so hopeless, not so afraid.

For once Nick was quiet. There was no prattling left in him. I could hardly see his face any more, though the track was easy enough to follow in the dusk. We sank down and rested for a bit, back to back, and he began to sing, in a croaky, tuneless voice.

'A frog could do better,' I told him.

He jumped up and stretched. 'We're tired, sir, and

hungry, and I'm sorry for us both. But we have to get on. We can't be that far from my quarter now. Food, that's what we want! Fish pottage and ale, and some of Grandmam's wet suckets!'

He began to run, and I loped after him, and then stopped, winded and tired. What good would it do, to go home with him? I didn't belong there. There was nothing more they could do for me. I slipped into a side alley, and into the maze of dark streets. I didn't want Nick to find me. I didn't want to go back to his house, to his family, to the chortling Widow Susan.

I didn't want any of them any more.

Attacked

I had no idea where I was going. I thought maybe I could find my way to Newgate from there, and somehow get a message to my father about Lord de Crecy. A misty sort of moon gave me just enough light to find my way down the alleyways, and I was glad of it. I slipped my ring off my thumb and fastened it back on its cord, for safety, then carried on. After a bit I had the nervous feeling that someone was following me, footsteps clattering, stopping, clattering, stopping. I paused, and the footsteps paused too. My heart started thumping loudly.

Before I could turn round, a hand came from behind and grabbed me round the neck, and another came over my mouth, and I was hauled backwards onto the ground. A thick-necked man with breath like a dog's was peering into my face. I saw him upside down, could just make out his face glistening with sweat, black hairs curling from his nostrils, his eyes bulging out of his head. He kept one hand over my mouth and flashed a dagger into my face, and he was laughing at me as he used his knife to rip open the top of my shirt. His fingers groped for the cord. He snorted with triumph as he wrenched it free. He held up my father's signet ring.

'That's a pretty trinket for a street urchin to be wearing! Where did you get it, you little thief? Could get you hanged for this! But I won't, cos I'm having it myself!'

'Please don't take it!' I shouted, grabbing his wrist. He punched my face so hard then that I smashed back onto the ground. His boot came after, grinding into my chest and then into my cheek. I clung onto his ankle, trying to bring him down so I could snatch back my ring. He thudded down, winding me as he fell. His knife flashed in his hand as he held it pointed above my face.

'I'll show you what happens to boys who fight back.' He raised the knife, poised, ready to plunge it down into my neck, but he was suddenly grabbed from behind and hauled off me. He stumbled away, and my rescuer stumbled after him. I staggered to my feet. I was too scared to run after them, too shocked and winded, and I had no idea where they might be in that maze of dark passages. I put my hand to my face and felt the sticky ooze of blood. I crouched down on all fours, dizzy and sick and frightened. I didn't know what to think, what to do, where to go. My life had been saved. But my signet ring had gone.

And the worst thing was, it was all my own fault. Why would anyone attack me? I was just an ordinary boy now. Whoever it was must have known about the ring. And this is what kept coming back to me, kept tugging at my brains like a fish tugging at a hook: the only people who knew about my ring were Nick and his family.

'Why do you want to help me?'

I pulled myself up onto my feet and swayed like a drunken beggar, trudging through the alleys till I could feel the cold air coming off the river. I made my way to the bridge where Nick and I had taken the boat to Greenwich. Little pinprick reflections of candlelight in houses and shops gleamed like eyes on the water. I sat on the river steps, folding my arms tight across my chest to try to hold in the pain. It was bitterly cold.

I kept thinking about Nick. He was just an ordinary boy, but he'd shown me more kindness than any other boy I had ever met. In the court, all the boys were jealous of each other; nobody trusted anyone else. At home at Montague Hall the only boys I knew were servants, and children of servants. My father had always treated them like members of the family. Yet sometimes with Nick I even forgot that he was a commoner. I needed him to look after me, he was right. But I needed him for something more than that, something deeper, and I couldn't understand what it was. It was almost like the way I needed my father, needed my sister. It was almost like the way I needed Matthew.

There was no way Nick would have sent someone to do this to me, I told myself. Not Nick. But if it wasn't

Nick, or someone from his family, who could it have been?

The receding tide had dragged itself away from the steps, leaving the stinking rubbish of the city behind: rotten, pulpy fruit and vegetables settling into the mud. In the moonlight, the bones of a dead donkey emerged from the slime. Its face was set in a hideous smile. 'What can I do, what can I do now?' I moaned aloud, and still the donkey grinned, and I couldn't move, not even to drag myself away from its stench.

It was there that Nick found me, hours later. It was day by then, tide coming back in, icy water lapping round my ankles. I heard feet pattering down the steps, and felt someone squatting next to me. I could hear the grin in his voice as he spoke.

'You're a slippery fish, sir, and no mistake. I was following you, and you just went and disappeared clean out of my sight. "Lost him," I said to myself. "Lost him good and proper now." And I hunted round all the nooks and crannies. No Master William. I was worried, I tell you. Then I followed my feet down here, and here you are, sitting like a sleeping duck with your head tucked into your belly. And, sir, I must warn you that you shouldn't be here. This is a dangerous place at night. You should never come here without Nick to look after you.'

I uncurled myself and lifted my head to look at him. He clapped his hand across his mouth.

'Who did that to you? I'm too late, aren't I? You've been set upon, and I should have been there to protect you. Your face is as black and blue as a starling's wing, sir. You've been kicked and battered and in no end of trouble, and where was I? Nowhere to be seen, that's where I was. Who did it to you?'

'I don't know,' I groaned.

'You can't do anything without me, sir. Remember that. Trust me. I won't let you down.'

I couldn't look at him. Did he know how many times I'd doubted him? 'Why do you want to help me, Nick? I'm just a danger to you, you know that now.'

'I told you. I like adventures. Besides, we're all right, aren't we? If I was in trouble, you'd help me, wouldn't you?'

I tugged at the fastening on my boot. When had I ever helped anyone? Nick prattled on as if he hadn't even noticed that I'd hesitated.

'A gentleman needs someone to look after him like a sheep needs a shepherd. Like I need my guardian angel.' He crossed himself quickly and glanced upwards as if he expected to see his angel there, wings spread out over his head like a tent in a storm.

'I think my guardian angel was with me last night.' I told Nick about the rescuer who had come out of nowhere. 'I don't know who it was, but he saved my life, and chased away my attacker. He didn't have wings though.'

'You sure it wasn't another robber, sir? They work in pairs, often enough, like dogs in a pack, only that second one saw that fine ring, and thought, *I'll have that myself*, and he ran after the first scoundrel and stole it off him.'

'I don't know,' I admitted. 'I don't know anything.'

The one thing I did know was that my father's ring had gone. Who would believe my story now, without it?

And I had no idea whether my father was still alive. I groaned and covered my face with my hands, and the pain inside me was worse, much worse, than the pain I'd got from the attacker's foot on my face and my chest.

'Oh Lord, don't do that, don't, Master Will!' Nick said. '*I'm* here! You're not all on your own, and you never will be.'

I didn't answer him. There was nothing he could do to help me now.

'Isn't there anyone left in England you can go to?'

I shook my head. I could feel the prickle of tears in my eyes, and I clenched my fists together. I had no idea where my Aunt Carew was now, but it was obvious that she would do nothing to save my father. Her own husband was the one who had caused him to be sent to prison, and she wouldn't do anything against Uncle Carew. The only friends of my father's that I knew of were staunch followers of the Pope. Most probably they were in jail themselves by now, like Lord de Crecy. Or hanged. And if they weren't, there was nothing they could say or do to help him even if they dared. There was no one in the world who loved and cared about him as much as I did.

Except my sister.

'There's Margery!' I said, sitting up. 'But she's miles away. And she's married to one of the king's friends. A real nobleman, in France.'

'France!' Nick's eyes widened. 'Where's that?'

'It's over the sea.' I was full of despair. France! It might as well be the moon. And the thought of the sea came lurching wet and dark at me, drenching me in fear. I sank my muzzy head down to my knees again.

'Sir, we can do it! We'll find a way! Ah, I'll be a sailor man at last, I'll ride the tides like a rich man rides his horse, I'll go to lands where the sun burns down all day, and other lands where the ice is as thick as castle walls, and I'll see great monster fish.'

I had to smile at him, even though it hurt my face to do it. 'You ninny, Nick! France is only a few hours sailing time away.'

'Then there's nothing to stop us, nothing at all. You aren't thinking straight, that's your trouble. Come home with me first, and Grandmam will mend your bruises with herbs. And when you're better, we'll go there. We'll sail to France. We can do it!'

He helped me to my feet, but I found I couldn't walk. He half-carried me up the steps, and set me down so we could both get our breath back. My head was spinning with dizziness, and the movement had opened up my wounds and set me bleeding again. I was shivering uncontrollably by then.

'You're feverish, sir,' Nick said. 'Let's get you home.'

'Home.' It was a good word to me that day, even though my fuzzy brain knew that he didn't mean the ancient golden walls of Montague Hall, nor my prince's red-brick palace at Hampton Court. They would never be home to me again, neither of them. Home was a simple timber and mud cottage with a sagging thatched roof, and if I'd gone there last night, none of this would have happened.

I needed to lean on Nick at first, because the robber had kicked my shins so hard and they had stiffened up while I slept on the cold river steps, but after a bit I wanted to walk on my own, and Nick let me. He kept glancing at me anxiously. I grinned at him to show him I was all right, but I felt strange – dizzy and cold, so cold.

Widow Susan tutted and fussed over me as if I was a child of her own family. She took some bunches of lavender that were hanging to dry in front of the window slit, and set to grinding them with a stone and steeping them in oil. Meg drew fresh water from the well and warmed it a little over the fire, so it wouldn't shock me too much, and gently bathed my face. Sarah Downey sat with baby Arthur at her breast, staring at me and gritting her teeth every time I winced. Then Widow Susan dabbed on the lavender oil, and though it stung I managed to keep my mouth shut. She sent Meg to fetch more water so she could bathe my shins, and tutting and hissing between her gums, she rolled up my hose and eased the blood-clogged cloth away from the wounds.

'I must go to France!' I murmured. It was all I could say. My teeth chattered together like stones in a riverbed.

'You won't be fit to go anywhere yet,' the grand-mother scolded. 'That villain nearly killed you, and I don't want him to kill you again. Not today, at least. I want you to lie down and get warm because you keep shivering as if you wanted to shake your skin off your bones, and I don't like that. You won't get up that ladder; you'll open up all those sores if you try climbing. Take my mattress by the fire, and I'll get some good barley broth going for you. If anyone can get you well, old Susan can, but you must stay calm and warm for the next two days.'

194

She shuffled me over towards the fire. I was feeling dizzy by then, couldn't stop shivering, I let her lower me down onto the straw and cover me with her rough blanket. I could feel myself fighting against the cold surge of the sea; I was rising and falling, grasping blindly at nothing, choking as my mouth filled with water. I was heaved into air, and I felt the heavy drench of water dragging me down and down. I was heaved up again, I heard my father's voice, calling, calling, 'Matthew. Matthew.' I tried to speak but my mouth was full of water. 'It's not Matthew. It's William.'

Then someone stroked my brow with something warm and sweet-smelling. I was home, with the fields golden with corn and dancing with poppies and daisies. I could hear the skylark churning and churning her silver song. I tried to open my eyes but my lids were heavy, so heavy, and at last the sweet herbs and the purring fire soothed me into a long, deep sleep.

'Who can make you well again?'

When I woke up again, Margery was sitting by my side, stroking my hand. I opened my eyes and smiled at her, and the shape dissolved and turned into someone who wasn't Margery at all, but just as gentle, just as sweet.

'Who are you?' I whispered. She drew her hand away and stood up.

'Grandmam, he's awake,' she called.

An old woman came and peered down at me, touched my cheek, and helped me to sit up. 'Take a sip of this,' she said, and nudged my lips with the edge of a spoon. It tasted bitter and I turned away, pulling a face. 'I've seen a dog smile sweeter than that. A little more, sir,' she laughed. 'Trust Susan. It tastes nasty, but it will do you good.'

Susan. I remembered the name, and who she was, and where I was. And so the girl who wasn't Margery was Meg, and yet she had been stroking my hand. How strange that she should do that, but how nice too. And then the memories of last night came inching back; Meg cleaning my face, Nick helping me through the streets, the cold bite of the Thames around my ankles. I could feel myself limping and lurching down the dark passages, and before that, a man's face leering down at me as I lay helpless on the ground. What happened? In a panic, I felt for my ring.

'It's gone,' Widow Susan said. 'Yes, sir, you remember it all now.'

She went outside, and Meg with her. I shouldn't be here; I should be with my father. I struggled off the mattress and limped to the door. They were sweeping the yard between them, turning over the old dry rushes that had covered the earth floor of the house, stamping on the mice that scuttled out. Meg had Arthur dangling under one arm. When I appeared Widow Susan looked round sharply.

'Oh, he's up and walking like a corpse come to life! Where do you think you're going, young sir?'

'To France,' I said.

'Nick!' Widow Susan called. 'There's a live skellington here! He's awake!'

Nick was hauling a cartload of firewood towards the house. He dropped the shafts and came running to me, a huge smile on his face.

'Are you better, sir? Oh, you look better, but you were so grimly pale before, I never thought you'd be moving about like this. Oh, it's good to see you, sir!'

'But if you think you're fit yet to go traipsing over the sea to France, you must change your mind,' Widow Susan scolded. 'Look at you, you can hardly walk! You need more of that tasty potion I made for you. See he takes it now, Meg. It will keep him strong for his travelling. Who can make you better? Only old Susan, remember that.'

'Be safe, William. Be strong'

It was true. My wounds were much better now, but I was still as weak and dithery as an old man. I let Meg lead me back indoors and sit me near the fire, and I drank more of the disgusting brew. She giggled at the faces I pulled.

'Grandmam says the worse it tastes, the better it is for you,' she told me.

'What is it?'

'I don't know. She's going to teach me her arts one day, but I don't know much yet. I know one, but it won't help you much! I know how to grind the bones of a mouse in a mixture of roses and honey,' she smiled. 'It's for earache! Grandmam keeps most of it secret, in her head. But she can make sick people better, and dying people live longer or die easily, out of pain.'

And that set me thinking and thinking. I glanced round at the bunches of herbs and jars of potions that she kept on her shelves. When the grandmam came back in again to take up her drop spindle, I blurted out my thoughts to her.

'Widow Susan, have you ever been to Newgate prison?'

She glared at me and crossed herself quickly. 'What a

198

question! I'm not a sinner, and if I was, I'm clever enough not to get caught. Newgate? It's death, that place. It's very death. It's worse than death.'

I shuddered. 'I mean, have you ever been inside it?'

She closed her eyes. 'Aye, I have. I had a brother there once. And that's why my heart goes out to you, knowing your father is there. I went to visit my brother with my mother and father, to plead for his life. We got nowhere with that idea. He was down in the pit they call Limbo. Bodies lying on top of bodies. Filth like you've never seen, and a stench to make you empty your guts out. And the place crawling with lice, and wriggling with rats. All we could hear down there was groans and screams, and it was so dark, we never even found our John. If we had, how could we have helped him? So we prayed for him to die quick and leave his misery behind, like we tug on the legs of our hanging friends. *Die, die*, we tell them. Death's better than life when you're in that state.'

Meg had come creeping in, and was crouching next to me. 'I'm sure things would be better for your father than that,' she said. 'He would have some money, wouldn't he? He could buy a little comfort.'

'Ay, he won't be in Limbo,' Widow Susan agreed. 'That's for petty felons, whether they're guilty or not.'

'I want to see him,' I said. 'Will you take me there, and help me to find him? And if he's sick, or weak—'

'As he will be. Make no mistake about that.'

I took a deep breath. 'Then I want you to give him some of your potions to make him strong again.'

'And be taken for a witch, and thrown on the fire?' she shrieked. 'Do you think I'm mad?'

'But it's going to take me so long to get help for him. You must give him something to keep him alive till I get back.'

She leered her toothless face at me. 'Keep him alive to suffer torture? Keep him strong enough to step on the hangman's trap? Is that what you want?'

'Please.'

Her chuntering stopped, her rhythmic spinning stopped. Her eyes gleamed.

'You know so much,' I whispered. 'You're so clever. Can you do it, please?'

Her grin turned from mockery to mystery, and at last she nodded. 'I'll do it. Meg, you'll have to help.'

She sent Meg running for water to boil and herbs to crush; peppermint and lavender, horseradish and others I'd never heard of, and all day there was grinding and boiling and muttering, and strange smells rising, and billows of steam like sails unfurling. I began to think she was truly a witch after all and that her mumblings were spells and curses, and I was frightened because of what I'd asked her to do. But there was no stopping her now, no hushing the croaking of her singing. Behind her the straw dragon's head that Nick had made leered at me out of the shadows, black smoke leaking out of its empty eye sockets. The fire sputtered and hissed under the boiling cauldron.

At last it was done. She poured potions into little bottles and Meg wrapped them in leaves one by one, and placed them in a rush basket, along with two stoppered jugs of Grandmam Susan's ale.

Then Widow Susan put on her cloak, and handed one to me. It was of brown wool, and she had made it for me herself, she said, while I was ill. It was for my journey to France.

'It's a long walk to Newgate for someone in your state,' she said. 'So we'll go slowly. But you'll have to come with me to point him out to me. I warn you, boy – he won't be a pretty sight to see. Don't speak to him. Don't cry out or grieve, or say anything out loud to show that he's your father and you're his son. Because if you do, they'll chain you up alongside of him and you'll never get out of there till you're on the hangman's cart. Do you understand me?'

I nodded. Fear rose up in me again, blinding my eyes.

Meg held out a little circle of twisted cord and slipped it over my hand onto my wrist. 'I've made you an amulet, to guard you against evil. Be safe, William,' she whispered, shy now. 'Be strong.'

Newgate Prison

As soon as we arrived at the stern black gates of the prison, Widow Susan told me to pull my hood over my head to hide my face and my hair. She led me in past the guard, saying she had to visit someone she used to work for.

'A kind man, with money.' She nodded knowingly at the guard.

'He'll be over on the masters' side, prob'ly. What you got for me then, sweetheart?' Spit sprayed out between his snaggly black teeth as he laughed down at her.

'Good ale.' She handed him one of the jugs. 'I made it myself.'

'Now you're a woman who speaks good sense.' The guard slurped back the contents of the jug in one go, belched, and waved us through.

'Masters' side is for the lucky ones,' Widow Susan hissed at me. 'Those who've got money to give these drunken goats their simple pleasures.'

We went past the guard into a gloomy hall. It was impossible to tell how big it was, it was so dark. The whole place stank worse than the river, and it was hot and sweaty with so many people jostled together, crying and screaming some of them, or just crouching, still and silent on the end of chains, like dogs waiting to die.

They'd had their legs or their backs broken on the rack, Widow Susan told me. I never thought any place on earth could be as bad as this. I just stood there, stifled and scared, peering out of my hood into that awful darkness, till she jerked my arm.

'Do you see him?' she muttered. 'Can't stand here gawping, there's a gallery for that sort of entertainment, but you have to pay.' She pointed up to a balcony where people were strolling, pointing and laughing at what they could see. 'I'm not staying here a moment longer than I have to, I tell you.' She took the bottle of peppermint water from her basket and breathed it in, splashing it on her forehead. 'I'm in hell, and not even dead yet.'

I looked round anxiously. There were so many people here, and it was so dark. How on earth could I find him? And maybe he wasn't here anyway. Maybe he wasn't one of the lucky ones, after all. I shook my head. 'He isn't here.'

'Then they've hanged him already, and that's a mercy. Come on. We're leaving.'

It was then that I saw my father.

He was half-naked, and his skin was striped with blood. He was standing, chained by his wrists and his ankles to a post, so he couldn't sit or lie down or even kneel. His head was bowed and his eyes were closed, and he was swaying as much as his chains would let him. His lips were mumbling. I knew he was praying. I couldn't bear to see him like that. I wanted to rush over to him and put my arms round him, to scream at someone to untie his chains. My father, my father.

My hand was trembling as I touched Widow Susan's arm. 'He's there,' I whispered, low with fear and dread.

She nodded. 'Stay here. Don't come any closer. It'll do you no good, nor him neither.'

So I did as I was told, but I was still nearly fainting with shock. How could they do this to him, my strong, tall father? But I had to do what Old Susan had told me, or it might be worse for him, much worse. Nick's family knew far more about how to stay alive than I did. I pulled my hood right round my face, leaving just enough of a gap so I could watch her. A keeper was sitting nearby, bleary-eyed with ale, cursing the prisoners for screaming so loud that they gave him a headache, and Widow Susan hunkered down next to him, and they chattered and laughed for so long that I thought she must have tricked me, and had just come to enjoy the sights of the jail after all. She pointed to one of the groaning prisoners and they both cackled like a pair of old geese. Then she took the second bottle of ale out of her basket and gave it to him. He took a swig from it and then put his arm round her and started nuzzling into her neck with his thick, slimy lips. I wanted to scream and drag her away. I wanted to slap her grinning face. All this time my father swayed on his chains and muttered soundlessly, as if the only part of him that was alive was his mouth. I felt all my hopes, all my world, slipping away from me then.

At last, the keeper slithered sideways, fast asleep and adding his snores to the other noises. Widow Susan stood up at once and went over to my father. She took out one of the phials of oil and began rubbing it gently, so gently, into his skin where he'd been bleeding. He winced in sharp pain and opened his eyes. She put a bottle to his lips and told him to sip from it. He drank slowly, and I could tell from where I was standing that the look of agony was clearing from his eyes. He could hold his head up, he could focus on her. She talked to him all the time, though I couldn't hear what she was saying, and from time to time he nodded, but still he clenched his face against the pain when she used more oils on him.

I couldn't bear it any longer. I pushed my way outside and stood gasping in the cold air. It was raining; I flung back my hood, letting the rain wash over me, wash away the stench and the horrors of the hell that my father was in. My tears were streaming down my face, mingling salty and hot with the rain drops. Horses splashed mud up at me as they trotted past; beggars jostled at my side, but I never moved from the spot until Widow Susan came and shook my arm.

'You've seen how bad he is,' she said. 'So don't hope for too much. I've done what I can for him. He's easier now, and he'll sleep well for a bit, even standing up like that.'

I wiped my face with my sleeve. 'What did you say to him?'

'I told him you'd sent me and that you were safe. That cheered him up more than any medicine. William, he kept saying. William.'

'Did he really? Did he say my name?'

'He did. And he thanked me deeply, deeply for the care I've shown him. He is a true gentleman, your father.'

'And I thank you deeply too,' I said. In that moment,

I knew she was greater than any of the ladies I'd met in court, in spite of her rough ways.

'Will he live?' I asked, my voice no more than a husky whisper.

'He might. Till they hang him.'

The long journey

On the way back to the cottage we saw Nick, whistling cheerfully as he pushed his empty handcart.

'Have you made any money?' the grandmother shouted.

Nick opened his hand and showed her a fistful of warm brown coins. She picked out half and closed up his fist again.

'I'll take the cart back home,' she told him. 'William's as well as he's going to get for a bit, and there'll be no peace from him now if he languishes in our cottage another night. I've been reading the stars, and they tell me now is as good a time as any for journeying south. Be off with you both.' And without any goodbye or other blessing, she took up the shafts of the handcart and heaved it away along the muddy, sticky lane.

'Have you found out how we get to Dover?' I asked. Nick's grandmam was right. I'd have gone there on my own if I knew the way, whatever the danger. I wouldn't stay a minute longer in London.

He grinned. 'Well, I know the road sign that points to Dover. I know there's always people coming and going down that road, carts and merchants and the like. The first bit was the pilgrim's way to Canterbury, so it'll be a clear enough road to follow. And I know the sea's at the end of it. We got this bit of money Grandmam gave us – we could buy some bread and cheese with it to keep us going, and I know we'll have to walk slow because you've got no speed in your legs yet. And that's it!' He shrugged. 'That's all I know, Master Will.'

'But how far is it?'

'Miles!' he grinned again, as if the prospect of walking miles was something to be cheerful about. But then, Nick was nearly always cheerful. 'So we'd better get moving!' He strode ahead, whistling. 'Thing is, we have to go past that Lordy Crazy's place again, in Greenwich! We might as well have carried on from there in the first place, and saved you a mugging and me a few days' work.'

'So we might,' I said. 'But I wouldn't have seen Father, I wouldn't know that he was still alive. And we wouldn't have had any money at all if you hadn't worked.'

I was already feeling more cheerful. I hurried beside Nick, matching my stride to his and even trying to whistle with him, though I wasn't much good at hurrying and whistling at the same time and it gave me hiccups. We passed Greenwich without stopping, and I was glad of that. I didn't want to risk seeing any more nobles. We spent the night in the woods, and the next, and creepy nights they were too, for me. Rooks croaked into the stillness and deer plunged through the thickets, scaring me out of my wits. Nick snored beside me, and when I fell asleep at last, screech owls like banshees tore my dreams in half. Nick snored on, hearing nothing. On the second morning we saw a hangman's gibbet through the trees, which I was very glad I hadn't seen the night before, and the grey stones of a castle. We met an old woodman with a face as brown as tanned leather, and he told us we were outside the town of Rochester, and well on the way to Canterbury, which was halfway to Dover.

'There was a time,' he said, leaning on his axe as if he had a whole day to spare, 'when this way would be full of Canterbury pilgrims, on their horses and donkeys, or walking barefoot, some of them. It was a sight to see, and a sound to hear. They'd be singing and playing instruments, folks from all over the place with their tales to tell. Hideous strange, some of them were too. I miss the pilgrims.'

'Why don't they still come?' Nick asked, and the woodman's old face creased up with surprise.

'You don't know? Do you know why they came in the first place?'

'To worship at Thomas a'Becket's shrine,' I said, not wanting him to think I was as ignorant as Nick.

'Aye, the blessed saint lay there four hundred years, till our own good king, Henry, had his bones dug up and thrown into the Thames. No pilgrims since then. No pilgrims for two years or more, and this lane is quiet now without them. Our king had his reasons, no doubt.' He swung his axe and smashed it so viciously into the side of a dying oak tree that I jumped away from him in fright.

We tramped on and on. Nick tried singing, though his voice wasn't getting any better. Now the lane got busier, with carts piled with heavy loads of vegetables and fruit on the way to a market. One of the carts lost some apples as it bumped along over deep ruts, and we stuffed our stomachs and then our pockets with them. We spent the next night in a barn, and a farmer's wife gave us some small ale to drink and a fistful each of beef to eat, and in exchange we broke some logs into kindling for her. Nick showed me how to do it, and this time I was glad to help him. Next day there was more traffic, all heading for Dover, all piled with goods. The carters called out to us cheerily as they passed us, and we walked and ran, walked and ran in turns, but by the end of the afternoon my boots were giving me blisters, and even Nick had lost the will to hurry. We trudged along, not whistling, not talking. Dusk was falling, the traffic was easing off. We heard a cart rumbling behind us and Nick turned round and waved his arms at the driver.

'We're weary travellers,' he called. 'May we ride with you for a bit, sir? We're heading for Dover.'

The carter jerked the reins. His old horse stopped lazily.

'Do you have money?' the man grumbled.

'A little,' Nick said carefully.

'Then I advise you to walk three more miles, where there's a tavern. You'll find many a merchant or carter willing to carry you to Dover from there.'

'Can we spend the three miles in your cart?' Nick asked.

'Aye, if you must, but you won't thank me for it.'

'We must,' I said.

The carter clicked to his horse to set off again, and Nick used up the last of his strength to vault into the cart as it drew past. He heaved me up and I tumbled in after him, yelping as I landed on something soft and squashy and reeking to high heaven.

'Phwaa! It's a dung cart!' Nick shouted. He tried to leap out again, but the driver pretended to be deaf and urged his horse on to a fast trot, which set us rolling round and round in the muck, laughing helplessly.

He set us down at the tavern, and there, in a cluttered yard, a huge carter built like a bull was unloading stuff. It was nearly dark by then, and although the man held up a lantern when he saw us, I don't think he realised how mucky we were.

'We're heading for Dover, sir,' Nick called. 'Can we take a ride with you? We've got a few pence, but not much.'

'I'll take you on.' His voice seemed to come from somewhere in his belly. 'I've some goods to unload here, and you can help me with that. And tomorrow I'm riding empty to Dover, so I'll be glad of your company.'

That night the man slept in the tavern and we rolled up in his empty cart, after he'd sent a toothy girl out to us with a bowl of fish stew and ale. She sniffed as she handed the food to us.

'What a stink!' she said, giggling.

When the carter came out in the morning he chased us off to the well to wash ourselves clean. 'Clothes and all,' he shouted. His voice boomed round the yard. 'They'll dry on the back of the cart, and you can wrap yourselves in these blankets till they do.'

'We thought you hadn't noticed,' Nick grinned.

'Took me a while,' the carter said. 'I'm used to smells. When I come up from Dover I'm usually carrying fish, so there's always a bit of a reek in my cart.

211

But you two last night! It was enough to turn the stomach of a pig!'

The water was clinking with ice, but I pulled off my tunic and hose and scrubbed myself down. As I was rubbing myself dry with the rough old blanket I noticed that Nick was trying to keep himself covered up while he washed himself. 'Go on, Nick!' I laughed, and gave him a shove towards the pail of water, and it was then that I saw what he was hiding. There was a cord looped round his neck, and dangling from it was a ring.

I didn't know what to say. Had Nick stolen the ring from me? No, it was a man – I remembered his stubbly face clearly. But was he something to do with Nick? But if he was, why was Nick travelling with me to Dover? I turned away, baffled and worried. Before I could say anything, the cart driver called me over and gave me some breakfast gruel and asked me to clean out his cart for him. There were the spines and bones and goggle-eyed heads of old fish stuck to the boards. I peeled them out as well as I could, and when Nick ran up to join us, raw-cheeked from the icy water, we spread our clothes out to dry over the back of the cart. We set off, huddled up in our blankets. Nick was sparky, full of chatter and jokes, and he and the driver gossiped away as if they'd known each other for years. The driver told him about two big ships that were moored just outside Dover, which were being loaded up with all kinds of things. 'Special things, that rich folks have,' he said.

'Who owns them?' Nick asked, but the driver shook his head. 'No idea. But they're big. They're important. And they're bound for Calais. That's all I know.'

'Calais!' Nick said. 'That's where we're going, isn't it, Will?'

I turned away from him. I didn't want to talk to him, didn't want to look at him. I had to think, think, think about that ring.

But at last, at long last, we could hear the screeching laughter of gulls, we could smell the salty tang of the sea, we could hear the fussy noise of people and carts in the town below us. We must be there! I kneeled up in the cart, peering round eagerly.

'I'll leave you here,' the driver rumbled. 'I've a family I like to stay with when I'm here, and there'll be a tasty fish pie for me. Here, you might as well take this.' He threw me a dead rabbit, still in its fur. 'They gave me this at the tavern, but it's no use to me. I only eat fish, breakfast, noon and supper. Lovely fish!'

We wriggled back into our still-damp clothes and shimmied out of the cart. Nick skipped round and round, waving his skinny arms in the air, and yelling, 'It's over! It's over! We've come to Dover!'

Then he grabbed my arm and I whirled round with him, singing out loud. I couldn't help it.

Dover!

The ring

We ran to the brow of the hill. The bells were chiming out three of the clock. Down below us, the little town was bustling with life. We could hear the trundling of cartwheels over cobbles, and the shouts of workers calling to each other. Dogs were sending up a frenzy of barking as if they could smell strangers in the town. People were milling everywhere, soldiers, merchants, traders with baskets on their heads and hips. We could see the harbour bristling with dozens of masts. Just beyond the harbour lay two huge, brightly-painted war ships. My spirits rose as high as a skylark.

'They'll be the ones the carter told us about. Going to Calais!'

'Can you see Calais from here? Can you see France?' Nick asked. He screwed up his eyes. However hard we scanned the horizon, we couldn't make out anything that looked like another country. But it didn't matter. It was there, we knew it.

'Is Mistress Margery's husband a Frenchman?'

'No,' I said. 'He's Richard Oakland, the Duke of Carlisle.' I felt proud, saying that.

'But why does he live in France?'

'Because he's the Lieutenant of King Henry's castle in Calais. It's an English town, but it's in France. We won it, hundreds of years ago, in a battle.'

'Right then,' Nick said. 'I probably knew, but I'd forgotten. I'll go and find us a passage, Master Will, on one of those big sailing ships!'

He set off at a run, turned round to grin at me, threw his hat in the air, did a somersault and ran off. I remembered the ring again, looped round his neck just like mine had been. 'Nick!' I shouted. 'Wait!' I started to run after him, and stopped. There was no chasing Nick, he ran as swift as a hound.

I was filled with that wriggling doubt again, squirming in my head like ants swarming from a leaf-pile. Why was he wearing my ring round his neck? What if he was planning to sell it? To show it to a soldier? I was lonely again, lost and lonely and worried.

If I never saw Nick again, I had no idea what I would do.

Slowly I collected together some wood and built up a fire. I set about skinning the rabbit the carter had given me, nicking the fur and peeling it away from the tight little body. Then I skewered it with a stick and built a frame to balance it over the flames. Soon its juices were spitting, and the familiar smell of roasting meat made my stomach rumble. I thought about Matthew, and how we loved to spend a day riding and hunting, and how Ned Porritt would make us a fire and skin and cook a rabbit or hare for us, just like this. We would sit as close to the crackling fire as we could, so our eyes were smarting with the wood smoke and our hands and faces were scorching hot, and then Matthew and Ned would tease me with stories of the headless knights who haunted the dark forests.

At last I heard Nick whistling. I jumped up from the fire and ran to meet him. His cheeks were bunched with smiles, and I knew he was in luck, and that he'd found a way of getting us to France. But never, never would I have guessed how we were to do it.

'The carter was right,' he called. 'Those two ships are setting off with the tide at first light tomorrow. And we'll be on one of them! The *Lion*, it's called. We're going as ship's boys, and there'll be plenty for us to do, because every deck will be packed with people. You won't have to worry, just keep your head covered, just do the loading and carrying you're told to do, and no one will even look at you.'

I gazed at the ships. They were very fine, I could tell even from here. They crouched on the water like hunting animals, with guns shining in the setting sun, and the tall masts draped with coloured banners that were just waiting for the wind to set them streaming. They were no ordinary sailing ships. They were surely ships of war.

'Nick, who owns those ships?'

'You don't need to know, Master Will.'

'I do!' I was angry with him for being so cocky and so secretive. How could I trust him if he kept secrets from me? 'I can go on my own,' I said quietly. 'I don't need you, Nicholas Drew.'

I had hurt him. I could see by his eyes. He nodded and turned away.

'I'll go then.' He didn't look at me. He started to walk away, his head held proudly high. 'If you don't need me, I'll go.'

'Nick,' I called. 'Tell me.'

He didn't turn his head.

A few feet further on, he stopped and stood, arms folded, looking down across the harbour to the open sea, darkening now with mystery as the sun was just tipping the last of itself under the shelf of the horizon. *One day, one day, I'm going to be a sailor like my father*, I remembered him saying that to me, the day we went to Greenwich together. *I'm going to sail round the world and see everything there is to see.* He was whistling again, a jaunty little jig that he used to fill up spaces between talking. It made me smile to hear it. I knew his head was filling up with adventures. I strolled over to him and stood by him. We still didn't look at each other.

'I will go to France,' I said. 'I'll get there.'

'You might be seasick. Who'd look after you?'

'*You* might be seasick. Who'd look after you?'

We both started giggling.

'So tell me, Nick. Who owns those ships?'

'King Henry.'

'*What?*'

He grinned at me, full of himself. 'Don't worry, he's not going on either of them. But there'll be plenty of courtiers on board, nobles and pages and lords and ladies-in-waiting, and hundreds of soldiers. Just look at those ships. Doesn't it swell your heart to see them so fine and proud? They're like floating courts, I'm told. The *Lion* and the *Sweepstake*, they're called. I never saw anything more beautiful in my life.'

'What are they doing here?'

I could see he was bursting to tell me now, but he teased me with silence for a bit, till he couldn't hold it in any longer.

'They're going to Calais along with a hundred pretty little escort sailing ships to greet the Princess Anne of Cleves, and bring her to England. And when she gets to England, King Henry's going to marry her. That's what they told me, down in the harbour.'

I could hardly believe what he was saying. King Henry was to take another wife! I spoke the names out loud. Queen Katherine of Aragon. Queen Anne Boleyn. Queen Jane Seymour. And now, Queen Anne of Cleves. And what would happen to my little Prince Edward now, if this new wife had sons too? All that the king cared about was having an heir to the throne. The prince was cosseted and cared for as if he was a weak sapling. Mother Jack had often said: 'His father wants him to grow into a mighty oak! It's to be hoped he does!'

I imagined the excitement and the gossip at court. I imagined the thrill the courtiers must feel at the thought of going to Calais to greet the future queen of England. The Duke of Norfolk would probably be among them, and the Howard family. My uncle Carew? Which of the ships would they be travelling on?

'You're never expecting me to go on one? With all those nobles? All those courtiers and soldiers? You're mad!'

But even greater than my fear of sailing on one of King Henry's ships, was my terror of the sea itself. I moaned aloud in panic at the thought of floating across it, with the brown waves reaching up their arms to pull me down and down.

Nick heard me. 'Master Will, it's more than that, isn't it? It's even more than being caught by the king's soldiers? You're real scared, even I can see that, like there's ghosts round you.'

I could feel my throat burning and bruised with swallowing. I twisted Meg's amulet on my wrist. 'I had a brother,' I said at last, 'and he drowned in the sea.'

'And you saw it happen, most like? That's what scares you.'

I shook my head. 'No. I didn't see it happen. One minute we were standing on a rock together. And the next minute, I was being pulled out of the sea by my father.'

'He saved your life.'

'But he thought I was Matthew. He wanted to save Matthew.' Now it was coming, and I swallowed hard. I didn't want to cry, I didn't want to cry in front of Nick.

'What would he have done? Your brother? If he was scared of the sea, like you?'

'He'd pretend he was a soldier going into battle. "Onward, ever onward!" That's what he used to say.'

'I like that,' Nick chuckled. He ran over to the fire I'd made and squatted down, turning the rabbit on its spit. The juices spurted into the flames, making them hiss, and he gave an 'Ah!' of pleasure. I stood next to him. There was another thing, nagging me like a sore tooth that needs to be jerked out.

'Nick. When you were getting washed at that tavern, I saw a ring under your tunic.'

He put his hand to his neck. I saw him clutching a cord.

'Can I see it?'

He dragged the cord over his head and thrust it at me. 'There,' he said. 'I've hid it as long as I could.' It was my ring. The Montague ring.

I could feel a kind of wild fury rising up in me. 'You had it all along! You stole it! It was you, that night. Or you sent someone to take it off me, to beat me up—'

'Sir, sir...' he kept trying to break in, but I was so angry and confused and upset that I didn't want to listen to him. I was like the little prince when he was having one of his tantrums. Nick said nothing else at all until my anger had fizzled away.

'I *was* there that night. When you slipped away from me I ran after you, trying to find you, and I saw that robber attacking you. I'd seen you looking at the ring when we were walking back from Greenwich, and I reckon he must have seen too, and followed us till you were on your own. I pulled him off you, and when he ran off, I chased him instead of looking after you. I should have stayed, but I knew how much that ring means to you.'

I kept swallowing, but I couldn't speak.

'I wasn't going to tell you about it, not yet. I chased after the man and I got the ring off him. I'm sorry to say I had to use my knife to do it, because he was bigger and stronger than me. I don't know what kind of state I left him in, and I don't really care. It was you I was worried about. I ran back, and I couldn't find you. I was panicking. And when I did find you, I was grieved with myself for leaving you and chasing the robber instead.'

'But why didn't you tell me? Why didn't you give me my ring back?'

'Sir, I didn't want anything like that ever to happen to you again because of this ring. I decided to keep my mouth shut, and to wear the ring myself, and to give it to you when the time comes. That's what I decided, sir.'

And I believed him, with all my heart. He was the one who had saved my life. My guardian angel.

'Do you want to wear it, or do you want me to keep it safe for you?'

Dumbly I handed the ring back to him, and he looped it round his neck.

'I dare go on one of those ships,' I said. 'I'll do it. If you'll come with me, Nick. I do need you.'

And then we tucked into that rabbit as if we were at one of King Henry's famous banquets. It was the best feast ever.

'Onward, ever onward!'

There were deck hands everywhere on the harbour side, shouting orders, running, bustling, and we were told there would no shortage of work for us to do; loading up little boats with boxes and barrels of stuff to be taken on board the king's ships. It was bitterly cold down there by the sea. Little waves chopped round the harbour wall like dogs jumping up to snap at us.

'Get off to the *Lion* now, you boys, and help unload,' a deck master shouted. Nick jumped lightly down into one of the little boats. I couldn't follow him. All my terror of the sea welled up again. The waves threw themselves up at me, ready to suck me down into themselves. Again and again they came for me, clawing at me with fingers of spray. I backed away, miserable with fear, and one of the sailors shoved me in the back.

'Get on, get on!'

I knew I had to make the hardest journey of my life, to take the step that left the land behind me, and to trust myself to walk above the sea. My hands were sweaty with fright. I closed my eyes. 'Help me, Matthew,' I whispered inside my head, and I heard a voice floating up to me, 'Onward, ever onward!'

I jumped, and landed on all fours in the rocking little boat, and looked up to see Nick grinning at me.

In no time we were out of the harbour and into the full swell of the waves. The nearer we drew to the king's ships, the huger they seemed, like timber castles rising out of the water. We could see the great blunt stern, like a wall of wood, and the lines of cannons nosing out of the hull, and the slope of the tumblehome, and the fancy balustrades and galleries. We could see the red and white flags of St George already fluttering from the mainmast, and the banners twitching from the two shorter masts. We could hear them flapping, even over the mutter of the waves and the screaming of the gulls. They reminded me of horses at the jousts, pawing the ground, eager to be off. I was as excited as Nick, too excited to be afraid any more, and I didn't need the snarling sailor behind me to urge me up the rope ladder to the deck of the *Lion* with a lash of a rope. He made me yell out loud, but it was with excitement as much as with pain.

'A snail would do better! We've got a tide to catch, and it doesn't wait for the likes of you!' He growled, and I levered myself out of the little boat and scrambled up the ladder hand over fist.

I had done it. I had really done it. I turned to see Nick grinning at me, and I knew I would never be afraid of the sea again.

Boatload after boatload, the courtiers and their servants came, shuddering with cold in spite of their fancy fur cloaks. And after came the king's soldiers, boat after boat, till there were so many people crammed on board that if a fish had leaped up and

223

landed on deck we'd have sunk. The tide was right, the sea was silver with morning light, our great ship, the *Lion,* was ready to sail. The little tugs rowed us out to sea. The men heaved on the ropes and the sails were hoisted, with much flapping and straining until they bellied out like huge birds' wings. The king's flags and banners were streaming wide now, bright as pheasants' tails. The ropes creaked, and all the timbers growled like snoring dogs. The little tug boats slipped their towing ropes and danced back towards land. Our ship cut through the waves, and cold raining spray showered over us all.

I ran to the side and looked across the water at our sister ship, the *Sweepstake.* Her painted prow gleamed golden in the sun as she cut through the waves, her full sails billowed. Dozens of little painted barges sailed with us, surrounding us, blazing with colour, and dancing on the waves.

'Isn't that a grand sight?' Nick said behind me. 'Like a charming flock of goldfinches. Even better, like angels, they are, every one, and we must be in heaven!'

How King Henry would love to hear you saying that! I thought, *Seeing as he thinks he's God!* But I daren't even whisper it out loud. My shoulders were still smarting from the sailor's rope; I didn't want to give anyone else an excuse to strike me again. I looked out at the boats, skimming as if they were alive on the water, creatures of the sea. And suddenly out of nowhere, the answer to one of Brother John's riddles came into my head.

'Got it! Got it!' I shouted.

'What?'

'Tell me, Nick. I have no sight nor hands, many ribs, a mouth in my middle. I move on one foot, I am swift as the wind. What am I?'

'What are you? You're a boy, same as me.' He stared at me, puzzled, and I wanted to laugh, but I held it back. 'Course you've got sight. You can see me, can't you?'

'Get moving!' a sailor shouted. 'There's some barrels here need lashing down. No time to admire the view. We've got six hours' sailing ahead of us, if the wind's kind.'

The wind wasn't kind. The wind was full of treachery that day, and soon after we left Dover and the gleaming white cliffs behind us, it tossed our boat about like a child's toy. But before it really took hold of us, before it threatened us with a cold swim, my day was spoiled by something far worse than wind or storm, thunder or lightning.

Nick and I were scrabbling on our hands and knees on the deck. Some barrels were rolling loose, and he and I were the only ones small enough to scramble behind them and tighten the ropes again. A group of young courtiers strolled past us while we were crouching down there. All I could see from my tight corner were the legs, smart in coloured hose and fancy leather shoes. I could hear their voices. They were jesting together about the king's castle in France, and how beautiful the women there were said to be.

'I know for a fact that a pretty young goose called Margery has flown over there this year,' one of them said. I started. They were talking about my sister.

And then came another voice; one that I knew. 'We could soon pluck her feathers.'

They laughed, and I went cold and sick inside. I ducked my head lower, and when they had passed I turned slightly so I could look up. One of the courtiers was thinner and taller than the others. He was holding his cap in his hand so the wind wouldn't take charge of it. His flapping hair was the colour of candle wax. There was no doubt about it. It was Percy Howard.

I sat back on my heels and groaned.

'Will?' Nick asked.

I couldn't put a voice to my anger and wretchedness.

'Tell me!' he insisted.

'I've seen the person who put my father in prison. The Duke of Norfolk's nephew, Percy Howard. He came snooping round our Hall and then he betrayed us to the king. And did you hear what he just said about my sister?'

'I've got my knife,' Nick whispered. 'And I'll drive it between his shoulder blades.'

I knew he meant it, and part of me wanted to cheer him on too, to see the end of Percy Howard, who hated me so much. But I shook my head. 'Kill Norfolk's nephew, and in front of his friends? You're mad, Nick. You'd be thrown overboard, and so would I.' Even so, my hand curled round the dagger at my belt.

'And if he sees you here, what do you think he'll do to you? He'll have you tied up and stored below till you can join your father. Let me do it now!'

'He'll never recognise me, surely,' I said. 'Not like this.'

I remembered the way I used to walk past the lower status people at the palace. They were nothing. I never looked them in the eye, unless they were among my servants. They had nothing to do with me. Someone like Percy Howard would never even notice a common ship's boy. He might know me by my red hair, but I had my cap pulled well down to cover it. The only thing he might recognise was my voice, just as I had recognised his. If I kept quiet, he would never know me. It was better that way. Yet because of him I had lost my home and my father. It would mean nothing to him if King Henry's soldiers found me and threw me on a bonfire when we reached Calais. Why should I care what happened to him? Why should I spare his life, when he had ruined mine?

But I did care what happened to Nick. He would die, there was no doubt about it, if he did anything to a member of King Henry's court. So I dropped my hand away, and my dagger stayed where it was. I put my hand on Nick's arm, and he let his own hand fall from his belt.

And it was then that the wind turned. The sea became a foaming beast, lunging and rearing, slamming the *Lion* from side to side, nearly tipping us overboard each time as we slid across the wet deck. And all those noblemen tricked out in their finery to greet the new queen were as sick as dogs.

I saw Percy and his peacock flock of courtiers crawling to the side of the boat and clinging to the ropes. Their servants could do nothing to help them because they were in the same wretched state. Nick and I were too busy to be ill, and maybe we didn't have any rich food in our bellies to bring up. The immense sky was black and fierce, day had turned into night. Green water streamed across the decks through the gun ports and washed this way, that way, whichever way the wind

227

heaved the ship. The sailors hauled on the ropes and loosed the sails, and tightened them again, and we were yelled at to give a hand, for God's sake, or we'd all be under the water. Nick screamed with excitement through it all.

'A sailor, a sailor, I'm a real sailor!' he shouted. 'God bless the wind and waves! God bless the sea!'

And, just as suddenly as it had come, the storm dropped to a fine breeze and the wind blew us steadily on course again. The wretched courtiers lay slumped on the deck, their faces as white as codfishes. If I didn't despise Percy so much I would have felt sorry for him.

One of the young courtiers with him saw me looking and shouted over to me. 'Boy, fetch me some ale to swill. My mouth tastes like stale cheese!'

His friends all laughed feebly. I called back that I didn't know where the ale was kept.

'Don't speak like that to me, dog!' the boy snapped.

'Sir, I am not your servant,' I said angrily, and turned away. I regretted it instantly. It was too late. He was on his feet and feeling for his jewelled dagger, but Percy was there first. He grabbed me by the shoulders and swung me round, and stared into my face. I tried to look down, but he cupped my chin in his hand and tilted my head back.

'I know your voice,' he said. 'And I know your face, grubby as it is, and your hair like a mat of dirty red wool.' He knocked my cap off and tugged me by the hair till my face was right against his.

I shook my head, not daring to say anything else, and Nick slid up to us across the wet deck and tried to pull me away.

'Leave him alone!' he shouted. 'If you know him, you know me too. We're brothers. Our father's a ferryman at Westminster steps. We've rowed you across the Thames many a time, haven't we, Peter?'

Percy stared at me, and then let me go, so I dropped back into Nick's arms. Then Percy staggered as a new turn in the wind brought the boat up onto its elbows, and he launched himself back to the ship's side, groaning and clutching his stomach.

'I wish I could die!' he moaned.

'Amen!' whispered Nick in my ear.

Strangers to each other

At last we drew into the port of Calais.

'We've done it! We're in France!' Nick tugged excitedly at my sleeve. 'We're proper sailors, we are!'

The little cottages with their queer tiled roofs shambled in a higgledy-piggledy jumble up towards the king's mighty castle. Its pale towers and turrets looked slender and ghostly in the rainy mist. The long grey arms of the harbour stretched out to welcome us, and little boats danced towards us like streams of unleashed dogs running to greet their masters. Gunners fired cannons, and the shots echoed from all the walls of the town. The king's flags and banners fluttered like waving hands.

Our anchor was lowered with a grumbling and groaning of chain and rope, and a mighty splash as it hit the water. An army of soldiers dressed in red and blue were the first to disembark, beating drums as they were rowed into the harbour. Next the nobles and other highborn were taken ashore, and they had so much to be carried by the way of gifts and fine clothes, so much to be heaped into the waiting row boats, and there was so much to do with ropes and sails, that nobody took any notice of us, scurrying backwards and forward like ships' mice. At last all the nobles were landed and strolling off to their lodgings round the town and in the massive castle that dominated it. The *Lion* and the *Sweepstake* lay at ease outside the harbour waiting for the future queen of England to be brought on board. Nobody knew who we were; nobody cared. Our captain was too busy to notice us. We jumped ashore with one of the boats, and hauled the last two wooden chests that were bulging with gifts onto the waiting wheelbarrows. Then we looked at each other, looked back at our ship and ran. We simply ducked our heads and scampered away – a pair of brown ship's mice, lost among the crowd.

Bells were peeling all round the little port, flags flying, trumpets blaring, cannons firing from the castle ramparts. Flocks of apprentices, merchants, women with little children jostled together, waving coloured ribbons and shouting excitedly. It seemed as if all the people of Calais had come out that day to see King Henry's ships put in, in spite of the chilly December rain squalling round their faces. I darted ahead of Nick, dodging between a group of apprentice boys dressed in the same brown woollen clothes as us. It was easy to mingle with them. Nick caught up with me at last, panting. 'You've definitely learned how to run!' he chuckled, gasping for breath.

The street was slippery with so much rain and so many scurrying feet, and I slipped and fell a couple of times, smearing myself with mud. I didn't care. I could see the huge main gate to the castle now, and nothing was going to stop me. I sprinted through in the wake of a pushing crowd of Calais schoolboys, straight into the cobbled entrance yard. And there, at once, like a gift from my guardian angel, I saw my sister.

231

I hardly recognised her at first. She was with a cluster of other girls: maids-of-honour, ladies-in-waiting, and young noblemen's wives. They were all giggling and talking excitedly, clutching one another's hands and laughing at private jokes. Margery looked taller than last time I saw her, and not so plump and awkward. She was jumping up to see over a woman's head, and then she clutched another girl's hand and ran to be at the front of the group. I had never seen her looking so happy. I ran forward, waving my hand and shouting 'Margery! Margery!' across the crowd. She turned her head this way and that, craning to see where the voice was coming from. She looked straight at me and away again. She didn't know me. I had changed as much as she had. We were strangers to each other.

As I struggled to get nearer, a bearded nobleman came up to her and put a warm cloak round her shoulders, lifting up her hood to hide her face from the rain. And she stood on her toes and kissed him, full on the lips, and pulled away, laughing up at him. I must be mistaken, I thought. This couldn't be my sister. This man couldn't be her ugly old husband. Crowds pressed between us, so I couldn't see them any more. I dodged round with Nick following close behind me. When I got to the front, the girl had gone, along with all her friends, like a flock of birds.

The man who had kissed her was still there, watching after them with a smile on his face. He turned to his waiting page and called, 'Make sure Lady Margery changes into dry clothes.' The boy bowed and hurried after my sister.

'It must be him!' I said to Nick. 'I have to speak to him. Now.'

'I wouldn't. Not yet,' Nick warned, but I was so excited that I took no notice at all.

'Give me the ring,' I insisted. I pulled it from his neck and looped the cord over my head.

'Be careful,' he called.

The man was already turning away. A flock of nuns passed in front of him, their brown habits flapping like cold sparrows. I pushed my way through them. I ran to him, and put my hand on his arm.

'Lord Richard of Carlisle?' I asked.

He shook his arm in annoyance and frowned down at me. 'There's a beggars' gate at the back of the castle,' he said. 'Go there for your scraps.'

'Lord Richard, please don't turn me away. I'm Margery's brother.'

He paused, looked briefly at me, and raised his hand. Immediately two soldiers moved forward. One grasped me, pulling my hands behind my back. Nick ran out of the crowd and tried to pull me away, and was immediately grabbed by the other soldier. They started hustling us away, and we squirmed and struggled to break free. Lord Richard walked off as if he was turning his back on dogs fighting in the street.

'I'm William!' I shouted desperately. 'She must have talked to you about me. I come from Montague Hall. Margery is my sister. Please, please let me speak to you.'

The soldier who was dragging me away flicked the back of his hand across my face. I shouted again, 'Lord Richard, I am the son of Robert Montague.' I struggled round, and saw that Lord Richard had paused. He still had his back to me, but his head was turned to one side. He was listening. The soldier kicked me on, and in desperation I shouted it all again in French. He turned and looked at me. I said it again in Greek. It wasn't good Greek, I knew, but it was more than an ordinary ship's boy could do. He signalled to the soldier to let go, and I dropped to my knees. Nick stood with his hands on his hips, glaring defiantly at the soldiers.

'Lord Richard, really and truly I am William Montague, grandson of Sir Henry Montague... brother of your wife, Margery.' I said the whole thing, and more, begging him to take me to my sister. I gave him her birth date. I told him she was afraid of dragons, that she wasn't a very good dancer, and I did it all in perfect Latin.

Lord Richard smiled and came back to me. He touched my bowed head and told me to stand up.

'How come a common boy like you is such a scholar?'

'Because I am who I say I am – William Montague, the grandson of Sir Henry, and son of Robert. My ancestor was Walter Montague.' I pulled at the cord round my neck. 'And this is my family's seal.'

Lord Richard took the ring from me and turned it over in his hand, curious and mystified.

'Take no notice of him. He's a thief and a beggar,' a voice came from behind me and I closed my eyes and sighed. I knew who it was, even before I turned to look at the pallid face of Lord Percy Howard. 'He stole that ring. The person he pretends to be is wanted for treason.' He laughed. 'My advice to you is to throw this boy into a cell, along with his grubby friend, and let him rot.'

He strode up to Lord Richard, put an arm round his shoulders and walked him away, whispering to him intently. For a moment Lord Richard turned and looked at me. Then he made a signal to the soldiers, and walked on with Percy. The soldiers dragged Nick across the yard as if he were a bundle of rags, and I ran after him, begging them to leave him alone, not to hurt him. They opened a heavy studded door and threw him inside a room, and bowed mockingly to me. I followed, and they shut the huge studded door behind us.

In the castle cell

'What did I tell you, Master Will?' Nick grumbled. He pulled his torn hose away from his knee, which was bleeding heavily where he had been dragged across the ground. 'You do things too quick. You don't think first.'

'I had to do it,' I said. 'It was my only chance. Here,' I kneeled down and tore a strip from my shirt and bandaged his knee with it. There was no window in the cell, and the only light to see by came from cracks around the hinges of the door. Nick watched me in surprise as I dabbed carefully at his knee, but he didn't say anything, and neither did I. And then I closed my eyes and sank back against the wall. It was all over now, after everything I had been through. If only Percy hadn't turned up at that minute. Everything was lost. I'd put us both in King Henry's hands, and there was no escaping now. Torture and death had been hanging over me for weeks and weeks. Thief, beggar, traitor – was there anything else I could be accused of? And the worst thing was, I'd dragged Nick down with me.

'Nick, I'm sorry.'

No one hated me more than Percy Howard, and he hated me for only one thing; because I was King Henry's favourite. He had despised me from the moment that King Henry had smiled at me and told me I had a look of himself. He had wanted me dead then. Well, he had his way now. I put my head in my hands. I had dropped into a deep well, and there was no way out.

I have no idea how long we sat there, saying nothing to each other. There was no more light in the room. It must have been well into the night when we heard footsteps, someone fumbling with the lock, and the door was pushed open. The light from a rush lantern flickered round our cell. We both leaped to our feet, alert, ready to run between the soldiers' arms if we could. But the light softened and spread, and we saw a small figure standing alone in the doorway. It was Margery.

She held her lantern high and stared at me, her hand to her mouth. She stayed in the doorway, not stepping any further, with doubt and horror clouding her eyes. Yet there was a flicker of recognition there.

'Margery,' I said softly.

'Will!' she gasped. 'It's really you! But you look so different – you're so grubby and your hair's matted like a wild cat's – and look at your bruises! What's happened to you?'

Someone stepped in from the night and stood behind her, and as he held his lantern forward I saw that it was Lord Richard.

'You're quite sure?' he asked her.

'I'm scared of the dragon,' Margery whispered, moving towards me.

'I'm scared of the bear,' I said.

And my sister flung her arms round me.

'These are very dangerous times, and I had to protect you, Margery,' Lord Richard said. 'Percy is greedy and ambitious, like most young men of his family, but I didn't know he was so treacherous. He'll be punished for his lies. I'll have him sent on a mission straight away; he won't be back till long after you've gone, Will, I promise.'

'Let me get a room prepared for you,' Margery said. 'And a servant will bathe you and dress you in clean clothes. Then you can tell us your news. Oh, Will, Will, I can't believe it's you, really and truly you, here in Calais!'

'And what about this young fellow?' Lord Richard said, turning to Nick.

'This is Nicholas Drew. He's my—'

'I'm Master Will's servant, my Lord,' said Nick firmly. 'I look after him, only I didn't do it too well this time.'

'Never mind, servant Nicholas. I'll put you with my own servants. You'll have a clean pallet by the fire, and you'll dine with them tonight in the great hall.'

'All my dreams come true, all in one day!' Nick's eyes shone. 'Wait till I tell Grandmam! But tomorrow, sir, I must go back to my ship. Master Will is safe now.'

A letter to the king

Nick did dine in the great hall, but I didn't. Lord Richard told me that it would be much too dangerous, for me and for him, and that I must stay in hiding until he had decided what to do.

So Nick, washed and tidied, went down to dine, his eyes bulging with fright and excitement. He sat at the servants' end of the trestle tables, and Margery told me later that she could see him eating and gazing round with wonder, and every so often babbling away to another servant. He wore himself out before the banquet was over and had to be carried over to the great fireplace and tucked into a straw pallet to sleep it all off.

It was my old nurse, Joan, from Montague Hall who brought me something to eat. All she had been told was that Lady Margery had a special visitor and that she must pretend not to know him. It was impossible, of course. She burst into tears as soon as she saw me.

'I can't believe it's you, Master Will! Look at you, thin as a clothes peg, and how tall you've grown! But you've still got that lovely rug of red hair. I love that hair of yours! But whatever have you been up to?' She came closer to me and dropped her voice right down to a whisper. 'I thought you were page to the young prince? What's happened? Oh, don't worry, not a word, not a word, Lady Margery has told me to pretend I don't know who you are, and that's my promise, but, Master Will, I don't know what to say to you till I know you're well and happy. I won't say a word. Not a word more.'

I think she'd have said lots more if she could, but Margery came in and sent her away so we could talk to each other. And so at last, in the rosy shadows and shifting firelight of her room, the whole story came out, though it hurt me to tell it and it hurt her more to hear it. I told her what had happened to Brother John, and to Father, and that Montague Hall had been burned to the ground, that our aunt had abandoned us and our uncle had betrayed us to the king.

'Why, why?' Tears rolled down her cheeks, and she didn't try to stop them. 'I didn't know anything about this. All this was happening, and I didn't know. I've been really happy here, and now I feel guilty. Oh, poor you, you've been through so much! No wonder you've changed.'

'You've changed too,' I said. I tried to find the right words to tell her how pretty she was now, and decided against it. 'You're taller,' I said. 'You're a lady!'

She smiled. 'My Lord Richard is the kindest man in the world. I was completely wrong about him. He *is* very old, but not quite so old as I thought. He's halfway past thirty, which isn't so bad, is it? And he isn't a bit ugly. We were married in the summer, but he says I'm too young to have babies, and he wants me to wait until I'm sixteen, and then he'll marry me properly, if you know what I mean?' She blushed. 'Then we'll have the finest wedding anyone has ever seen, and probably hundreds of children. But, oh! I'm being selfish again, telling you how happy I am.'

'I watched you this afternoon. I saw you with him.'

She glanced away from me. 'I love him, Will. That's why I'm so happy. I can almost forgive Aunt Carew for being so harsh with us, because she taught me how to be a lady and she brought me here. And Uncle Carew gave Lord Richard a fine dowry with me too. Really, I have such a lot to thank them for, and it's so hard to hear what they've done to Father, and to our home. Oh, I can't even think about it.'

I didn't tell her what was obvious to me, that the only reason why they had made such a good match for her was because the title, Lady Margery of Calais, wife of Lord Richard of Carlisle and Calais, would bring honour instead of shame to my uncle's family. Wealth and power, that was all the Carews cared about.

'Oh, and guess what!' Margery laughed, bright as raindrops again. 'Aunt Carew stayed here till last month, and then she told me she was going back to live with her husband in England because she is having a *baby*! At her age! "Now I can shake off the Montagues for ever," she told me. "Don't expect to hear from me again." She was so triumphant, Will! She'll have a proper Carew after all, and I hope she has dozens of them! So that's the last I'll see of her. No more Aunt Carew!' she twirled round, laughing and clapping, and then stopped still. 'What am I doing? Father is waiting to die in Newgate, and I'm dancing! Poor, poor Father. I can't bear it!' Tears splashed down her cheeks again. 'I'll speak to my husband as soon as he comes from the great hall. Surely, surely, there's something he can do.'

*

Next morning I woke to hear the wind and rain squalling round the castle walls. I lay inside the red-curtained cave of my bed, warm and safe, and then I remembered where I was and why I was there. A servant arrived to dress me, and though my instincts now were to send him away so I could do it myself, I knew it was impossible. For one thing, I didn't want to do anything to offend Lord Richard. For another, the doublet was so heavy, and with so many laces to fasten at the shoulders and the neck and the waist that it was impossible for me to dress myself. So I held out my arms and allowed myself to be dressed, and all the time I was dithering inside with impatience. At last I was ready, and the servant bowed and said that Lord Richard wished to see me.

I was taken straight to his study, where he was sitting at his heavy oak table with a quill in his hand, writing. Margery was reading by the window and Nurse Joan was sewing, squinting as she threaded her needle. It was very peaceful in there, after all the turmoil of the last few months. In spite of the storm outside, pale streaks of sunlight fingered their way through the window slits, lighting up the stone walls and the richly coloured tapestries. A huge fire in the hearth purred like a sleeping cat. Margery glanced up and smiled at me and Lord Richard asked me to sit on the stool by his table. I watched him while he wrote, and my jittery nervousness began to calm down. He was younger than my father; though his dark hair and beard were just silvering at the temples; when he looked up at me his eyes were kind; worried, sad and kind.

'William, I don't know if I can help, but I'm going to try. I have to say our king is a very great man indeed, a very powerful man, but it's impossible to read his moods. When he is angry, no one knows how to appease him.'

I nodded, twisting again and again at the little amulet that Meg had given me.

'This is what I'm going to do, and all we can do is hope. We have one very small chance. He owes me a favour. I found soldiers for him some time ago, when he was at war, and my army won the day for him. He promised me land in return. I don't need land; I have enough for my future family.' He smiled across at my sister, and I felt my throat going tight, the way her cheeks blushed, the way she smiled back at him. 'I can't come to England to speak to King Henry myself; it's impossible at this time. We have many visitors coming to the castle, and my duty here is to entertain them on His Majesty's behalf. So, I've written him a letter asking him to release your father to my care, instead of giving me the land he promised.'

I wanted to fling my arms round him. Instead, I remembered my court manners and bowed deeply. 'My Lord, I am eternally grateful.'

'It may not work.' He heated a stub of wax in a candle flame, dropped it onto the letter to seal it, and pressed his ruby-studded signet ring into it. Then he handed the letter to me. 'You will have to give this to King Henry yourself. No one else must do it. You'll have to be very brave.' He stood up and put his hand on my shoulder. 'I wish you well, William. With all my heart, I wish you well.'

Anne of Cleves

The next day Anne of Cleves arrived. It was just after dawn. Nurse Joan covered me up with a brown hooded cloak and hurried me outside to watch her arrival. Margery's husband would be the first to greet the princess, along with the Lord Deputy and the Knight Porter of Calais, and then there were great horses and men at arms in red velvet coats and gold chains, and all the archers of the king's livery. I couldn't help thinking how proud my favourite knight, Sir Andrew, would have been to be one of them. And he would have been there, if he hadn't led me down to the wherry on that last afternoon.

There must have been a hundred or more noblemen in the procession that followed the archers, all dressed in purple velvet and satin and with high, gold collars round their necks, and twice as many as that of yeomen in the king's colours, and then came the children of honour and the people of Calais, all dressed in their best in spite of the early hour and the awful wild weather.

When Her Grace, Princess Anne of Cleves, came to the lantern gate she paused to look out at the king's ships, with their hundred banners of red and gold, and all their flags flying. From the decks came such a blaring of trumpets and beating of drums that the screaming voices of the gulls were lost inside the noise. All the guns were fired at once, and they created such a thick black smoke that we were all blinded for a time, and I had to grasp Nurse Joan's arm to check she was still there. When the smoke cleared, we saw hundreds of soldiers in the king's livery lining the street, making a lane for the future queen to pass through to her lodgings.

All I wanted to do then was to get back onto the *Lion* and to sail back to England. But we were not to sail that day, or the next, or the next week even. Winter storms made the sea as treacherous as wild horses.

'There'll be no taking the Princess Anne over today,' Nurse Joan sighed every morning, day after day, and I was reckless with impatience, brooding all the time.

'I can't wait any longer. I have to get back to Father. Any ship, any boat will do,' I said. 'A fishing boat!' But nothing at all was risking the sea between Calais and Dover. And I had to keep myself hidden. The only time I went into the main quarters again was during the Christmas celebrations, when a banquet was held for all the visiting courtiers. The hall was decorated with hundreds of muslin flags that were sewn with tiny bells. They tinkled and chimed as the dancers moved around. We had to wear masks, and we could only see through narrow slits. My mask and cap were deep velvet green, made for me by Nurse Joan.

'I like this colour,' she said. 'It suits you.'

I remembered that my uncle Carew had bought me a green doublet and hose because it was King Henry's own favourite colour. He thought it would make the king like me. I remembered how afraid I had been that day, the day I was taken to meet the king of England.

How different things would have been if the king had never even noticed me. How I wished he hadn't. Percy Howard was welcome to him, I thought. All this favour and honour amounted to nothing; nothing at all; I knew that now. It could be snatched away in a moment.

I could see through my mask, but it was hard to recognise anyone else behind theirs. Apart from the very tall people and the very fat ones, everyone looked much the same, which was strange. I knew Margery by her familiar laughter but I didn't see her husband at all, though I knew he would be there. I searched for someone who looked like Percy, but no one was quite lanky enough, no one had quite the same pale yellow hair. I recognised his cousin, Kathryn Howard, who had come to be a maid of honour to Anne of Cleves. She flirted with every man in sight; I'd noticed her before when the court came to Hampton. She was easy to recognise by her easy manner and her high-pitched giggle. She always behaved like that.

I kept myself hidden in shadows. I stood watching the strange sweeping hoppity dances that they did in this castle, and saw Margery in the middle of all the dancers, as light and graceful as any of the girls there. Aunt Carew had taught her well, after all.

I wasn't the only one standing alone. I saw the future queen of England, Anne of Cleves. She was tall and thin, and a bit plain-faced. She was solemn and unsmiling, and she and the maids she had brought with her from her own country were all dressed in country brown; dull and ordinary among all the peacocks. She reminded me of a brown hare in the grass, watching, still, silent. She refused to dance, though her English maids fluttered round her like summer butterflies. Kathryn Howard chattered away to her as if she was doing her best to make friends with her, but Anne of Cleves just frowned from time to time and said nothing back to her. I had heard that she didn't speak French or English. I wondered if she was any good at Latin. Perhaps she was as anxious to get away from the court as I was. I expect she was nervous about being late for her wedding.

At long last the weather calmed. Nick sent someone with a message for me: The *Lion* was being prepared to sail. Would I go with him, or would I travel with the courtiers? I sent a message back: 'With you, of course.' I asked for my brown shirt and hose to be returned to me, and disdainfully my servant bowed and smiled; the curled-lip smile of court.

'It has been given away at the beggars' gate,' he said. 'I did not think you would need it again.'

'I'll see to it!' Nurse Joan said, when I stormed into my sister's room. 'I'll find you something to wear, even if I have to make it myself. That brown wool is easy to get hold of.'

'Make it mucky, and put a few holes in,' I told her sulkily. And then I added, 'Please.'

'Ooh, manners at last,' she smiled, reminding me of Grandmam Susan, and I laughed.

As soon as my clothes were ready, Nurse Joan helped me to unlace myself from my satins and velvets. She strapped the letter to King Henry round my waist, inside a purse of coins from Lord Richard. Then I slipped the brown woollen jerkin over it and became a ship's boy again. It was strange, but I felt easy then, at home with myself.

'Take care, Will!' Margery begged. 'Oh, but do what you can for Father. Tell him, tell him, if he's still alive...' She couldn't go on. Tears streamed down her cheeks. I pulled myself away from her hugs, and ran like the wind down to the port. Nick was hopping about anxiously, waiting for me. We were on the very last of the little boats to leave the harbour for the *Lion*. I was put to work as if I had never set foot inside the king's castle, and it felt good to be busy again. I'd had enough of hiding.

Just as we set sail to leave, I saw a young man on the quayside, waving the plumed hat of a courtier. It was Percy Howard, and to my great joy, he had missed the boat.

This time the passage was smooth and swift. Fifty boats sailed with us to escort us to England, and their little lights danced on the grey water as the day ended, like the fireflies on the marshes around Montague. We drew into Dover on the evening tide, and it was cold, with piercing arrows of rain. I saw Princess Anne waiting to disembark, and I thought how weary she looked, and how anxiously she turned to her maids, not knowing what to do next. She was a stranger in a foreign land, and I think she was afraid. I was given a flaming torch to light her way to the chairlift that would swing her down from the deck, and for a brief second, before I was pushed aside by her page, I stood so close to her that I could have touched her. The torchlight softened her face, making her look younger, pale and tired, a little frightened. She glanced across at me and smiled a kind thank you.

I could have put Lord Richard's letter into her hand and said in Latin, 'Give this to my lord His Majesty for me.'

But I didn't. I daren't.

Yet for that tiny moment when our eyes met I knew I liked her. She had looked a scruffy ship's boy in the eye and hadn't turned her head away. And we were both scared at the thought of what we had to do next. I hoped King Henry would like her too. I hoped he would be kind to her, and that she would make his wild, cruel heart a gentle place instead of a lion's den.

Then she was gone into the rain and the darkness, and I was being shouted at to get on with my work, and Nick was yanking my sleeve as though he was pulling me awake out of a deep dream.

With some of Lord Richard's money we paid for a ride home to London. We had to get back as quickly as we could now. I sat at the back of the cart, my head down against the driving sleet. I needed to be on my own. On the boat I'd been too busy to think properly, what with all the jobs I had to do and Nick sparrow-chattering in my ear. The Christmas banquet at the castle in Calais had given me an idea. I was hatching a plan. It was so daring that I didn't want to speak about it to anyone – not yet.

If I was going to do it, I would have to pretend to be someone else – someone as fearless as Nick.

The king's masque

The great hall of Greenwich Palace was decorated with bunches of holly. Their scarlet berries gleamed in the candlelight like drops of garnet set in emeralds. The floor was strewn with sweet-smelling rosemary, and a huge log fire burned in the hearth. From all over London, musicians and players had been invited to perform to the court, and there was a trembling of nervousness among them, giggling and grinning and dithering. A small group of mummers and musicians stood among them, just inside the hall, close to the studded entrance door. In the middle of them was a boy with a rustling cape of rushes round his shoulders. He wore a dragon's head made of straw. Another boy dressed in green stood at his side, hopping from pointed shoe to pointed shoe with nervousness and excitement. The musicians behind them were in a little huddle, trying to remember how their first tune went, humming the start note to one another, as fidgety as rabbits because none of them had ever set foot inside a palace before.

At the other end of the hall stood the new queen of England, Anne of Cleves. Her ladies-in-waiting swanned round her in their poppy-red and forget-me-not-blue dresses, flashing their jewellery and their smiles at everyone, but she was tense and still. She wore a dress of silver cloth, and pearls and chains of silver were looped in her long brown hair. Her hands were clasped together as if she was praying. Around her tense stillness the whole room buzzed, like the inside of a beehive, with excitement.

There was a rolling of drums and a fanfare of trumpets. The court fell silent. The boy in the cape of rushes stiffened. His lips moved with silent prayers. The boy in green craned his neck and stood on tiptoe to see over all the heads. The great door at the very end of the hall was flung open and a company of players ran in, all dressed in green and gold and with masks over their eyes. They capered round the ladies, making their dresses sway like flowers in the wind. Queen Anne started in alarm. One of the players was taller and fatter than any of them – a huge swollen figure of a man. He pranced up to her like a limping bear and took her hand. Her head was bowed now; she had no smiles for him or for anyone. He lifted her chin to look at her, to make her look at him. Then he pulled off his mask and threw it to the ground. It was King Henry, and everyone gasped, pretending they had never for a moment guessed it was he.

But it looked as if no one had warned Queen Anne that this might happen. She looked startled and annoyed, frowning deeply at him, not understanding that this was his favourite game and that she was supposed to laugh and clap her hands with surprise. Perhaps she was even expected to kiss her new husband. But she screwed up her face and scowled at him instead. And King Henry turned away from her and stood with his legs astride and his arms akimbo and said loudly, 'I don't like her.'

At that very moment, in a fit of nerves, the musicians at the back of the hall lifted up their instruments and began to play a bright, cheerful jig. The dragonboy tried to stop them, to tell them that the moment was wrong, but it was too late. As they danced forward, the courtiers made way for them like a parting in the Red Sea. Tumblers somersaulted the full length of the hall, tiny bells jingling on their wrists and ankles. Singers clapped their tambourines and sang lustily.

The musicians and mummers stopped right in front of King Henry. He glared at them with rage and astonishment. His queen was white-faced, her head turned to one side. She wasn't even watching the procession that was being held in her honour. The lad in green bowed awkwardly. Every muscle of his body was quivering with fright. The boy in the dragon mask bowed, slowly, deeply. The fiddle player tucked his fiddle against his waist and began to play; the man with the long red beard pressed his wooden flute to his lips, and the dragon boy began to dance, very slowly, very carefully, letting the strands of his rush cloak swirl round him like the rustling leaves of autumn. All around him the courtiers clap, clap, clapped, like the pattering of falling leaves, and the sound rose and swelled and filled the hall, as if they were all willing the tension to break and the party to begin. But the moment the dancing dragon boy swirled to a halt and bowed again to the king, the music stopped. The clapping stopped. Nobody moved or spoke.

252

The queen turned her head. The king was completely silent. His eyes never left the dragon boy. The boy put his hand inside his rustling cape and drew out a scroll of parchment. He held it out to the king. Instantly a guard stepped forward, his hand on the sheath of his sword, but the king motioned him away and took the scroll from the boy. He broke the seal and unrolled the letter, and read it very slowly. His eyes narrowed. He frowned and looked up sharply.

'Take off your mask!' he snapped.

And I did. I drew the straw head up over my face.

For I was the dragon boy. I was the king's favourite. I was William, son of Robert, descendant of Walter Montague, the beloved favourite of the Plantagenet King Edward of England.

Yet also I was the runaway page of the Tudor Prince Edward. I was the son of a traitor. I was a boy without a home.

I kneeled down in front of His Majesty, and waited to be dragged away to my death.

'What do you think of this, madam?' the king asked, thrusting the letter towards his new wife. She frowned, and he tutted and read it out to her.

'*My most gracious Lord and king of all England, I beseech you in the name of our friendship to forgive this boy, who has acted only out of love for his father, as any boy would and should. He loves his father so much that he has risked his life for him. I beg you to forgive him for anything he has done to cause you displeasure. And I beg you to find it in your heart to grant pardon to his father Robert Montague, who has always been your loyal servant. You have graciously blessed my marriage*

253

to his daughter, Lady Margery. Humbly I ask you to release him and place him in my care. I will never, ever expect another favour from Your Gracious Majesty, though I remain humbly and always at your service. I am Lord Richard of Carlisle, Lieutenant of Calais.'

King Henry rustled the letter in front of his wife's face. 'I ask you again, madam, what do you think of this?'

It was obvious that Queen Anne hadn't understood a word, but she did understand his anger and my terror. She did something so wonderful then, that you could feel the 'Ah!' as every person in the hall drew in a breath at the same time. She stepped up to the king and put one hand on his sleeve, the other on my shoulder, and curtsied deeply to him.

Then another extraordinary thing happened. The pretty lady-in-waiting, Kathryn Howard, fluttered her hands like a butterfly caught in a net and kneeled behind her mistress the queen. The king watched her in astonishment, but she braved a smile at him. She had no idea whether she should stay there or stand up again. I saw his lips twitch a smile in return. One by one the other ladies-in-waiting frowned at each other and then kneeled behind their queen, their robes swishing like soft rain. The queen kept her head bowed. I ducked my head then, and closed my eyes. I knew the king would want to remind her and all his court that he was a mighty and strong ruler. He had just announced to everybody that he didn't like his new wife. Would he want to show her how cruel and powerful he could be? One nod from him would send my father and me to our deaths. Or would he want to show her that he could be a noble and generous king? He could forgive us.

Like the flick of a coin, heads or tails at a cockfight, he could choose one way or another.

'William Carew. Why did you run away?' he asked.

'Forgive me, my most gracious king.' I spoke as clearly and as bravely as I could. 'I wanted to help my father.' My heart lurched like a trapped bird inside me.

Nobody moved. Nobody spoke. It was as if a sleep of enchantment had been cast over the whole room.

'You love your father?' His Majesty asked at last. His voice was very low.

'I do, My Lord,'

'How much do you love him? Eh? How much should a son love his father?'

I had no idea what kind of answer he expected. This quiet anger in his voice frightened me more than the bellowing fits of rage I had seen in him before. I thought of what my aunt Carew had said. *The king loves you as much as he loves his own son.*

'A boy should love his father as much as a subject should love his king,' I stammered.

'Look at me, William.'

I raised my eyes, but I couldn't look into his.

'Do you love your father enough to change places with him? If I release him, as Lord Richard asks, will you take his place in my prison? Will you take his punishment for offending me so deeply?'

I did look at him then, with a start of shock. I thought of the sweltering darkness of Newgate prison, with its smell of vomit and fear. I thought of the stripes of blood on my father's side. There was a long, agonising silence.

'Yes, Your Majesty,' I said. 'If you ask me to, I will.'

'Go,' he said at last. 'Take your father to France. You are released, both of you. But never come back to England again, as long as I live.'

Father

We stumbled out of Greenwich Palace into the freezing white frenzy of a snow blizzard. Jack Downey the flute-player and Buttons the fiddler and Nick, the boy in green, wrapped me up in my brown cloak to try to stop my shivering.

'I never knew a boy as brave as you!' Nick kept saying. I could hardly speak for relief and joy. Grandmam Susan and Meg were waiting for us with a handcart, along with Sarah Downey and Button's wife. They were all convinced that they would never see any of us again outside of Newgate.

All the time we were in Calais, Grandmam had been visiting the prison with herbs and lotions for my father, bribing her way in with her jugs of ale. 'Thank the Lord I won't be visiting you in there too,' she said. 'Get him out of that place quick. We'll wait at home for you.'

Meg, Nick and I hurried to Newgate as though hounds were snapping at our heels. It was bitterly cold; the streets were grey with ice and the river was frozen so hard that we were able to push the cart right along it. It seemed to take for ever to get there, and when we did there was a bundle propped against the gate and I knew it was my father, dumped like a bag of dirty laundry. I rushed up to him, and kneeled down, and put my arms round him. He held me tight, tight.

'I thought I would never see you again, Will,' he said, his voice choking. 'I thought they were bringing me out to hang me!'

I was so full, and there was so much to say, that I couldn't do anything else but cling to him, but Nick gently eased me away and helped Father into the cart.

Meg tucked the blanket round him. 'You're free!' she told him. Her breath smoked away from her in the frosty air. 'You're really, really free.'

When we got to the cottage, Grandmam Susan ran out to help us. Between us we half-carried Father in. He gazed round the humble, dark room as if it were the finest of the king's palaces, and bowed to Widow Susan as if she were the new queen herself. He couldn't stop thanking her for everything she'd done, and she told him off for talking so much.

'Save your strength for getting well,' she said. 'The sooner you're out of this country, the better.'

Every day she brewed up more potions for him, and cooked nourishing stews so that he would be strong enough to ride to Dover. I had given her all the money that was left from Lord Richard, and she used it to buy the best meats for Father. She never ate with us during this time, and I think my father had her share of everything. She made up a straw bed for him by the fire, and I slept beside him, keeping him warm. I sent Nick to Calais with a letter for Lord Richard and Margery. He had no trouble working his passage across, and a week and a half later he came back with a purse of money for Grandmam Susan, and a bundle of good clothes for my father and myself. My sister sent pages and pages of ecstatic letters, and a bag of ribbons, and a willow-green cloak for Meg. She put it on and swirled slowly round in it, so the rushes whispered under her feet.

'You're fit to be a lady in the queen's privy chamber,' I told her. She was even prettier than Kathryn Howard, but I didn't tell her that.

She giggled. 'Serve the queen? Not me. Not ever. I know where I belong.'

*

Every night I stood outside the cottage and watched the stars, and prayed for a sign that it would be safe for us to leave the country.

'What you looking for?' Nick whispered, standing at my side with his head craned back, watching with me. 'Your guardian angel?'

'Maybe,' I said.

'He's up there. I know it. Only he doesn't show himself till the right time comes. And then he'll shine like fire and he'll bring a message from God. You go to sleep, Master William. I'll watch out for him.'

And one day, we saw it together, the miracle sign that I had been waiting for. A shower of shooting stars cascaded down the blackness like a shimmering waterfall.

'Your angel has opened his wings, sir,' Nick announced. He turned to me, and in the starlight I saw his face tense and unhappy. 'It's time for you to leave us.'

Widow Susan made a chicken pottage for us that night, with plenty of her favourite herbs chopped into it.

'I have never smelled anything so good,' my father told her. He waved Meg's hand away and walked to the table without her help.

'Don't eat too much,' Widow Susan warned him. 'We don't want your stomach to pop now, do we?'

'I'll have some of your good ale, too,' my father laughed. 'But first, if I may, I'll bless this welcome meal, and this fine house, and thank God for everything you've done for me. I've never been in better company.'

Widow Susan pretended to choke with surprise and scorn, but her eyes were bright, and her sallow cheeks plumped up with smiles. My father blessed the food, and we all sat down together: Meg, with little sleepy Arthur on her knee, Nick, his Grandmam, my father and me, and we ate with a quiet, thoughtful silence. It would be our last meal together. The night was huge with all our memories, all the things that had happened in the last few weeks. Although the air was sharp we had the door open to draw out the smoke from the fire, and through the doorway we could see the stars as bright as eyes.

'Guardian angels,' Nick whispered. 'Lots of them, all taking care of us.'

We could hear the fire crackling, and the cows of the neighbouring cottages lowing to each other, pigs snuffling, hens muttering as they settled down for the night. Out in the lane, owls were hooting to each other. It was the sort of night when sounds come to you from far away. And we heard a voice, we all heard it, shouting from a distance, and then coming nearer: 'Where lives Widow Susan? Where lives Widow Susan?'

Nick jumped up so quickly that his stool knocked over a jug of ale. He raced out of the door, sending grey smoke folding round us like wings. Meg gasped aloud, thrust Arthur into my arms, and ran after him. Father and I stared at each other, shocked and afraid. We had no idea what had happened, or what we should do.

Then we heard the sounds of their voices, Nick chattering, Meg laughing, a man's gruff voice, and at last they came into the yard; three figures clinging to each others' arms as if they were one single shape. They squeezed into the house and stood in front of us.

'My father's found us!' Nick shouted. 'My father's come home from the sea!'

A fine son

And so we were ready, and we went to France, my father and I.

As we left, Grandmam Susan and Meg were laying out sheets on the grass to dry, and Sarah Downey was holding Arthur. It was just like that very first morning that I had stumbled into their yard and demanded help. They had done so much for me, and there was nothing I could do for them in return. My father must have heard my thoughts.

'Be sure, there will be messages and packages from Calais. You'll have as much money as you need to make yourselves comfortable, I promise you,' he said. 'We will never be allowed to return to England. But you will always be in our thoughts.'

'You have a good lad here,' Grandmam Susan said. She put her hands on my shoulders. 'A fine son.'

'You still have my amulet,' Meg said to me.

I glanced down at my wrist, pretending to be surprised. 'So I have.'

'Always wear it.'

I nodded. I didn't know how to say goodbye. Neither of us did.

Nick's father pulled up with a horse cart he had hired for us. He wanted to drive us to Calais himself.

Nick scrambled up beside his father, and I climbed into the back with mine; and we were away, waving and calling till the little thatched cottage was out of sight.

When we arrived in Dover, we stood together on the quayside watching our sailing ship being loaded up. The little boat that would take us out to it was ready, waiting. It was time to go. I turned sadly to Nick.

'Goodbye, Master Will,' he began. I shook my head.

'I'm not your master, Nick. I never was. I'm your friend.'

He stared at me, and then he nodded, grinning. A moment passed, an embarrassed moment when neither of us knew what to say. Then he piped up with, 'Before you go, can I ask you something? I've been puzzling a long time about what you told me when we were sailing on the *Lion*. And I'm still puzzled. You said you only had one leg or something. It made no sense to me, because you've got two, same as I have. And you said you can't see, either. But you *can*.'

I looked sideways at my father, and he smiled. 'Aha! Brother John is still in our hearts. He taught me that riddle too, when we were just children. *I have no sight nor hands, many ribs, a mouth in my middle. I move on one foot, I am swift as the wind. What am I?*'

'Now *you're* one of those things too?' Nick said. 'But look at you, you *have* got hands, sir.'

His father gave a big guffawing laugh. 'Nicholas Drew!' he said. 'You're the son of a sailor, and you want to be a seaman yourself, and you don't know the answer to that one! Look at the ships on the water! Just look!' Nick's eyes widened in amazement.

He moved away from us, muttering and counting on his fingers. We were hurried to our boat then, too quickly for last goodbyes. As soon as we climbed on board the sailing ship, the rowing barges began to tug it out to sea. I rushed to the side of the deck. I could still see Nick and his father, side by side on the quayside.

'Goodbye, Nick!' I shouted at the top of my voice. My father and I took off our hats and waved them in the air, and when Nick spotted us he threw his own hat so high that the wind took it and bowled it into the sea. In all the screaming of gulls and shouting of crewmen and passengers, I could hear his voice.

'I know what you are! You're a ship!'

'He got it!' I laughed. I waved both my arms in the air, and jumped up and down like Nick.

'Goodbye! Goodbye! Goodbye, Will Montague!' came his voice. 'Remember me!'

My father put his hand on my shoulder. 'The people we love stay with us for ever. Your mother, Brother John, our dear Matthew, your good friend down there. They never leave us, and we're made strong by remembering them.'

I turned away at last from the receding white blur that was Dover.

'I thought I'd lost everything when Matthew died,' Father said. 'There was nothing left to live for.' He twisted his ring, the Montague ring.

'You had Margery,' I reminded him.

He smiled down at me. 'Indeed. And I had you. Widow Susan is right, but she didn't need to tell me. You're as fine a son as any man could wish to have. I'm proud of you, Will. I always was, and I always will be. You know that, don't you?'

I nodded, but I couldn't make any words come.

I don't think my father expected me to, either.

Thank you to all the people who talked to me, lent me
books and shared their knowledge about Henry VIII,
Tudor houses, costumes, customs and Catholicism
under Henry. They include Derbyshire Libraries,
Caroline Davenport, Judy Oldroyd and Jean Parker of
Bramall Hall, Shelagh Gregory, Liz Maude and
Julia Bruce, and special thanks to my partner
Alan James Brown.